"Tani. You're Having a Nightmare. Wake Up!"

"What is it, Aunt Kady, is something wrong?"

"You screamed as if you were being tortured to death, and kept on screaming," Kady informed her. "Everyone on the ranch is outside this door wondering who attacked you."

"Uh, no one." She shuddered, remembering. "It was just a dream but it was really gruesome."

"How did it start?" Kady kept her voice quiet.

"Something was hunting, I think, but I could hear it coming. It got closer and closer. I could feel the hunger. It jumped at me. It bit me here"—she touched her throat—"and I couldn't move. I was bleeding and it was drinking the blood, then it started—it was eating me *alive*—I couldn't move or scream but I was screaming inside. I was screaming and no one came. . ."

TOR BOOKS BY ANDRE NORTON

Beast Master's Ark (with Lyn McConchie)
Beast Master's Circus (with Lyn McConchie)*

The Crystal Gryphon
Dare to Go A-Hunting
Flight in Yiktor
Forerunner
Forerunner: The Second Venture
The Gates to Witch World (omnibus comprising
Witch World, Web of the Witch World,
and Year of the Unicorn)
Here Abide Monsters
Moon Called
Moon Mirror
The Prince Commands
Ralestone Luck
Stand of Stars
Wizards' Worlds
Wraiths of Time
Grandmasters' Choice (Editor)

The Jekyll Legacy (with Robert Bloch)
Gryphon's Eyrie (with A. C. Crispin)
Songsmith (with A. C. Crispin)
Caroline (with Enid Cushing)
Firehand (with P. M. Griffin)
Redline the Stars (with P. M. Griffin)
Sneeze on Sunday (with Grace Allen Hogarth)
House of Shadows (with Phyllis Miller)
Empire of the Eagle (with Susan Shwartz)
Imperial Lady (with Susan Shwartz)

THE SOLAR QUEEN
(with Sherwood Smith)
Derelict for Trade
A Mind for Trade

THE WITCH WORLD
(Editor)
Four from the Witch World
Tales from the Witch World 1
Tales from the Witch World 2
Tales from the Witch World 3

WITCH WORLD: THE TURNING
I Storms of Victory (with P. M. Griffin)
II Flight of Vengeance (with P. M. Griffin & Mary Straub)
III On Wings of Magic (with Patricia Mathews & Sasha Miller)

MAGIC IN ITHKAR
(Editor, with Robert Adams)
Magic in Ithkar 1
Magic in Ithkar 2
Magic in Ithkar 3
Magic in Ithkar 4

THE HALFBLOOD CHRONICLES
(with Mercedes Lackey)
The Elevenbane
Elvenblood
Elvenborn

THE OAK, YEW, ASH, AND ROWAN CYCLE
(with Sasha Miller)
To the King a Daughter
Knight or Knave

CAROLUS REX
(with Rosemary Edghill)
The Shadow of Albion
Leopard in Exile

THE TIME TRADERS
(with Sherwood Smith)
Echoes in Time
Atlantis Endgame*

*forthcoming

BEAST MASTER'S ARK

Andre Norton and Lyn McConchie

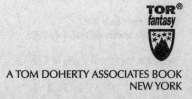

A TOM DOHERTY ASSOCIATES BOOK
NEW YORK

BEASTMASTER'S ARK

Copyright © 2002 by Andre Norton and Lyn McConchie

All rights reserved, including the right to reproduce this book, or portions thereof, in any form.

Edited by James Frenkel

A Tor Book
Published by Tom Doherty Associates, LLC
175 Fifth Avenue
New York, NY 10010

www.tor.com

Tor® is a registered trademark of Tom Doherty Associates, LLC.

ISBN: 0-765-34009-7

First edition: June 2002
First mass market edition: July 2003

Printed in the United States of America

0 9 8 7 6 5 4 3 2 1

To our good friend Sharman Horwood,
who also loves the Witch World,
this book is affectionately dedicated.
And to Jean Weber (Australia) in memory of Minou.

Chapter One

Behind the desert the Peaks framed a sky that would be a soft lavender when the sun rose. It was the end of the dry season and even in the dark of night the heat was stifling. The strange puff bush blossoms like plumps of cotton wool hung limp. It was the season where nothing hurried that wished to live, and certainly not in the searing desert. But it was there where a beast ran. It had come from the Peaks country that lay behind it, into desert fringes, and it was now out into true desert. But it had reasons.

Just within the boundaries of the great desert and jagged rocky mountain area humans called the Big Blue, a lame frawn ran desperately. It was a strong animal but it was starting to stagger. Its hoof, split by a stone, slowed it, but behind the reeling beast terror came scrabbling, so the frawn ignored the pain. It could not ignore the need for water. But in this place there was none and the animal's weakness grew. If it ran hard it could leave the hunters far behind, but they traveled steadily. When the frawn stopped to rest they closed in again. At last it could run no longer, every part of it craved water. Its strength drained away and it sank to its haunches. It would fight.

But the horror that followed was too great and it stood again to stagger on. The hunters did not care. They had little but the instinct to follow and kill. They would do one relentlessly until they could do the other. How long the hunt continued did not concern them. They flowed over the barren lands, crossed dry watercourses, and clicked past dry brush. They hunted and nothing would turn them from the hunt.

Ahead the frawn suddenly stopped. It staggered, sank slowly to the ground, and stretched out. Too little water, heat too great to bear, so far to run and the heart had given up. The frawn died mercifully as the first of the hunters reached it. But the flesh was still warm. The blood still flowed. They feasted, though the feast would have been more to their taste had the flesh been yet living.

On a great ship sailing the depths of space and heading for the planet on which the frawn had run the hopeless race, one worked. Her head was down as she concentrated. Orphaned niece of the two scientists who led the crew of the ship, she was a hard worker and just now she was fascinated by what she did.

Tani was splicing genes in her small laboratory when her uncle Brion entered. He peered over her shoulder, then smiled approvingly.

"Good, we need more meerkats. They're a clan animal." His gaze dropped to the tiny dice lying on the gene chart and his eyebrows rose. "What are these for, my dear?"

Tani giggled happily. "Your fault, Uncle Brion. You said that genes combine at random, so I've been throwing the dice and splicing that combination where it's viable." She enjoyed creating meerkats, anyway. Meerkats were a type of mongoose and killers of snakes among other small prey they favored. A meerkat's looks were its fortune in the human world. They were long and slender-bodied. A shape akin to that of a mink. But the meerkat had a yellowish-colored rougher fur and their eyes were large, with the rings of dark fur about them making the eyes look larger still. Humans were programmed to react favorably to that large-eyed look. Meerkats lived in affectionate family groups, stood up often on the hindlegs to scan territory, and would fight only if pressed. However, if they must fight, they do so effectively and as a group. All traits that attracted humans, and had delighted Tani.

Her uncle grinned cheerfully back at her. "Whatever works, sweetheart. But don't let Jarro see you doing that. The idea would give him a heart attack." He noticed the faint shadow flit over her face and said nothing. Their colleague was a pompous little stuffed shirt who didn't get along too well with anyone on the ship and Brion had an idea the man was being especially hard on Tani.

He hid a sigh. It was understandable. Jarro had worked hard for his qualifications and saw the inclusion of Brion's young part-qualified niece as unfair. As well Jarro's people had been first-in settlers on Ishan. Being from a first-in family gave status normally but now that planet, with Terra, and much that had been Terran, were gone. Like many others left stranded by the deaths of their home worlds, he suffered.

He patted Tani's shoulder. "Don't work too hard. We land on Arzor in another few hours."

"I won't, Uncle Brion. I just want to get this last pair of meerkats started in the embryo tanks."

Brion studied the list beside her and nodded. "That's good. Three more females and four males. With the genetic material from the other meerkats on Arzor we can build a viable gene pool again." He smiled down at Tani. "That's another species we've taken back from Xik destruction."

Tani's voice trembled. "I know, but we lost so many. Even tracing the surviving Beast Master teams, and some of the Beast Masters are just selfish." Her voice broke into a wail. "That one on Fremlyn who wouldn't let us take his animals or even take samples from them. He said it would distress them. And Marten took his side."

"I know. But Marten's gone and we did get the samples. Finish up what you're doing. Just think. Once we touch down we'll be on Arzor at least three months. You can fly Mandy and the coyotes will have desert to run in." He smiled down at the head bent in sudden industry. Sometimes he wondered if they hadn't been wrong to keep the girl. He left the laboratory wondering about that. His sister had been Irish as he was. Well, unmixed blood anyhow, even if the last three generations had been lived in Arizona.

But Tani's father, Bright Sky, had been of unmixed blood as well. Cheyenne from a long line of warriors, and medicine men who had not all been fakes. He'd been chosen as a Beast Master just after the birth of Tani and a year after his marriage to Brion's sister. Alisha had loved him and accepted his odd calling. She'd accepted his beast team as part of him, but it had been Tani with whom the team bonded, as well as with their human leader.

The child had known the team from her earliest days. She'd rolled on the ground with the two wolves, teased the African eagle, and romped with the mongoose pair. Then, in one night of attack and defeat as the Beast Master team attempted to retake a world from the Xik invaders, all were gone. Team, husband and father, and half of Alisha and Tani's world.

Tani had been five. Too young to understand the reasons that the Terran High Command had used up men so recklessly. Her mother had understood, but in grief and pain akin to madness she'd turned her back. Being a Beast Master and fighting, using one's animals for that war, was bad. From that it had been a small step to a slow warping of Alisha's truth. Only her loved husband, Bright Sky, had been a good Beast Master. The others were not. They wasted their animals, threw away the gifts they had been given. Alisha had been killed two years later in a Xik breakthrough raid on Terra. She'd been a medic and had died still trying to save lives. Brion wasn't sure how much of Alisha's twisted teaching Tani remembered, or had accepted.

The girl was both her parents. She had the black hair and animal-empathic abilities of her father, Bright Sky, and from Alisha, the eyes changing from green to gray and fierce love of life. She wasn't pretty, except to Brion and his wife, Kady, who loved her.

Brion shrugged. His niece was healthy, clever, and hardworking. He could hardly ask for more. It had been just under twelve years since Alisha had died. That reminded him. He headed for his office. Tani would be nineteen a few days after they landed. He must discuss a suitable present for her with Kady. He'd keep that in mind as he reviewed the planet they'd reach very soon.

He sat back in his cabin, reviewing the Arzor tapes. One Beast Master had settled here, a Navajo named Storm. Hosteen Storm. Judging from the dates, High Command had added later material as it came to hand. The man was stepson to Brad Quade, a descendant of one of the First Ship families. Quade had large holdings in the Basin, one of the most fertile ranching areas. Storm's mother had died on Arzor, leaving a son by Quade, a boy named Logan who was the Beast Master's half-brother. Storm had taken his team to Arzor with him. An African eagle, two meerkats, and a dune cat. He eyed the latter item thoughtfully. They had DNA from several of those, but more would help widen the gene pool.

He just hoped this man wouldn't be as difficult as the Beast Master on Fremlyn. The Beast Master there had refused to allow Brion to take samples unless they provided mates for his remaining team. Brion had refused, the idea was unacceptable. A series of new animals spreading out into a world where they had not evolved could be an ecological disaster. A pity Marten had taken the man's side. They'd obtained samples by court order, one of the animals had been injured, it had subsequently died, and Marten had quit.

He'd argued they could have given the Beast Master infertile mates for his beasts. At least the animals would have company. Ridiculous, of course. The Ark wasn't traveling between planets to provide a lonely-hearts service for animals. It was there to preserve everything it could of Terran species. To collect samples where they could be found. Marten had stayed with the Ark for several weeks while he tried to convince them to at least provide infertile mates for the Beast Master team. He'd failed. Brion had arranged to have the animals of the team darted and samples taken. He'd returned to Marten's anger and a formal resignation slapped down on Brion's desk. Brion had regretted his inflexibility later on.

They could have escaped all the problems if he'd only agreed to the infertile mates. He wouldn't make that mistake again if only this Beast Master would be sensible and cooperative in return.

Brion ran the tapes a second time, making notes as he slowed and reread portions of the information. Kady entered to lean over his shoulder reading what he was writing.

He looked up at her. "Have we talked to the Government yet?"

"I made contact an hour ago."

"And?"

The news wouldn't please him, Kady knew. "They say that there is nothing in their laws to force a Beast Master to allow his team to be used as specimens. If Beast Master Storm refuses, then we must persuade him or do without samples."

She saw his face cloud with anger and laid a hand on his arm. "Brion, don't lose your temper with them. It will make things worse. It was Marten who's caused this." Her voice overrode his angry questions. "I'll tell you, just listen. He sent Arzor a message, telling them that on Fremlyn you'd taken genetic samples by force and injured a team animal that died after we left. Fremlyn saw those beasts as one of their last links with Earth. The authorities there are furious. I had a personal message from Marten, too. He's been given a huge grant and retained to clone and gene-splice a new pool of the team beasts. The Government is setting aside a large island as a reservation for them."

Brion smiled sourly. "So he's done well for himself, and left us wading in the mud he's thrown."

"And mud sticks. We have to be very careful the Arzoran people don't see us as intruders, taking what we want and ignoring the consequences. Arzor is somewhat primitive, a ranching world, they live by animals. From the way the man I talked to spoke about it, this Storm is very well thought of. He's the one who broke up a Xik holdout group on Arzor two years ago."

Brion laughed suddenly. "Tell Tani to be nice to him then. Maybe she can talk him into letting us take samples."

"You could also consider something else." She reached over to scroll back a tape. "Look at this report. Arzor would be right for a viable expanding meerkat population. They used to have rinces that filled the same niche. They were filthy little beasts, cannibals, and with scent glands even worse than the Terran skunk. The settlers killed a lot, then some kind of plague came. Most of the rinces died and the rest couldn't sustain a population. They breed too slowly and they're dying out. It's causing problems with that life chain. I'd have to do a workup of the ecological balance, but I think meerkats would fit right in there. How many has Tani done?"

"Seven," Brion said absently as he studied the tape. "Eagles breed very slowly. Arzor does already have a similar bird-predator species and the authorities would have to take care eagles did not grow so numerous that they competed with the zamle. Otherwise I'd see no harm in allowing the man's eagle to have a viable mate. So long as we emphasize he must let things happen naturally. He is not to incubate eggs or aid in the survival of weak eaglets. Two breeding naturally would help expand a breeding pool we can use next time we stop here."

Kady looked at him affectionately. "Good idea. Shall I tell Tani to make a start on a male eagle? With forced growth he'd be old enough to hand over before we leave."

"Do that. Just to be on the safe side she could also start cloning a male dune cat from our tissue samples. We can study the situation further and it can always be sterilized before we hand it over. It will all help to convince this Storm that we aren't unsympathetic. I must get on. We're landing in a week and I have a million things to do."

He hardly noticed the slight hiss of the closing door. He was already immersed in a study of his genetic material lists.

The week passed quickly for Tani, who was very busy as well. On Arzor it seemed to pass more slowly. On the Quade holdings Hosteen paced and worried. Would the incoming Ark provide him with mates for Hing, Baku, and Surra? He suspected they wouldn't. He'd heard about the Fremlyn debacle. But Hing in particular needed a mate. Meerkats were sociable animals, they lived in a clan. Things had been all right so long as Hing's mate, Ho, was alive. Luckily she'd been in kit when Ho died. Now she had four barely adult youngsters to provide a clan. But there was no mate to provide more, and worse, of the babies, three had been male and fights were beginning.

He desperately needed mates for Hing and her clan. He'd talked to his father's friend at Ecology Headquarters. They'd run tests. The meerkats could be allowed to breed and spread out in their family clans. They'd take the niche the rinces had once filled. Now if only Arzor could persuade the Ark people of that.

The Ark had been a wonderful idea. No one had heard about it for several years after the destruction of Ishan and Terra. Then word had begun to spread through the worlds that still thought of Terra as home in many ways. An Ark to carry genetic material from one world to another. Making sure that the vast cornucopia of possibilities from any one world did not have to be lost again.

Somehow they'd been tied in with the Beast Master Headquarters, Hosteen thought. On the Ark were samples from all of the improved species that had been used in Beast Master teams. The Ark had been built in orbit as a transport. It had been an unarmed merchant ship of a type too thin-hulled and underengined to be useful in the war. The merchant family that owned it had left it mothballed in orbit, waiting for the war to end. Some wise woman had seen a possible future and quietly convinced the High Command to cover their bets both ways. The transport had been transformed. Into its broad belly had flowed samples of genetic material from millions of Terran species. The finest laboratories had been built inside its walls. A husband and wife scientific team had been placed in charge and when all was complete, the Ark had left to work quietly in a sector devoid of inhabited planets.

Seven months later the Xiks, with whom the Terran Alliance had been fighting a desperate and savage war, had broken through the Terran defense. Now Terra orbited as a burned-out cinder. A symbol about which every planet settled by humanity had rallied. Ishan too had died before the Xiks were thrust back—and back. Until at last they were beaten.

Not that all Xiks accepted their defeat. They were a species who believed no other race was their equal in civilization, warlike abilities, or rights. Particularly the latter. To the Xiks, their rights and wishes were paramount. Over a year ago Hosteen himself had discovered that. A Xik holdout team had been secretly on Arzor, in league with several human renegades, stealing stock and shipping it off-world. More dangerous yet had been one of the near mythical Xik apers, a Xik, altered by their own surgeons to appear human, and used to destabilize governments, to cause strife and dissension amongst small populations. The holdouts, Storm believed, had been only a sideline. It was the aper who'd been important. Those enemies had died but there were still rumors of other holdout groups as well as plans some believed the Xik leaders had for a resurgence. Hosteen glanced up at the sound of footsteps.

"Logan, good to see you. How's the herd?"

His younger half-brother smiled. "The herd is fine but Dumaroy is flapping his mouth again."

"What else is new?"

"It isn't like that this time, brother. This time Dumaroy may have trouble. He says that there's something moving in the Blue. Nothing to do with the Norbies for once."

Hosteen came to attention. Dumaroy had a fixation about the natives, but he was a good rancher. He knew the land and the frawn herds that moved over it. The natives were broadly divided into two peoples. The more civilized Norbies who traded with the settlers and often worked on the ranches, and the Nitra, the wild tribes of the lands further from the settler areas. A people who lived in the old ways and intended to remain that way. Both peoples were divided into smaller clans that held their own territories.

"What does he say?"

"Frawns are dying. Along the edges of his land where it runs into desert. Just one here and there, but they're finding skeletons."

Hosteen stared at him. "Frawns do die."

"Yep," Logan agreed. "But you don't usually find a clean skeleton where there wasn't one the day before. Dumaroy says something is killing frawns and stripping them to the bone overnight. That isn't Norbies, it's something he's never met before." He grinned. "An' he says it's something he doesn't want to meet on any dark nights, either."

Hosteen nodded. "I don't know of anything that can do that here. How sure is Dumaroy that the skeletons have appeared so quickly."

"Says he wasn't sure at first. Just sort of noticed there seemed to be a couple more around than he'd seen before. But then he was camped right over at the edge of desert. He'd ridden out after some fool yearling frawn an' didn't find it. Next day he rode out after the frawn again and there it was. A man doesn't miss seeing a skeleton right under his horse's hooves. An' Dumaroy says that he had a good look at everything. The frawn was lying right across his tracks from the day before."

"Did he backtrack it?"

"He says so. Says there were signs it had run for miles right out into the edge of the Big Blue and then circled for home range again. The thing that is bothering him is that he couldn't see tracks of anything else. It must have been chased; no frawn is stupid enough to head out into waterless country just for the heck of it. But he couldn't find tracks and that upset him more than anything. You know Dumaroy."

Hosteen smiled a little. He did. He also knew the man was right. The Big Blue was the name the settlers had given to an area in which little grew, since there was no open water. It was a great area of desert bounded at the back by jagged foothills rising into mountains, equally arid. Over much of the desert and over the mountains in particular the winds and updrafts were so fierce that no air transport could survive. The few that tried over the years had all crashed.

"Yes. Dumaroy tracks well enough, but the Norbies track better. He doesn't want to call on them for help?"

Logan's answering grin was broad. "Nope, he doesn't. So he's asking for you and Surra. A comcall came in just before I left the house asking if you'd take her over there an' see what you can find."

He saw the look of surprise and sobered. "I know. If Dumaroy asks for your help then he's a lot more worried than he lets on. Will you go?"

"Yes. If Dumaroy's animals are dying, how long before whatever is causing it spreads?" Logan nodded slowly. "So, call Dumaroy. Tell him I'll be there tomorrow."

"What about the Ark. I thought they were landing a shuttle tomorrow. You wanted to talk to them about the team. They want to see you, too. They might take offense if you aren't there to meet them."

"If something new is killing frawns, that's more important. Tell them I'm sorry but I've had to ride out. I'll be back as soon as I can." He looked at Logan. "Just keep them away from Hing and her family. I don't want them doing anything until I'm there. From what the Fremlyn people say this Brion Carraldo thinks anything he wants to do is his right because he's a scientist."

Logan snorted. "They won't get near Hing. Even if they do get a look at them I'd stun the man before he laid a finger on them. Go and see about Dumaroy's trouble. I'll tell Dad where you've gone."

With that Hosteen was content. Brad Quade, his stepfather, would smooth over any ruffled scientific feathers. He had to have mates for the team, yes. But frawn ranching was what kept the planet of Arzor solvent. Frawn hides were not only beautiful, they were solidly durable. Frawn fabric was lovely, hard-wearing, water-repellent, and lightweight. Moreover, the Norbies relied on the frawn as Hosteen's own people had once relied on the buffalo. The Native Protection Agency at Spaceport would have something to say if the frawn herds were in danger, quite apart from what ranchers like Dumaroy would say and do.

He decided not to waste time. If he called in a copter he could be at Dumaroy's ranch house in hours. Surra was used to copter travel and he'd take Baku as well. He used the com to call in. Then he prepared. Brad arrived shortly before the copter touched down.

"I must go, Asizi." Storm used the Navaho word meaning respected chief. His stepfather had only become really known to Hosteen in the past couple of years, but by now a strong bond of affection had grown between them. Family was paramount to the Navaho and Storm had been raised in that tradition.

"Logan told me," Brad Quade returned thoughtfully. "Ride wary. If there *is* something out there that can kill a frawn and strip it to bones in a night, I'd rather you didn't run into it. Logan says there are no tracks?"

"None Dumaroy or his men could find. That isn't all.

Frawns are fighters. One wouldn't just roll over. Either what killed it was so terrifying the frawn ran until it dropped, or it did fight. So where were the bodies? If whatever attacked it was big, it would have left tracks. If the attackers were small, then the frawn should have killed some."

Quade's face twisted into worried lines. "It doesn't sound good, son. Watch out for Dumaroy. You know him. Ten to one he's already started to wonder if this really isn't some new Norbie trick. It's only a step from that to him making trouble with the natives."

"Not this time, I don't think. Logan says he's honestly worried and even Dumaroy can see the Norbies could be worse off than ranchers if the frawns were destroyed."

From outside came the sound of the copter landing. Hosteen was ready. Brad watched in silence as the man he thought of as his son boarded with two of his Beast team. Baku didn't like copters, she preferred to use her own wings. The eagle ruffled a little in mild protest as Storm carried her aboard. Surra flowed silently up the lowered steps to place herself in a comfortable position on the floor between the seats. She knew when hunting was afoot and was only eager to get on with it. In contact with both, Storm was aware of their emotions. Unconsciously he reached out with his mind to calm the eagle, to assure the big cat that they would hunt soon. He hardly felt the sudden lift as they ascended. He was too busy wondering: What was it that came out of the Big Blue and killed?

The copter landed at their destination; Hosteen swept his team out and kept his face impassive as Dumaroy ran up.

"Two more fresh skeletons. I've got one of the men out riding to check. Take your pick of horses and let's go."

Suddenly Storm was as eager as the big rancher to leave. He swung his arm up, issuing a mental command. The eagle soared upward to circle the ranch buildings.

"Show me the horses. Do you have travel rations ready?"

"Yeah. I need to supply a couple of the line camps on the way, so I've loaded a cart. The cat can ride when she needs to." He shrugged. "It's a fair way. We'll be riding most of the day to the first camp. After that we can night over and be there by midday."

"What about your man?"

"Mirt Lasco's kid, Jarry. He said he'd stay at the Big Blue camp. That's about an hour's ride from where he found the frawn skeletons."

Storm glanced up sharply. "That's a risk."

"What?" Dumaroy snorted. "Nah. No man's ever been hurt or nothing. An' the Norbies'd be kicking up a fuss if any of them'd been killed. I reckon it's safe enough. Anyway, you can't tell young Lasco nothing. I said he should come in to the trail camp an' he reckoned he'd just have to ride all the way back again."

"His choice," Storm said shortly. He was worried but there was nothing he could do about it now. "Where are the horses."

He was led to a small corral where several ponies waited. Even with the urgency Storm halted a few seconds to look them over. They must be some of the mounts Put Larkin had sold after culling. They were good, but not as good as that herd of Put was going to be in several more generations. This bunch hadn't the Astran duocorn blood Larkin was adding these days. Nice animals, though. He selected a gray with a black mane and tail, a little larger than the others. Dumaroy handed over a bridle, then a saddle with filled saddlebags attached.

"Canteen?"

The rancher nodded. "Here. Two, an' water purification tablets just in case. Never go far without them." Storm had the horse ready in minutes and waited. Dumaroy swung up and led off. Behind him rolled the ranch cart drawn by a small but strong mare. Surra had leapt up to lie comfortably atop the load. Storm followed.

They rode in silence most of the day and it was close to dusk before the trail camp came in sight. It was a sturdy log building, plain and square, half tucked into the rise of a small hill. Inside there was a fresher, a com caller, and a stable connected deeper into the hillside. With the earth above, the stable would stay cool through even the hotter days. They ran their mounts into the waiting stalls, provided food and water, then returned to the main cabin to stow most of the supplies from the cart.

Baku came to Storm's mental call. She sideslipped in to land on his shoulder, accepting the offered chunk of raw meat. He allowed her to move to the branch he'd placed across a cabin corner. She'd be fine. Surra was settled on a bunk and Storm brought her water. She drank eagerly, then ate before falling asleep, sprawled along the soft bedding. Dumaroy looked as if he'd have said something, glanced at Storm, and kept it unsaid.

They were moving again at first light. This time at Storm's insistence they moved more slowly. Surra ranged out at first ahead, then on either side of them. A thread of interest from her caught Storm's attention. He sent Baku in that direction. The picture he received had him pulling up the gray pony hastily.

"Dumaroy! I thought you said there's been no frawn skeletons found this far into the good lands?"

"That's right. Why?"

Without answer Storm sent his pony trotting in the direction Surra had gone. They rounded a clump of brush and boulders to find her circling a skeleton. Baku floated lazily above. Dumaroy cursed savagely.

"Another one gone. This is costing me."

Storm turned to look at him. "There's more." He nudged the pony along a frawn track and into a small gully. At the end of it lay a jumble of new-stripped bones. At least six frawns, maybe seven. Surra had trotted ahead and reached over to sniff the skeletons. She wrinkled her face in an expression of disgust and spat. Above Baku ranged out further. Surra sat waiting as Storm dropped lightly from the gray and checked the bones.

"Fresh." He drifted around, widening his path in a spiral. He paused and looked again. "Rig, see what you make of this."

The big man plodded over to search the ground where Storm pointed. He blinked. "Dunno. It sorta looks as if it rained here, doesn't it." He considered the tiny, almost invisible marks. "I can only see them when I look from the right angle. You reckon whatever made them may have had something to do with the frawns dying?"

"I don't know, but it's worth remembering."

Dumaroy nodded. "Yeah. An' there's something else. Guess I should have made that kid come in to the trail camp no matter what he said. These here frawns are well outside of the Big Blue. Fact is, they're closer in than where the kid woulda camped."

Storm gave the signal for Baku to scout. Surra obeyed as well, all business now that she knew there was danger. Storm pushed his mount into a canter. "We're either in time or too late. Nothing we can do but ride."

Chapter Two

Tani was angry. It was an insult to the Ark and to her uncle, she thought. That Beast Master had said he'd meet the shuttle when it arrived. Instead here was some man telling them Storm had decided to go off into the desert. He'd given them a long tale about the local animals dying and this Hosteen having taken two of his team to look for the cause. It was *rude*, that was what it was. She was surprised Uncle Brion didn't say something about it. Instead he was chatting about conditions here just as if it were nothing.

She slipped away, back to the shuttle. Mandy would like to be outside. Tani hauled out the perch the paraowl used and set it solidly into the earth beside the ramp. With that ready she marched inside to return, carrying the big bird. Mandy hopped up happily onto her perch, checked that the food and water containers were full, and stared about. The Azoran man with Uncle Brion came over to admire her.

"She's beautiful. An Ishan paraowl, isn't she?"

Tani softened toward him. Mandy *was* beautiful. "Yes, they were considering using them as special messengers for the Beast Masters."

He nodded. "I thought she must be augmented.

Paraowls aren't usually happy out in the daylight."

Tani was happy to show off her friend. "Mandy enjoys the daylight. And she can carry really long verbal messages without making mistakes. That's why the first settlers on Ishan called them paraowls. It's short for parrot owls, because they are such good mimics and because they only flew at night. The slang name for them was 'ghosts.' " She grinned up at him. "That's because they were completely white and flew without making a sound."

He smiled back. "But your Mandy isn't white."

"No." Tani stroked the paraowl who gave her small purring cry. The feathers were white, overlaid by a stippling of fawn shading into quite a dark brown. "Mandy's camouflaged. If she sits on almost anything without moving you can't see her. A few of them were born like that. On Ishan the other wild ones usually killed them because they were different. They showed up too much against the snow. We incorporated the gene for it, so now they're all like this. Mandy still flies without any noise, though. Give her chest a scratch, she loves that."

Brad Quade cautiously offered his hand to the bird. That was one of the most powerful beaks he'd ever seen. Mandy nibbled his fingers gently as he petted her. He could see that the feather pattern was such that looking directly at it left his eyes feeling blurred. He sighed. "She is lovely. I hope you have plenty of material. It would be a shame for her kind to die out."

Tani laughed. "We have tons. Well, a lot. And they aren't going to die out. There's a big demand for them." Brad raised his eyebrows in query. "A year before the Xiks destroyed Ishan a shipload of scientists from there went to look over DuIshan. That's the desert planet a few parsecs from Ishan. They came back to say it was uninhabited, people could live there, and there were quite a few things that could make it commercial."

She giggled a little. "Ishan had three shiploads of settlers on the way almost before the scientists had finished giving their report. Another three went out the week before the Xiks hit Ishan. Since then DuIshan has started ranches and they're using the paraowls as comcallers where they don't have the money. Or where a ranch hand is on the move reporting in each evening."

Her eyes laughed up at Brad. "It's like your horses here. Self-replicating, cheap fuel, and don't require off-world parts to fix when they break down."

From the corner of her eye she noticed Uncle Brion nodding. Many of the paraowls had been bred and sold from the Ark's laboratories. The darker variety was now predominant. DuIshan, or the second Ishan, had a climate similar to Arzor. DuIshan ranched sern, large dimwitted birds like Terran ostriches, which were native to the planet. To guard them they used coyotes, again bred from Beast Master experiments. That reminded her. She concentrated a moment and saw sharp-eared heads appear at the top of the ramp. Brad Quade saw them almost as quickly.

"Coyote?"

Tani called them silently. They trotted down to stand beside her as she introduced them. "This is Minou and Ferarre." There was pride in her voice, as was right, Quade reflected. They were handsome animals. Both had fur brindled in a light and dark gray. They'd vanish like the paraowl the minute they stayed still. The gaze of two sets of golden eyes rose to meet his, the light of more intelligence than even the coyote's age-old wisdom shining up at him. He could see why they'd be a real advantage on DuIshan. He admired them openly and with honesty, watching Tani's face glow with pleasure.

She'd been clearly hostile when Storm wasn't here to meet her uncle. Perhaps she'd felt the man had been insulted. But it was more than that. There'd been a tiny note of contempt any time she mentioned Brad's stepson. He studied her unobtrusively. Good bones. She wasn't pretty but in later life she'd be elegant. Her thick black hair was tied back in a long tail that fell across one shoulder. He couldn't make up his mind what color her eyes were. Sometimes they looked green, other times a cooler gray. She'd be about eighteen or nineteen, seven or eight years younger than the twenty-six-year-old Hosteen. The relatives were Irish but Tani looked different.

From comments her uncle had made, he and his wife had mostly raised the girl. That was a worry. Children took their opinions from their family. If the Ark's leading scientists were antagonistic to Beast Masters, then Storm's hope of mates for his animals might be in vain. That Fremlyn affair hadn't sounded good. He chatted on until he believed he'd smoothed over any anger at his son's absence. Storm should be back tomorrow. Surely this business at Dumaroy's couldn't be too serious. He bit back a sigh. In his experience things were often even worse than you'd expected. Anyhow, one should plan for that. He hoped Storm was doing so.

•   •   •

Storm hoped his planning for dangers would be sufficient, too. Baku was soaring, shifting out in a search spiral further and further. Storm stayed in contact. Surra, too, was moving, slipping quietly along a trail she was following, her face wrinkled in disgust at the—to her—rank stench of it. Dumaroy sat his mount restlessly as he watched. The rancher wanted to be up and doing something, and he was worried about young Lasco. Dumaroy's trouble was that he tended not to think before acting. Storm saw that the man's fidgets were getting worse. If they didn't move soon Dumaroy would start off half-cocked and without him.

"Whatever's doing this to the frawns may not leave many footprints, but it leaves a trail Surra can track."

Dumaroy lowered his head like an angry frawn bull. "It's takin' too much time. I reckon we should check out the kid before we run too far down any trails."

To his surprise Storm agreed. "I think so. Which is the quickest way there?"

"Down that canyon and across the mesa at the far end of it. The temporary camp should be a few miles beyond if that dumb kid's stayed where he said he would." The voice was almost casual but Storm wasn't fooled. Dumaroy was genuinely worried.

Without speaking, he sent his horse down the sloping canyon side. The rancher followed, pushing his mount to move into the lead. Gradually their speed increased until both were riding at a slow canter. The harness mare shifted to the same pace to stay with them, the cart bouncing over the ground. Surra squalled her indignation, jumping down to run on her own four feet, after one rough jolt.

Once her breed had been a smaller big-pawed big-eared cat that ranged desert wastes. Scientists had taken them and produced something that was still sand yellow, with the fox-like ears and muzzle. But now the breed was three times as large, with broad feet that kept them from sinking in soft ground. They retained the keen hearing that made them so effective as hunters, and in the Beast teams it had become an asset in war. One trait had remained completely untouched. They still did not like sustained effort. Surra would come on after them at her own pace. He reached out to reassure her, soothing her anger.

Follow, then, he mind-sent her. She dropped back, shifting to her own preferred speed. She'd catch up when they slowed or halted.

It was plain Dumaroy had no intention of stopping until they reached the line camp. He was holding his mount to a canter still, but every sign was that if he found what he feared he might run crazy after anything he could blame. Storm had better have a trail to point the man down when that happened.

Trouble, always trouble. Storm had hoped this season, once the work was up to date, to take time off and investigate further the sealed caves deep into one side of the far mountains across an arm of the desert. Some other race, not native to Arzor, had either carved out or expanded and made use of caves they'd found there. To both the Norbies and the Nitra the area was sacred. They had not created the caves and to them the area was a place from which to stay away. The cave's creators had not interacted with the natives, but they'd left an indelible impression of power.

Storm had been into the caves twice. By accident the first

time and for sanctuary. The second time Storm had gone in following the lost son of a rich off-worlder. The cave system was huge, miles of tunnels and vast high-ceilinged caves. There were a few Forerunner artifacts to be found there, but on Arzor there was little money available to be spent on investigating such things. Nor would the natives appreciate humans digging into the places they held taboo.

He linked with Baku as he rode. Nothing. Trotting far behind now, Surra too could report no scent she did not know. He linked tighter to the eagle, sending her ahead to where the camp should be. His body relaxed, balanced automatically in the saddle. His mount would follow the other. The link tightened further. Now he could see fuzzily in the shades of gray that was full link with the team's eyes in the sky.

There! The camp. No sign of horse or rider, and the door was shut. He bit back a sigh before sending Baku swinging out again. He could see no tracks, but Surra could follow the trail. He dropped out of the tight linkage with Baku and reached for her. As soon as she came to the camp she should follow the bad-smelling tracks if any were there. She spat in disgust, but she'd do as he wanted. Now to slow Dumaroy if possible. The harness mare was starting to fall behind.

"Rig!" There was a snap in the voice, which demanded attention.

"What?"

"I think we should leave the mare back here. Then we circle the camp. Come in from the Big Blue side. That way if the enemy is still around we could have them cornered against the desert."

"What about Jarry?" The voice was harsh with strain but the rancher's horse had slowed.

"If he's dead and they're gone, hurrying won't help. If he's dead and they're still there, better we try to ambush them. Find out who or what they are. If he's still alive we're more likely to save him if we aren't known to be around." Storm was relying on Dumaroy's background. The man was a hothead but he'd been a good soldier and served his time against the Xiks. Putting the plans on a war footing reminded the rancher of that.

It worked. Ahead of Storm, Dumaroy pulled his horse to a walk. He dropped to the ground and tethered the sweating harness horse. "If we circle from here we can have cover all the way. We can come in direct from the desert side. Temporary camp's an abandoned Djimbut burrow. We shored up the sides an' roof, split the area in half an' put a door in an' a pair of bunks. The open half's for the horses. That's it, pretty basic, but it's only used for the night now an' again. We leave stores an' spare bedding in a steel soldier's trunk at the back."

"There's cover all the way in from the Big Blue side?".

"There is. I lead." The last was a flat statement. Storm nodded in agreement.

"Your territory."

Dumaroy remounted and loosed his reins, setting the pony into a faster walk as they circled. Behind them Surra was closing fast, cutting toward the camp across the circle the riders were making. Unobtrusively Storm slowed them again. The dune cat reached camp and he felt the shock of her emotion as she struck along the trail she could scent. She would keep clear of the incoming riders, too. They broke through the screen of brush and Dumaroy gave a hoarse cry.

"Hello the camp! Jarry? You there?"

Storm moved out wide of the man. He allowed his pony to drift forward, watching the area all the while. But he could slow the rancher no longer. In a flurry of sand the man was heading for the hut. Storm received quick impressions from the hunting pair. Baku had the dune cat in sight and was ranging ahead. Surra was trailing with caution but swiftly. Neither had seen or scented danger, but they were old campaigners and stayed wary. By the doorway Dumaroy halted. He bent down, pulling the door open to look inside, then reined back his pony hard with another cry.

Storm walked up slowly. He could guess what the man had found and he was right. Two jumbled skeletons lay inside the cool shelter. Of Jarry only bones remained. The horse too was only bones, but beside him the saddle was untouched on the saddle peg. Jarry's hat, boots, and belt lay undamaged by the bunk. Storm moved past the stricken rancher and examined the bunk. He looked up sharply.

"Dumaroy, check the trunk, did Jarry use the blankets?"

The rancher shook his head without moving. "Nope. The boy had his own sleep sack. Pretty good one his ma made him. Padded an' with a liner she could take out an' wash."

"Then where is it?"

The big man stared vaguely around. "I dunno." His grief and puzzlement were about to flare into fury. "Why's it important?"

Storm bent to pick up a tiny shred of material. "Look. Frawn fabric. Was Lasco's sleep sack made of that?"

"Yeah, so what?"

Storm was examining the bunk structure itself. He straightened slowly. "Look here, Dumaroy. This wood's been damaged." He saw the rancher was about to explode and held up a hand. "Listen. I think this has something to do with whatever killed the boy. There's shreds of the sleep sack on the floor. The wood across the center of the bunk looks almost as if someone took a drill to it." He paused. "Or some mighty funny teeth."

The rancher swore savagely. "What?"

"See for yourself. Listen. Lasco died here but there's no blood. If he died in his bunk, what would blood soak into?"

Dumaroy stared at him, his face suddenly blank. "The sleep sack, the middle of the bunk, but that's . . ."

"What's missing or damaged," Storm finished.

"You think whatever killed Jarry went on to eat anything with blood on it." He bent to examine the scored wood again. "Good teeth. Hope they choke on the splinters." As Storm had expected, the rancher's mood was turning to rage. "I'm gonna get whoever it was an' when I do . . ."

Storm interrupted. "Surra has their trail. What say we follow it. At least get some idea of the direction they went."

"What are we waiting for?" Dumaroy was outside and back on his horse in seconds. Then, as he reined the animal into a turn he gaped. "Storm?" His voice had gone hoarse with horror. "Storm, the kid wasn't stupid. He'd shut the doors. They aren't wrecked. How'd they get to him?"

"Underneath." The answer was quiet.

"But . . ."

"Think about it. Something too light to leave real tracks.

What they do leave is a million tiny marks you can barely see even with the light on them. They get into a hut through a shut door and don't wake the man inside. I figure a lot of somethings, light, small, fast, and likely cannibal."

Dumaroy looked sick. "Cannibal?"

"We never find any of their bodies. I suspect they eat their own dead before they leave."

The rancher jerked upright in his saddle. "I saw a vid once. Made on Terra. Some wildlife program about soldier ants. You think it was something like that?"

"Maybe. It fits." The other was shaking his head. "I know there isn't anything like that on Arzor—that we know about. But how long have we been here?" He knew the answer, as did Dumaroy. It had been almost one hundred and thirty years since the first trio of ships had set humans down on Arzor. Six generations. In that time they'd barely scratched the surface of what they could learn of the planet.

The natives had evolved here, born and bred to live in the vast semidesert lands. Tribes and the clans held large territories each. The land gave little food unless there was a wide territory in which to hunt. With the coming of humans had come horses as well, and both Norbies and Nitra had taken to those like a thirsty frawn to clean water. Settlers herded frawns in ranches, Norbies bought, traded, and occasionally stole mounts, their lives changing in consequence.

Dumaroy knew Arzor's history as well as any settler, that is to say, the basics as humans knew them, which wasn't a lot. He made no direct answer, turning his mount's head toward the desert.

"If we're gonna trail them, let's get going." He spoke

again after several miles. "Maybe they do come from here. Maybe they was in those sealed caves. Maybe we should blast the whole lot open an' clean them all out."

Storm said nothing. It was a possibility, and even if it were true it would be quite a while before Dumaroy was in a position to try. But he considered the idea. They had found one cave that contained over a hundred plots of plants native to very many worlds. Another where it seemed there had been some sort of interworlds zoo.

Perhaps there had also been a collection for insects or whatever stood in for them on some worlds. If a cave like that had been breached through accident or design, what could now be breeding and growing free unknown to natives or humans on Arzor? He'd talk to the Ark scientists when he returned. They might have ideas that could be useful. They could stop at the camp again on the way back. Maybe there'd be DNA left on the shreds of material or on the scored bunk slats, which would give the scientists something to work on.

Dumaroy was keeping his mount to a fast walk. But Surra had a good start. With luck it would be dark before they caught up to her. Dark. The thought was worrying. These things preferred to hunt at night. They seemed to be able to run down a frawn. That meant that even if they weren't very fast they could keep going. Out in the Big Blue there were no water holes. They had only their canteens for themselves and the beasts. Storm made up his mind.

Ahead Surra raced down the trail as fast as she could for several more miles. At the edge of a wide deep gully she halted, then she moved to shade and lay down. Dumaroy nudged his mount to move faster and Storm allowed it. They came up with the dune cat an hour later.

"Why's she waiting?"

"I told her to, Dumaroy. We knew the direction they're taking. If we go deeper in we could get trapped. Those things hunt at night. You want to wake up and find them all over you?"

The rancher shuddered. "Nope. Guess we go back. I gotta tell Mirt about his boy, too, an' see the kid's properly buried. All right, Storm. We go back, but this ain't the last of it."

Storm shook his head slowly. "No," he said softly. "I'm afraid it isn't. There was something else you didn't see, Rig. Surra found a couple more skeletons on the way here. I had her scout around. I can't be sure, but it looks as if those things, whatever they are, know animals circle to get back to familiar territory when they're chased."

Dumaroy looked at him with an odd kind of dread in his eyes. He waited.

"Surra found where the things split up. One lot kept following. The other half of them waited and the frawn ran right into them. I won't say they're intelligent, Dumaroy. It could be just instinct. But that trick is dangerous either way. That's why I wanted to turn back now."

"We don't circle like that," the rancher objected.

"Don't we? We'd run straight for home. Do you want to land them there?" Storm asked.

"Hell, no!" He glanced over. "Guess I'm out of my depth in this one. I like something I can fight, straight up." His face twisted in bitter humor. "I can't blame this on the Norbies. For once the goats are out of it."

"Not out of it, Dumaroy. They could be in more danger

than us humans. Let's just get back and make war talk. Those scientists from the shuttle may have a better idea of how to deal with this."

They kept to a steady walk the remainder of the day. By nightfall they had collected the mare and cart and were past the camp where Jarry's bones lay on the gnawed bunk. Storm had shreds of the sleep sack, and a broken slat from the bunk in his saddlebags. They made camp in a cave large enough to take them all, and in an unbroken half circle around the opening Storm made a fire. The beasts slept peacefully, but both men only dozed lightly and in turns. They kept the fire burning until dawn. Then they let it die. In the soft lavender half-light nothing stirred.

Chapter Three

Quade had strolled off, still talking to Uncle Brion. Tani stayed, making a fuss over the coyotes and stroking Mandy. She teased the big bird with a length of grass stem, tickling her chest feathers as Mandy attempted to grab the stem. The bird was enjoying the game.

"I've been neglecting you lately," Tani told her. "I know Marten took good care of you while I was so busy building more of your breed for DuIshan, but it isn't the same. I missed you and it's a lovely afternoon to be outside."

She tickled Mandy's breast feathers and gasped as the bird commented. True, the words had been in another language, but Tani had been around enough to know the meaning even though that wasn't a tongue she spoke. Marten had, however, and she knew how bitter he'd been. Maybe she was jumping to conclusions, though. An hour later she knew she wasn't. Marten had known he wouldn't be continuing with them long before the Ark left Fremlyn orbit. She'd thought it kind of him to volunteer to look after her team while she was so busy.

He didn't appear to have done any harm to Minou or Ferarre, but he'd taught Mandy a number of trigger words. Then to each he'd added a phrase or sentence either in the gutter argot of a world or in one-speech, where it was translatable. If Mandy heard the trigger word she would utter the comment.

He'd chosen common words, such as morning, afternoon, evening, pleasant day, and probably others Tani hadn't yet discovered. The one Mandy would say in reply to the word "afternoon" was a suggestion that the hearers should go and perform some very specific sexual acts on themselves and each other. The one for "evening" was so obscene that Tani blushed for her bird. The response to "morning" was a cheerful request to insert a digit in a difficult place and depart the immediate area. That one was in the Galactic one-speech.

Tani groaned. Mandy could be retrained but it would take time. If only she'd heard this earlier. But she'd been so busy even on the voyage that she'd spent less time than usual just hanging out talking to Mandy. Her aunt and uncle greeted her with the old Irish phrases. And on a ship using the twenty-four-hour clock and lit all of that time in the main rooms, few people used the terms for times of day. They tended instead to list specific hours. This little surprise had been intended to arrive once they'd landed and talked to locals. Tani said a few words the paraowl hadn't used. If she had that Marten here now she'd teach him something involving boiling oil or anthills.

She left Mandy where she was. It wasn't her fault and it wasn't fair to make the poor sweet stay inside. Tani would just have to remember to warn Uncle Brion about talking to visitors in front of the bird until Tani had made time to retrain her. She sighed. And that Beast Master still hadn't shown up. She just knew Uncle Brion would want her to provide him with meerkats. More animals he could use up and throw away. His stepfather, or whatever Mr. Quade was, had said the male meerkat had been killed accidentally.

Tani knew what that meant. It was Beast Master code for "I took a chance and one of the team died instead of me." Her mother had taught her all about it. Of course her mother had been a bit strange on the subject after Tani's father, Bright Sky, was killed. At times she'd left her small daughter quite confused. Tani had the Beast Master gifts, but Beast Masters were bad. Did that make her bad? she'd asked her mother. Alisha had sighed quietly. Having the gift was fine, she'd told her child. It was the training to use the gifts for war that was wrong.

Tani had seen records. There'd been less than a hundred Beast Masters and teams ever trained. Most of those got themselves killed during the last Xik push against Terra, doing crazy things. It was bad enough for humans to do that, but they had no right to make animals march into certain death with them.

Now that the war was over they could all settle down to sharing life again. Animal teams had worked well with Survey as first-in scouts, and with settlers opening up new worlds like DuIshan. She stroked Mandy and smiled. It was nice to think of the paraowls and coyotes on DuIshan. It was their kind of world and the settlers cherished their assistance. She tickled the paraowl's breast feathers, and the powerful beak that could have bitten off a finger as easily as Tani crunched a carrot reached down to nibble her hand affectionately.

The girl laughed. "I suppose you'd like a lastree nut?" The paraowl gave an affirmative croon. "Hold on. I'll find you one." She left Mandy waiting hopefully and went into the shuttle. There'd been a few of the nuts stored in the supply room there, she was sure. There were and she emerged holding two. With a happy squeak Mandy accepted the first and began to strip the steel-hard husk, a claw revolving it as she worked. Tani leaned against the perch. Mandy was luckier than she knew. Lastrees had been planted in groves on DuIshan as well, which was fortunate, since their original home was no more.

She glanced up. Almost midday. She'd leave Mandy out here to enjoy the sun. No one would be by until evening and she'd have retrieved bird and perch by then. It sounded as if Uncle Brion was planning to make the Quade ranch their planet headquarters for a while. She'd like that and so would the team. The ranch had horses. It had been almost a year since she'd ridden. Most of the settler planets used horses. They didn't have unobtainable expensive parts to break down. Often other worlds didn't have suitable items that could be used for fuels. Horses replaced themselves and they saw to their own fuel, as she'd said to the Arzoran. Sometimes it took a scientist to tweak horse genes so that the animals were able to live on native grasses, but mostly that could be done easily. According to the records, Arzoran grass was edible by horses without alteration, and horses loved the wide empty lands there. Tani had ridden a lot on DuIshan; it would be fun to ride again on Arzor.

On the Dumaroy ranch Storm was riding, but not for pleasure. He was weary and dusty, and the harness mare was lagging again. It was blindingly hot and Surra was unhappy about it. They reached the Dumaroy ranch house and the big cat collapsed in the shade. Storm brought her water while Dumaroy was at the comcaller. Storm was watering Baku when the rancher reappeared.

"They're sending a copter. Kelson is coming to talk to us both personally."

Storm nodded. Kelson was the right man. He held a loose mandate of liaison between ranchers, Native Protection, and Peace Office these days. It also looked more and more likely that his idea of a Ranger Force to patrol and check the wilder lands was going to be allowed. In which case Storm's younger half-brother, Logan, could be involved. That might keep the boy from infuriating their father so often.

"When?"

"Half an hour, he said. We're to wait."

Storm grunted. He'd spent the ride back thinking hard and he didn't like some of the conclusions. The wild tribes lived out in the Blue. If these whatever-they-were started killing the Nitra's animals or even the Nitra, the wild tribes would be on the move. With nowhere else to go but onto Norbie lands, that would start more trouble than any human had seen in the six generations since landing. The Norbie were the more civilized tribes—but they were fighters. They lived for it, with a regular point system for the hunters of dangerous game—and for warriors.

Squeezed by Nitra, the Norbie clans could start pressing into rancher-staked lands. Dumaroy and some of his kind would be the first to howl. They'd spent a lifetime blaming the Norbies for everything from missing horses to Yoris lizard attacks. Dumaroy had been proved wrong so often, few but those of like-minded listened anymore. Others would start listening again fast enough if the tribes moved in on their ranches. Storm could see big trouble coming. He'd like to get to that shuttle, talk to the scientists. Apart from any suggestions on the frawn killer, he hoped they might provide mates for the team. In the distance he could hear the copter droning in. He stood to walk to where it would land.

"Kelson!" Storm shouted his acknowledgement over the noise of the copter.

"Good to see you, Storm."

Dumaroy pushed in angrily. "Kelson! You gotta do something about this. There's something out there in the Blue eats frawns." He choked. "And Mirt's kid—he's lying out there, just bones." His voice went hoarse. "How'm I gonna tell Mirt? You gotta do something!"

"I plan to," the liaison man said quietly. "Just as soon as I have some idea of what that is. Right now I want you to come with me to the camp. We'll pick up what's left of Jarry and you can take him back for Doc Rendel. She may be able to tell us something quickly. Storm, I want to talk to you but not now. I'll swing by the Quade ranch in the morning."

Dumaroy was already in the copter waiting impatiently. He leaned out as Storm spoke. "Rig, can I borrow the cart. Surra's all in?"

"Yeah, yeah. Go ahead. She did good." He jerked back as the copter's engine started to growl. Kelson called to Storm from his seat in the copter.

"Forget the cart. There's another copter on the way to collect me. This one will take Jarry's body and Dumaroy straight in to Doc. It'll leave me at the cabin to have a look around. I'll be there in a few hours so the new one can stop off here and take you and the animals back to the ranch first, before it picks me up. I'll tell them to do that while we're on the way."

Storm's thanks were lost in the noise as the copter lifted. Kelson had arrived in one of the old slow copters. The incoming one would be one of the newer, faster type. Maybe the pilot would drop them at the Basin ranch rather than Storm's own staked lands. He could leave Surra to rest and ride in to the spot where the Ark's shuttle had landed. If he moved fast he could be there by late afternoon. The pilot was willing but at the Basin Brad Quade wanted to discuss all Storm could tell him.

At last he sat back. "I hate to say it, son. But you're right. If this thing spreads into Nitra territory they'll try moving away from it. That'll start real trouble with the Norbie tribes. If they start getting squeezed, some hothead will begin to look at the ranches. The real problem is that we hold our lands by treaty. The Patrol could argue that the original inhabitants have a better right to the land if it's a matter of survival."

"Then it's a pity we didn't have a Patrol in the eighteen hundreds," Storm said acidly, remembering ancient Navaho grievances.

Brad smiled reluctantly. He was part Cheyenne himself. "I know." He glanced at the large ornamental chrono on the wall. "Who knows about this so far?"

"Not too many, but one of them's Dumaroy."

"Who's probably on the comcaller right now telling the whole world," Brad said in exasperation.

Storm shook his head. "He's out with Kelson collecting the body. Kelson will make sure Dumaroy keeps his mouth shut. For a while, at least."

"Hummm. Yes. Rig made quite a fool of himself over that Xik holdout business. Then he cried wolf over the tribes moving last year."

"Kelson will remind him of that. Besides, Dumaroy said to me that he couldn't blame the Norbies for this, and I think he meant it."

"I'm sure he did," Quade nodded. "Until he realizes his ranch could be in danger. Bister led him by the nose during that holdout trouble. Dumaroy's never thought ahead for more than two minutes. He'll make a bad situation worse and wonder how it happened."

Storm grinned savagely. "Except that Bister isn't around anymore." He stood and stretched. "Nothing we can do right now. Kelson will muzzle Dumaroy for a while. I'll take a horse in the morning and go into the Port, maybe talk to those scientists. There's something strange about how those things kill. I can't make out how they're doing it. Jarry, I can understand, they had him and the horse trapped in the cabin. But how do they kill frawns?"

Brad nodded thoughtfully. "Soldier ants kill animals that can't move for some reason. They don't hunt them down. If you're right about the tracks Surra followed, those creatures hunted almost like a dog pack. Talk to the scientists about that too."

"I will. Where's Logan?"

"Hunting with Gorgol and the Shosonna clan again. He'll be back day after tomorrow. I'll tell him about this then."

●　　　　●　　　　●

Storm slept poorly. He kept seeing that pathetic heap of bones and wondering what the boy's last minutes had been like. By first light he was riding away. The ranchers almost always used horses on Arzor; fuel for vehicles was imported and very expensive. As his mount plodded down the last slope, Storm saw the port and the Ark's shuttle ahead. He felt on edge still.

Tani, too, had slept badly. Jarro had criticized her work on the meerkats. Well, not on them so much as the way she'd selected the genes to combine. Uncle Brion had said she should put the dice away. She'd meant to, but with worrying about Mandy she'd forgotten. Jarro had walked in without knocking, stood behind her and seen what she was doing. He'd been pompously unpleasant. He'd implied she only had this job because she was niece to the Ark's departmental heads. It wasn't true. Uncle Brion did run the administration and genetic supply and Aunt Kady was head of research, but Tani did good work. She had preliminary qualifications and had a lot of practice.

Anyhow, it wasn't as if there were dozens of people on the Ark. There were fewer than twenty and they were always shorthanded now that Marten had gone. Brion and Kady were her only living relatives; it was logical she live and work on the Ark. She paid her way.

Jarro was a patronizing pig who'd never done anything original or interesting in his whole life. Uncle Brion had said she should keep the dice out of sight, but when a person made a habit of sneaking up and never knocking it wasn't easy. Tani dressed and stamped out of her cabin. She'd put Mandy's perch out and spent time with her team. That would make her feel better.

She did so and the delight the paraowl displayed made it worthwhile. As Mandy peeled a lastree nut, Tani called the coyotes. She'd take them for a walk away from the ship. Not far, just so they could play with a ball and relax for an hour. But although she enjoyed the game something niggled at her. She really should go back to work before Jarro managed to walk past and sneer about kids wasting time. She was still feeling unusually ruffled as she rounded the shuttle's side to find a man walking toward the ramp.

Storm had left his horse at the edge of the port's plascrete apron. He could see the shuttle but had no idea Tani was close by. The port's bustle blanketed her steps and she was hidden by the shuttle as she approached.

He did see the paraowl. He slowed to look. He'd seen them once or twice at Beast Master training stations. This one was a beautiful specimen.

He approached it, speaking softly. The bird crooned a reply. Behind him Tani gasped. He had no right to talk to her bird. The way Mandy was responding indicated this could be the Beast Master. The prejudices taught her by her mother surfaced. Without thinking she snapped at him furiously.

"What are you doing? Leave Mandy alone."

Storm spun. It had been years since he'd been surprised like that, and his voice was cold with abrupt embarrassment. "I was doing nothing. I wished to speak to someone from the Ark. If you would tell me where I can find them this morning . . ."

Mandy took her cue, cutting in to deliver her order with

disastrous clarity. Storm listened to the words openmouthed. It was too much coming on top of the previous day's tension and a night of little sleep. He rarely laughed aloud, but this time he was unable to help himself—or to stop. It was the result of stress, but Tani had no way of knowing that. In seething silence she removed Mandy from her perch, stamped up the ramp, and paused at the top.

"I'll tell someone you're here."

It didn't help that the first person she saw was Jarro. Then an idea came to her. He didn't like settlers. He said they were uncouth and ignorant. She'd teach that man to laugh at her and Mandy. She smiled politely at the pompous young scientist.

"Jarro, there's a settler wanting to see someone. I suppose he doesn't know to make an appointment. But he's a bit insistent." She saw Jarro draw himself up. "I'm sure he thinks whatever it is must be important and I certainly can't speak for the Ark. Maybe you can talk to him."

She watched Jarro as he headed for the ramp. That would fix the man. Jarro would be his stuffed-shirt self. The settler wouldn't get anywhere near Uncle Brion or Aunt Kady and he could just go away and laugh at someone else. She left the paraowl on the perch in her cabin and went back to collect the larger outside perch by the ramp. Jarro *had* managed to wipe the smile off the man's face. She lifted the perch free just as he turned and walked away. Jarro smirked after him.

"Very sensible of you to have me speak to him, Tani. Imagine. That man expected us to produce mates for his team. He said he was worried over his meerkat. She lost her mate and it distresses him."

"He *is* a Beast Master." Tani felt triumphant.

"So he claimed," Jarro sneered. "He said he should speak to your aunt or uncle. He called them our 'Leaders.' Said there was some kind of unspecified danger here. Some rural rumor, I gathered. I told him they were too busy to listen to idle gossip. No manners, these settlers. He just walked away."

Jarro followed suit, departing up the ramp to leave Tani looking after the figure in the distance. She felt slightly guilty; perhaps she shouldn't have sicced Jarro onto him. But he shouldn't have laughed, either. She comforted her conscience with the thought that if he really wanted to say something important, he'd be back.

Right now Storm didn't care if he never saw the Ark or scientists again. He knew Jarro's kind. The sort of person who believed his own work so important, and himself so important for doing it, that no one else was an equal unless they were in the same business. He slowed his steps as he remembered. There'd been that technician in the sealed caves. He'd almost started a war just to prove how great he was. Storm knew better even if genetech Jarro didn't. Brad had found the Ark people pleasant. Storm could return and ask his stepfather to speak to them.

He recalled the paraowl's comment and the horrified embarrassment on the girl's face. Involuntarily he started to chuckle again. No wonder she'd been furious. Who could have taught the bird that sort of language? Although she'd approached him as an enemy in the first place, he'd seen the way she'd looked at him, as if she guessed he was a Beast Master and thought that Beast Masters were somehow bad. As if she were afraid he'd hurt her paraowl in some way.

He reached the ranch just as Logan returned. While he greeted his half-brother, then busied himself in admiring Logan's hunting trophies as Logan cared for his weary pony, Storm calmed. He walked inside with Logan to find their father waiting.

"How did you get on at the Ark?"

"Not well. I didn't see the Carraldos, only some tech who said they were too busy. Oh, and a girl."

"That would be their niece. She had her paraowl outside when I was there."

"They were still there," Storm said, his lips twitching.

Logan grinned at him. "Share the joke, brother?"

"Well . . ."

Even Brad laughed as the tale ended. Then he sobered. "I'll talk to Carraldo again. I think he might be sympathetic if I can take the ecology unit studies showing meerkats would fit into the niche where the rinces used to be. Having the meerkats breeding wouldn't upset Azoran ecology. I had the impression he was wavering on mates for Baku and Surra as well. But this Dumaroy trouble is more important. You didn't leave the samples?"

Storm was frustrated and angry. "I tried to explain about them. The man I spoke to made it clear he thought I was some backwoods idiot jumping at shadows. I asked him to take them and he just said they were all busy."

Brad looked grave. "I'll go there early tomorrow morning. Kelson is arriving here at first light. I'll com him now for those ecology reports. He can take me onto the shuttle and with him there maybe we can get them to take it seriously."

Logan glanced up. "Wrong tack, Dad. Think about it. They don't care about your problems. But what are they most interested in?"

"Genetic materials!" Storm snapped. "And keeping their heads in the sand."

"Sure, so you get their heads up by hinting this trouble might be some kind of animal unknown to Terran science. New genetic material."

"On the way back I was thinking about the sealed caves," Storm said slowly. "There was one for plants and one for animals. There could have been one for insects."

"So. Say that. Get them involved."

On the other side of the table Brad smiled to himself. At least Storm had lost that tightly controlled look he'd had. The idea was a good one. You always caught scientists' interest with bait in their specialty.

But they were losing time. He rose quietly. He'd com the liaison man now and make arrangements. Brion had seemed interested in the offer that he and his family should stay on the Quade ranch while they were on Arzor. If the girl liked to ride, then Logan and Storm could take her riding. She could bring her animals.

A pity she and Storm seemed to have gotten off on the wrong foot. Logan might be more to her liking, as a friend anyhow. They were about the same age, maybe the boy was a year older. He spoke to Kelson briefly before returning to the dining room.

"Kelson says he'll bring the papers and talk to the Ark. I've asked the Carraldos to stay here. If they agree they may come back tomorrow evening with me. Logan, run a few possible mounts into the corral for the girl to look over. Com the line cabins and tell the Norbies to move the stock further into the Basin. I want the frawn herds closer in case there's trouble. Storm, you'll come with us. Kelson wants you to tell your story and hand over those samples. He agrees with what Logan said. Genetech scientists should jump at the chance to find new material."

Storm nodded. The one he'd spoken to hadn't jumped, but then he hadn't had it explained to him that way.

"Yes, Asizi. I'll be ready." And if his medicine was good they'd meet with some scientist other than a pompous idiot or a furious girl.

Chapter Four

This time all three of them rode down to the shuttle. Storm riding Rain-on-Dust, his favorite mount, whose sleek coat was a light gray spotted with rich red dots like bright coins. Rain's spots were clear on his hard-muscled rump, fading toward the chest, but his mane and tail were the same warm red. Logan rode the tough wiry little black-spots-on-gray pony he preferred, while Brad was on a steady sensible black gelding. Tani saw them coming as she was taking Mandy out to the paraowl's perch again. She recognized Quade and Storm. Hastily she dragged the perch out of position by the ramp and hauled it well away toward a clump of trees some hundred yards from the shuttle entrance.

That damned Marten. If she could ever get her hands on him she'd do something drastic. It would take weeks to retrain Mandy, and Tani didn't have the time right now. She'd have to find it, though. Aunt Kady had said they could be on Arzor for three months or more, and Tani didn't want to be blushing every single time some local said "good morning" when Mandy was around. She jacked the perch into the hard earth, emptied the water and food bags she'd bought into the perch containers, and turned to walk back to the ramp.

"Ah!" Her small yelp of surprise made Logan smile at her.

"Sorry. I didn't mean to sneak up on you." He held out a hand. "I'm Logan Quade. Is this your paraowl? Dad said she was beautiful."

Tani was trying to edge him away from the bird. "Yes, that's Mandy." Please don't let him say the wrong word, she thought.

Logan stepped around her. "She really is lovely. I heard they can remember long messages and repeat them to specific people, is that true?"

Again Tani tried to move him along to the ramp. "It's true. They were bred to be messengers in the field when ordinary coms were either jammed or too dangerous to use. They can also double as attack birds, although they don't enjoy the work."

Logan had moved around her again and was admiring Mandy. "Maybe not, but they sure have the beak for it. Whooeee. I bet she could take a real bite with that. Her claws aren't bad either." He bit back a broad grin at Tani's attempts to shift him away from the big bird. "What do they normally eat?"

"On Ishan they used to eat insects. Of course the wild birds were a lot smaller. On DuIshan they eat lastree nuts, and the insects are bigger, too. The paraowls like the wire worms and fleetie grubs there. On the Ark I feed Mandy lastree nuts as a treat and a special mix we make up for her regular meals." She reached up to stroke Mandy. "She does love a lastree nut. I haven't given her one yet this nine."

Logan beamed. "Why not. It's a lovely morning." He waited. Mandy obliged with a pungent suggestion similar to the one that had convulsed Storm the previous day. Tani went red, waiting for this boy to start laughing. He just looked at her sympathetically.

"Did someone teach her that?" Tani nodded, too embarrassed to speak.

"On purpose?" She nodded again. "To be mean?"

That unlocked her voice. *"Yes!"*

Logan saw her distress and was suddenly angry at a corrupter of innocent paraowls. "That wasn't kind. How could they do that. Why did they do that, anyhow?"

Tani glanced up at him. He was nice. He hadn't laughed at Mandy and he really seemed to understand how horrible Marten had been to teach Mandy awful things to say. She began to explain about Marten. Behind her, Aunt Kady and Uncle Brion were talking to the other two. The Beast Master had looked over toward her twice. Maybe he didn't like her getting along so well with his brother.

Brad was talking to Kady. "So it looks as if we may have something previously unknown. The possibility exists that these things are insects of some kind released from the sealed caves. There certainly existed collections of plants and animals there, so insects are a possibility. My son tried to talk to you yesterday about this and to give you the collected material that might bear DNA. He was turned away by some young man who didn't appear interested."

Kady was furious. "Just how long has this possible material been detached from the donor?"

Brad calculated. "About sixty-five hours minimum now."

Kady used words in several languages. "That means by now it's breaking down. We may not be able to get anything. If we'd had it last evening there'd have been a better chance."

She turned to glare at Storm. "Describe the man who spoke to you."

Storm obeyed.

"Jarro! That idiot. I'll have him washing beakers for a week."

Brion intervened. "Kady, Brad has suggested we transfer to his ranch. It's much closer to events and we could use it as a base if we can drive the mobile laboratory over the road. Tani could stay there with us. Brad says the natives would take us into the field for samples and he has a few of the sealed cave plants growing on his ranch as well."

Kady's face lit up. "Anything from Ishan or Terra?"

"A few items," Brad assured her. "A few from other planets, too. A couple where we can't identify the planet of origin. Kelson has had us growing tiny plots outside to see what can live here. I do assure you we're careful, though, the plots are outside, but we prevent seed or genetic material escaping to cross into indigenous species. But if any of the foreign plants can survive Arzor weather and parasites, then we check to see if it is medicinal, edible, or useful in some other way."

"And have you found anything?"

He nodded. "One of the unknown plants yields a sap." He laughed suddenly. "It dissolves glass. They found out when it dissolved the beaker that was holding it. In concentration it can be used to reshape plascrete, or the heavy-duty clearplas." Brion whistled. "Yes, that's something that surprised us. Clearplas that has had time to set and cure usually requires a special saw to cut or shape it after that. In the right concentrations the sap can be used to etch glass or to cut it in exact shapes. A couple of artists are experimenting with it. Apart from that we've only found edible items, but two of them will grow here if they're hand-pollinated. They'll be a valuable export item for Arzor."

"And you'd have no objections to letting us take samples from anything?" Kady cut in.

"Of course not. Just so long as you keep us informed of anything you discover." His eyes twinkled at her and Kady smiled.

"We promise." She moved to take Brion's arm. "I think moving to Mr. Quade's ranch would be an excellent idea. Tell Tani to start packing."

"I will and you'd better do the same, my dear. But I think we will leave Jarro behind in the shuttle's laboratory. He can make a start on trying to extract DNA from the samples he so unwisely refused. It will be a boring and tedious job, but it may help to remind him he doesn't run the Ark the next time someone asks to speak with one of us."

By the paraowl, Tani and Logan were talking horses. "There's a gray and black mare that would do nicely for you. She's half-sister to my fellow here," Logan was saying. "Put Larkin has been breeding for a horse that will stand up to conditions here all year round. A lot of mounts don't handle the Big Dry very well. Put brought in some Astran duocorn crosses and the first foals from that mix seem to like the heat." He sighed. "Only now their hooves don't do so well in the Big Wet. Astran soil is a lighter sandy stuff, it doesn't hold the damp, where here the land really does."

Tani looked thoughtful. "That's only one gene complex. I could isolate it, choose for sex, and produce a couple of female embryos that would have everything this man has bred for plus really hard hooves."

"Would it breed true?" Logan asked with interest.

"It should. The complex would be a dominant. If we're going to your ranch I can take a look at the horses. Talk to your friend."

"You should talk to Storm as well. He knows a lot about animals. He's a Beast Master."

Tani's voice was sharp. "I'm sure he does. But I'm looking for a gene to keep hooves hard, not heads."

Logan opened his mouth and shut it again. There'd been an animosity in that which he was at a loss to understand. Maybe it had been the way Storm had laughed at Mandy. If it had been his bird he might have been pretty furious, too. Not that it was Storm's fault. He'd been really strung out with young Lasco's death and all. Logan had found Mandy's bad habit funny, too. He'd just known in advance not to laugh.

"Come on, let's see what the olders have decided." Tani grinned at the latest noun for those older than the speakers. It was used a lot by city teenagers speaking one-speech, but it felt odd to hear it here on the ranch.

Brion looked over as they strolled up. "Tani. Good. We're relocating to the Quade ranch for a while. We'll take the mobile laboratory, you pack whatever you think you may need, and put your things with that. Kady is talking to the others."

"Who's coming with us?"

"Only the three of us will be going. I want you to make sure that everything in the laboratory is in place. Brad tells me that while the first part of the road is easy, it gets rougher further along. I don't want to arrive and find items damaged. When you're ready come and find me. Kady and I will be talking to the others in the ship and leaving them with work schedules." His voice went grim. "Particularly Jarro."

It all took time; it was two days before the mobile laboratory with Brion at the wheel and Tani beside him crept slowly along the final stretch of the main road to the Basin. The even rougher stretch from main Basin road to the Quade ranch took another whole day.

Brad was present when they drove into the wide front yard, but Logan had gone to see a friend. Storm had vanished to talk to other ranchers, so Brad said.

"He'll be back later, but you've made better time than we expected. If there isn't anything useful from the ranches, he plans to talk to the Norbies. Shosonna, and the Zamle clan in particular, are friends. If they know anything they may tell Storm."

On the far side of the Basin, some miles into the semidesert, Storm sat watching the hand signs of a native Arzoran. The clan had known things, but nothing he'd wanted to hear. Opposite him sat an old friend. Gorgol had been one of the first natives to befriend Storm when he arrived on Arzor. Gorgol was still young but an accomplished hunter and warrior. His sleeveless tunic reached down to upper thigh; it was split over each hip and belted at the waist. The tunic was of undyed frawn leather, the belt of yoris-lizard skin.

The native stood far taller than any human. He was hairless and on his head he bore the two small curving horns that had originally brought the nickname of "goat" from some of the more foolish or arrogant ranchers. About his neck he wore a great wide collar of yoris-lizard fangs and Mountain Flyer claws. Red tattoos surrounded several warrior scars, showing his growing status within the clan.

Gorgol's hands flickered in the swift finger-talk. Native throats were not designed to speak a human language, nor were human throats designed to utter the odd, high-pitched twittering that was the native tongue. However, the sign language used was versatile and formed an excellent means of communication.

"Some of the Nitra clans are moving. They say strange things happen in their lands and it is better they are closer to ours and away from the trouble. Norbie clans are not pleased with this."

Storm's fingers flicked in turn. "Strange things?"

"Dead frawns, dead horses. Twice they have found a dead herder child. No one sees or hears any enemy. They only find skeletons where children were alive a day before. The bones say the child died without moving. The Nitra will fight an enemy they see. How can they fight an enemy none see? The Ones Who Drum Thunder speak of evil in the night." Storm winced. If the clan's shamans were already saying that sort of thing, trouble was brewing.

Gorgol rose to his inhumanly slender seven and a half feet as he stood. The small horns that crowned his hairless head curled back ivory white. His hands flickered as he continued.

"Nitra press now against our lands. This is not good for our clans."

Storm stood too. "True. Evil things in the night killed one of our people also. Many frawns have died and the ranchers are angry. If we hunt together we may find this enemy. Learn whatever weakness it may have, then kill it."

"A good trail. Tell us how Zamle clan may aid in this?"

"Wise ones of our kind come. It may be they know the ways of strange enemies. If you see any signs of this Death-Which-Comes-in-the-Night and the signs are close, send for me. I shall come swiftly, learn what I can. To know the enemy is to defeat it."

The Norbie's head nodded twice in the sign they'd learned from the settlers. "Very good. I listen for news from any clan, send word to you if any comes to my ears."

He was gone in a patter of unshod hooves as his mount scrambled up the slope. Storm stood, his face blank in deep thought. So the killers were on the move. Or perhaps they'd been on Nitra lands before they'd reached the edge of Dumaroy's place. It would take a long time and a number of deaths to spook the Nitra. The wild tribes must have been convinced from the beginning, too, that this wasn't some Norbie or Settler trick. If they had believed that, they'd have already been at war.

If he could talk to Norbie medicine men he might be able to get peace poles up to enter Nitra lands. Not for himself so much but for the scientists. They needed fresh samples. In the four days since they'd agreed to come to the Quade ranch, word had been relayed from the orbiting Ark. On the shuttle, too, Jarro had run every test he could think of and many that his fellow scientists had suggested. All DNA had been broken down completely in the too long a time it had taken for the tests to be done. Jarro had found nothing—if there ever had been anything to find, his comcall had added nastily. Storm had stopped at any of the line-camps with a comcaller. His stepfather, Brad, had kept him constantly informed of what was occurring.

Finally Storm moved. He must return to the ranch. The Carraldos would be arriving shortly. Brad would want him there to welcome them, family to family. Hing had been left back there with her family but both Baku and Surra had come. He rode back slowly, there was no hurry. He was bringing no good news. He came in sight of the ranch below just as the large vehicle that housed the Ark's mobile laboratory crawled down the final stretch of ground. It seemed to settle into position. Tani jumped out, the coyotes whirling about her in excitement.

From a little in advance of where Storm sat his mount, Surra's head rose. Then she was gone, flowing in a silent rush toward the oblivious trio. Storm's mind lashed out. There was a flicker of reassurance, then the big cat was down the slope and throwing herself at the girl. Tani landed on the seat of her jeans with a thump and a yell of delight. Her arms went out to hug the dune cat to her. Around them Minou and Ferarre seemed to be dancing a welcome.

Storm allowed Rain to pick a steady way along. It seemed that Surra knew the girl. Tani appeared to know the cat as well and to be delighted to see her again. He arrived to find the tangle resolving into Surra, purring friendship as Tani rubbed under her jaw. The girl's eyes were alight with happiness, but they changed as she looked up at his words.

"You know Surra?"

"I was at Terra station when she came in with you."

That explained it for Storm. It had been three years before, on another world when he'd been badly injured in a commando raid and Surra, too, had suffered minor injuries. They'd been transferred to Station Twelve for surgery. Tani must have been the person who'd cared for his team member while Storm himself was also hurt. He'd known someone had but had never been told a name. That after three years Surra had remembered the girl with affection showed that Tani must have been kind as well as done her job. He amended that as he saw the affection between them. More than kind. They had liked each other, there was trust there.

"I thank you on behalf of Surra," he said formally.

Tani snorted. "Surra thanks me herself. I don't need thanks from the person who dragged her into a mess and almost got her killed."

"I obeyed my orders."

"So it was orders that got Ho killed as well." The girl's voice was angry. "I saw the records on your team. You risk them as if they were nothing, then come to us for replacements."

Surra butted her gently, distressed at the human emotions. Tani shut down her anger. It wasn't fair to upset Surra. She gave the cat a final hug, then stood and walked away, turning her back on Storm in relief.

He stared after her, eyes hard. What experience had she ever had? Cocooned in the Ark, cared for by doting relatives, handed a priceless team to play with just because she knew the right people. His snort echoed hers. Let her walk away. He had no time to fight with ignorant spoiled children while people were dying on Arzor. He had to report to Brad. He wished he had better news.

Brad was with the scientists and all listened in silence. Kady was the first to speak. "Whatever it is, it's spreading. It's essential we get samples to identify."

Brad nodded, his face worried. "Yes. But so far anyone who has seen it has also died. Can you suggest a way in which we can get these samples in safety?"

Brion and Kady looked at each other, communicating silently. Brion shook his head. "To ensure safety we need samples to know what we must guard against."

They sat thinking before Storm stood again. "I've sent word with Gorgol. The Norbies will let us know if the thing moves onto their lands, and maybe we can talk to the Nitra. I'll ride the line cabins for a while, so I'm easily found if any of them wants to talk."

He went to pack in his room. At the corral he roped out a fresh replacement for Rain and a gray pack mare. Tani was there with Logan but he ignored them. He had no time for arguing now.

Tani stared after him once his back was turned. Storm really had no manners. He'd walked past them without even a word to his own brother. He was going riding, but did he ask if she'd like to come along? No, she answered herself. He didn't. Well, she didn't need him. Logan would take her out into the desert. He'd said he would. It wasn't as if there were any real danger. According to the ship's information tapes, the natives here were friendly and she'd have her team.

An hour later, Logan saddled the mare he'd mentioned as suitable for Tani, once she'd suggested they ride together. He led out, talking of the plants and animals of Arzor. He showed her the puff bushes, the feefaw birds nesting, and agreed she could ride any horse she chose once he'd had time to see that horses obeyed her eagerly. Hing and her family made it a habit to spend time with this girl who knew just where to scratch. It angered Tani that they had to come to her for attention and affection. Storm should have taken them or stayed. Between riding with Logan and petting the meerkat family, Tani worked. She isolated the gene complex as promised and looked forward to the arrival of a bunch of young horses. Once they arrived she could move on to the next stage and try for embryos that would grow into hardhoofed mares. It would show Storm she didn't just sit about enjoying herself.

For a week all was quiet—at least so far as the Quade ranch was aware. But it was merely the lull before the tempest. During that week Tani found herself sleeping badly. Not all night, just at brief intervals when some alert in a deeper part of her brain seemed to be calling her awake. Afterward she would sleep again but not immediately. It irritated her until on the sixth night she accepted something from Aunt Kady. That night she stayed asleep—through a nightmare that became so horrific that she woke everyone else. They rushed to her room, crowding to see what was causing her to scream as if she were in agony.

Kady pushed them out again and gently woke the shrieking girl. "Tani, Tani, dear. You're having a nightmare. Wake up." She watched in concern as her niece opened bleary eyes.

"What is it, Aunt Kady, is something wrong?"

"That's my question," her aunt said dryly. "You're the one waking us all up."

"I did? What did I do?"

"Screamed as if you were being tortured to death, and kept on screaming," Kady informed her. "Everyone on the ranch is outside this door asking each other who attacked you."

"Uh, no one." She shuddered, remembering. "It was just a dream but it was really gruesome." Her voice dropped as she started recalling her nightmare. "It started like the others but I always woke up before." Kady sat, arms around the girl, but Tani did not see her aunt's eyebrows go up in interest. So, that was the reason for the wakeful nights. This nightmare had been coming regularly, but each time it began the girl had wakened before she was drawn too far in.

"How did it start?" Kady kept her voice quiet and smooth.

"Something was hunting. No, I was hunting." Tani shook her head. "I don't know. Something was hunting, I think, but I could hear it coming. It got closer and closer. I could feel the hunger. I always woke up before, as soon as it was close. This time I couldn't wake up. It jumped at me. It bit me here"—she touched her throat—"and I couldn't move. I was bleeding and it was drinking the blood, then it started—it was eating me *alive*—I couldn't move or scream but I was screaming inside. I was screaming and no one came . . ." She bent over the edge of the bed, retching helplessly.

Kady held her, patting her arched back. "Just a dream, dear. It was only a nightmare." She continued to pat and soothe as Tani gulped, still retching. "Brion?" she called softly. "Bring me some of the dristanacin."

On the other side of the door Storm had heard Tani's gasped-out story. He drifted quietly away as Brion returned to enter Tani's bedroom, bearing the medicine that would help calm Tani's stomach. Her aunt and uncle would see to the girl. He arrived at the corral fence and hitched up to sit on the upper rail. Somehow he didn't think that was just a nightmare Tani had dreamed. He had the very unpleasant feeling that somehow she was hooking into the frawn killer's emotions. If that was right it went a good way to explaining why Jarry Lasco's skeleton was found where he'd lain down to sleep.

It sounded as if the bite of the killer produced paralysis. Storm felt like retching himself. Paralysis but not unconsciousness or loss of pain. You'd lie there, unable to move or make a sound while you were eaten alive. Probably the victims died in five minutes or less—from shock, or blood loss. But for the one dying it would be a five minutes that felt like five hours. During the time when Tani was awake she sensed nothing of the killer. With sleep her barriers lowered to a greater degree and she picked up more.

Without drugs to hold her asleep her own mind normally woke her as soon as the link became too distressing. But drugged she'd slept on and picked up an emotional overload. He suspected that at the last she was picking up both the ravening hot blood and live flesh hunger of the killers as well as the agony of the victim. It was the combination that had sent her retching. Deep in her mind she knew that the sating of one was the cause of the other. If he was correct, then she could locate the killers. There were drugs that could open her mind while she was awake.

He walked back into the house. He'd talk to his father about his suspicions. As he passed Tani's room he paused. Kady was sitting by the girl's bed. Tani was asleep. Her face a little flushed but so young looking. Like a small child after an exhausting day. Storm felt a surge of protectiveness. There had to be another way. Besides, if she was forced while awake to live the death of someone dying, eaten alive slowly while in link to her, it was possible she too would die. Too deep a link had killed before.

There'd been those training to be Beast Masters who'd been caught in deep link when one of the team died. Sometimes they'd died with them from the shock. He caught at that thought. Beast Master. Tani had a team. Clearly she had the gifts. Had she ever been tested and if not, how strong were her abilities? It would do no harm to talk to the Carraldos about the girl. He could make it clear he had no wish to abuse her gifts, but they might save a world. He climbed into his bed again an hour later, but that night there was little sleep for Storm. In the early morning he dressed and went out to the laboratory vehicle to find the scientists.

Chapter Five

Tani was sleeping in, exhausted by her night, but Brion and Kady Carraldo were up early, sorting out supplies and setting up tests in their laboratory. Storm ate swiftly. Outside Rain waited, saddled and ready. Storm would ride once he'd finished his meal. He was just leaning back with a cup of swankee when they arrived to breakfast. He allowed them to finish most of it before he looked at Kady.

"How is Tani this morning?"

"Still sleeping."

"Are her team with her?" He'd been unable to see that. As he passed the door had been closed. The meerkats were missing and Storm suspected they'd be with the girl, too, if her team was there.

Brion looked surprised. "Yes, why?"

"They'll help," Storm said briefly. "Was Tani ever tested for Beast Master abilities?"

Kady sighed. "Is this something to do with her nightmare, Storm?"

"It is." As they listened, he explained his theory. When he was finished both looked at each other and Brion nodded.

"I suppose I should tell you some of the background. Tani's father was Bright Sky . . ."

"I met him once," Storm broke in, surprised. "He was a Beast Master and a very good one. He was Cheyenne."

"Yes. Tani's mother was Alisha, my sister. We're of the old Irish blood. Now and again certain gifts appeared in our line, empathy mainly. The gift of sensing another's emotions when they are strong. Alisha was a good nurse. When the war became worse and doctors were in short supply she trained on as a medic. They used her and others like her to go as first-in paramedics after Xik strikes and once the Xiks were cleared out again. She saw some terrible things."

Storm nodded slowly. He'd seen some of those things as a commando Beast Master himself. In occupied territories the Xiks showed no mercy. It had been this knowledge which had made Ishan fight to the last so their world had been destroyed in retaliation. The final strike that had destroyed Terra had been intended to end the war in the Xiks' favor. They'd believed wiping out the home world would break the heart of Earth's Federation. Instead it had worked the other way. Other worlds had been settled from Earth for as many as ten generations. Arzor could count six generations born here. They could survive the emotional trauma of losing the home world and they had. But their rage had been the greater and in the end the Xiks had been beaten.

Brion was looking at him. "I daresay you know, yes. Well, Alisha saw things. So did Bright Sky. They came home and cherished Tani all the more. They were a close family. When Bright Sky was killed it hit Alisha hard." He sighed. "She responded by blaming the Beast Masters' command. They'd thrown her husband away to satisfy some paper plan.

She saw less of Kady and me through that time. We didn't know, but talking to Tani has shown us that perhaps my sister wasn't completely sane after Bright Sky was killed.

"Afterward she apparently taught Tani that all Beast Masters except her father were bad people, killers who wasted their teams to keep themselves safe. Tani was told she should grow up to keep the teams safe from war training and let the Beast Masters find their own ways to survive. When Alisha was killed it was tragic for the child. It reinforced some of what her mother had been saying."

"What happened?" Storm asked.

"There was a minor Xik breakthrough on Terra. They hit a big area down in Texas, flamed a lot of good people. Paramedics were coptered in to find and care for the injured. Someone didn't listen. They'd been told that minor Xik strikes were often used to concentrate valuable people in the wrecked area to be targets for a second strike. It was on the record that they were warned and ignored it. Worse still, when a couple of the medics said they wanted to wait to be sure the Xiks were gone, the officer in charge of sending them in threatened to have them shot for cowardice in the field.

"The Xiks did come back again and Alisha and over fifty medics we couldn't afford to lose died in the attack. Of course the idiot who'd refused to listen was court-martialed. He was demoted and sent to Fremlyn. He was killed there a year later. That still didn't bring back the people who'd died because he didn't want to be told. Alisha had named us as Tani's guardians if anything happened to her. We'd just begun to work on the Ark project."

Storm looked at him. "I thought that wasn't started until after Ishan?"

"There were two projects. Kady and I worked at Beast Master Headquarters. Our job was to choose suitable species from different Federation worlds for teams, and then improve them genetically. On other worlds there were a number of Beast Master stations. They had been built originally for Survey and their first-in scout teams. With all the major work concentrated in one place on Terra it was decided that this could be dangerous. If the Xiks wiped us out we'd lose all the records, knowledge, and the people and teams in training. Command decided to have complete sets of records and samples plus embryos duplicated and transferred to a couple of stations on other planets."

Kady looked at Storm. "We had all that in readiness when Ishan was destroyed. A great Lady at High Command saw that if it could happen to one planet there was nothing to say Earth was immune. She convinced others to accept her orders, promising she'd take all the blame if she was caught. She'd say they were acting under her orders. What she did was illegal. She could have been shot for it. She didn't have the power to act on her own but she went ahead anyway. She diverted funds and staff, and persuaded whole senior schools to assist in collecting genetic samples.

"In six months she had the Ark stuffed with material, a small select group of scientists, ample funds in a secret account on another planet for us. And she'd even raided animal parks and other places that still held some of the flora and fauna of Ishan. The original Ark was quite small. Too small for what we were doing. She was head of an old merchant trader family. She commandeered the biggest ship they had—a freighter unsuitable for war conversion, which had been mothballed—falsified the orders, and rebuilt that.

"With Ishan destroyed, and the Xiks breaking through to strike at Earth more and more effectively, the chain of command was often in confusion. She knew she'd have to answer for what she'd done if she survived, but she believed that what she was doing was not only right but essential."

Kady looked down at the table. Her fingers went out to touch a fork, lining it up neatly. "She was right. Tani worked with us during that time. She knew what Efana risked. It made her dislike Beast Master Command even more. The new Commander there changed his mind about the project to save Beast Master team samples. He wouldn't listen and we had to steal and clone samples we needed from them. Tani helped. We gave her an unofficial team to work with. That was a mistake. The Commander saw they worked for her and tested Tani, she scored high. So he tried to insist that she take the official training."

She picked up the knife, lining it up with the fork. Her fingers suddenly shook. "You know how hard it was to find people with the Beast Master gifts. The command was desperate. It was just two months before the final Xik breakthrough. Beast Masters and teams were dying everywhere trying to keep the Xiks from our throat. Tani refused but they said she was sixteen and old enough. If she didn't agree they'd conscript her and if she still refused she'd be given to the psychtechs. They'd convince her or break her, it would be up to Tani which she preferred.

"Tani has both the stubbornness of Alisha and Bright Sky. She was also a very confused child then. Alisha taught her that going into the field of war with her team was bad and wrong. If High Command had approached her more carefully she might have considered the initial training. Once she began that she might have accepted the rest of it. But the threats convinced her to reject it all."

Storm nodded. He had that stubbornness himself. The refusal to be forced into a path not of his own choosing. "I notice she always speaks of her parents by name?"

Kady shrugged. "That's because Alisha used to call Bright Sky by name after he died. Tani picked that up from her. Later on we both talked of them by name. She started doing it, too, although at the time she did call them Mom and Dad."

"How did she get out of the Beast Master training?"

"Efana was furious. She knew Tani would die but she was on a different chain of command. She couldn't help directly, so she cut us orders to take genetic materials to Terlaine. Then she had papers forged for Tani and helped smuggle her and her team on board. We took off. The final Xik attack came weeks later."

"Your friend?" Storm asked.

Kady shook her head as Brion answered. "Efana died with Earth. We had a message from her when it was clear Terra could not survive the final attack. She said we should tell Tani none of the beasts would suffer. She told us to remember that our work was for all the worlds. That soon we'd be needed for reasons of peace, but we should always remember that it might take two to make a war, but it took only one determined enemy to make a massacre. If we must fight to protect ourselves or a world, then we should do it knowing it was right."

"What did she mean about the teams?"

"Efana had the cages rigged. If the Xiks reached Terra, then she had only to press a pendant she always had. The teams would die in seconds from a lethal painless gas." Kady had tears in her eyes. "She always said it was the last gift we could give to those we loved. She knew that if the Xiks broke through it would be to destroy Terra. There'd be no way the teams could fight. The Xiks would use flamers from just beyond the atmosphere to burn Terra to a radioactive cinder."

Storm was silent. The Xiks had done so but it had taken time. Only a little time, an hour, while their fighters held off the desperate remnants of Earth's fleet. In that hour, as temperature soared and people burned alive, the teams too would have died horribly if not for this Efana. In his mind he saluted her. It also explained the small lettered name by the Ark's main ramp: EFANA'S LEGACY. And he could understand the girl better. She'd lost her father, his death warped in her mind by Alisha's pain. Then she'd lost her mother because of the horrible mistake of a fool, and she'd only just escaped mind-breaking by the aid of a woman who died heroically. He'd judged her as the spoiled child she'd seemed to him. Instead, she was a wounded survivor of the war with the Xiks.

"So you see," Kady was continuing, "Tani has reason for her attitudes. She tested high as a possible Beast Master. We are gradually teaching her that a team cannot live forever. That even in Survey, team members may be killed. She does know Earth and the Federation did everything to prevent the Xik war, it was the Xiks who would not be persuaded to keep the peace. Please, Storm. Try to be kind to her. She has improved in the time since Terra was destroyed."

"I will remember," Storm said as he stood. He nodded politely before leaving to collect Rain. He rode up toward the Basin rim still thinking of Tani. It was all very well to understand the girl, but her ability to hear the menace could be all that stood between Arzor and destruction. How understanding was he to be if she was prepared to let Arzor die rather than do something she found distasteful. His head came up at a long twittering call. Gorgol!

He swung to Rain's back and ran the stallion up the hill to where the Norbie signaled. Storm's fingers raced in the swift sign language.

"What happens?"

"Much trouble. One of the Nitra tribe has come into Norbie lands. They have taken the waterhole of the clan nearest them. The Nitra say death hunts in the desert lands. They stay here now. They refused the tribe water from what was their own waterhole. The two clans fought and there are dead to be avenged. The Nitra lost the battle and fled away. They have gone toward the Peaks."

Storm groaned. Dumaroy. His land was in the Peaks and nearest the desert. If the Nitra started trying to move in there Dumaroy wouldn't bother to talk. He'd fight.

"The Nitra have gone toward Dumaroy's land?"

"I think that is so. I have ridden here as fast as I could. Zamle clan does not wish war. Krotag said I should warn you of what has happened. You will warn Kelson?"

The Chief of the Zamle clan was no fool, Storm reflected. If Kelson could drop a copter between Dumaroy's spread and the advancing Nitra he might be able to prevent a war, which, if it involved an attack on a human ranch, could draw in far more than the original combatants. He dropped from his mount, handing the reins to Gorgol and taking in return the reins of the native's leg-weary pony.

"Go back to Krotag. Tell him I'll send word to Kelson.

Tell Krotag my father says, if war comes to Krotag's lands the Zamle clan is welcome here, always."

The Chief would accept that as an honest offer. Logan had been formally adopted into the clan several years earlier. As Logan's father, Brad's offer to share land in time of war was an offer of kin to kin. The Shosonna could take it without loss of face. Apart from that the old Chief would understand. The Norbies had a saying. Two brothers who stand together are thrice as strong as two who stand alone. The Basin ranches would agree. In the Peaks country Put Larkin, Dort Lancin, and their hands and families would agree as well. But not Dumaroy, who had always distrusted the natives. Not Dumaroy, raw from the loss of a rider who'd also been the young son of an old friend. Dumaroy would be itching to blame someone.

Storm pushed the fresher Norbie mount hard. When they pulled up at the ranch house the horse was lathered and blowing. Storm was off his mount and into the house as the tired animal halted by the front door. He dropped into the seat in front of the comcaller and flicked switches with flying fingers. Kelson was there, luckily. Storm talked fast. He heard Kelson yelling orders and the clatter of feet before the liaison came back to the com.

"Did Gorgol say why the Nitra have suddenly started this?"

"The killers have hit them hard, I'd guess. They said death hunts in the desert, so they're moving out so far as I got it from Gorgol."

"If they hit Dumaroy that'll be all he needs to paint for war."

Kelson grunted. "Too true. I'll be going. Maybe I can

stop this business before it gets ugly. I'll com you once we've sorted something out and I get back here." The soft hum of an open line died and Storm sat back. He'd better get outside and care for the horse, then maybe he should find Brad and bring him up to date on all this. He did so and was just sharing the bad news with his stepfather when Kelson called back.

"You can relax. The Nitra tribe turned off before the Peaks. They angled around and dropped down into an unclaimed valley there. I've had a word with Dort Lancin; they're closest to his lands. His people will keep an eye on them. I've left a consignment of G34 gas with Dort. He's steady. He won't use it unless he has to, but if he does at least no one should get killed." His voice faded a moment, then came back strongly.

"Storm, if you have any ideas about this thing now's the time to use them. We were lucky today."

"I know." Storm was terse. "I'll see what I can do. Quade ranch out."

Brad had been listening. "What have you got in mind, son?"

"The big problem is that without knowledge of the enemy we can't formulate a defense. Somehow I have to find the enemy and bring enough of one home so that the Carraldos can examine it."

"Ride carefully. The Nitra aren't children and they knew something was out there. They must have continued to lose people. Enough to scare them into moving off ancestral lands. For Nitra to do that they'd have to be . . . well."

"They'd have to have tried every offense or defense they knew and nothing's worked," Storm said flatly. "And if that's happened to one tribe, it'll keep happening. The other wild tribes will be starting to move against the Norbies soon. The Norbies will fight back and the Nitra will decide that we might be easier to take."

His stepfather looked tired. "I know. I've been talking unofficially to the Peacekeeper Command. If the natives are driven out of their lands, then our treaty rights could be revoked and ranches handed back to the natives. I've argued that all that will do is buy time. We have no reason to think that whatever is causing the trouble is just going to stop on the edge of our lands and leave the natives in peace. The time to do something is now, before a decision like that sets settlers against the natives, and the Peace Officers as well. Apart from that the planet can't afford to compensate ranchers for their land. If the Patrol comes to insist we have to leave and lose everything without compensation, then most settlers will fight."

"Will you, Asizi?"

"No, it would be futile. We couldn't win against the Patrol. But if we can find out what is causing all this, then we may be able to prevent the Patrol from arriving. Go and talk to the Zamle clan, son. Talk to Ukurti. He's a medicine man, maybe he has ideas."

Storm nodded. "I'll ride now. I won't hurry so I can take the team and scout on the way. Tell the Carraldos I'll see what I can find in the way of tissue samples for them."

He went in search of the meerkats. Hing was sunbathing by the side door. She was all he needed, but he sent pictures to her. "Your kits, where?" In return came pictures of the four other members of her family, all clinging to Tani. Along with that were flashes of emotions. Tani was warm, kind, security. Nice person. Storm cradled Hing. She was nice person too, of course Tani was kind. He received a picture that rocked him with amused surprise. It was himself standing by Tani. Linking them were a trio of meerkat kits with human heads and a query.

Storm tickled the meerkat's stomach. "No," he said aloud. "No, I don't plan to mate with her. Now go to Surra. We're riding."

Soon after, Storm walked a fresh pony up the slope. With him trotted Surra while Baku soared overhead. In a framed saddle pouch Hing chittered to herself, grooming her fur carefully. Atop the Basin edge Storm paused to look back down the land. Two dots in the distance to the east must be Logan and Tani. He'd known they were riding today. The girl was the key. Once he returned they'd have to talk. His mount plodded over the Basin rim and down the winding track.

That night as Storm laid out his sleep sack a thought occurred to him. If Tani could sense the enemy, what of Storm himself? He'd been trained to the team bond, perhaps if he went to sleep with the idea in mind—he did so, to wake sweating with horror and disgust. He slept and woke again. This time he stayed awake by the small fire. It seemed that he and Tani had that much in common. He too could touch the killers when he slept.

He rinsed his mouth from the canteen. The emotions had been sickening. No wonder the girl had reacted so violently. She had never fought; Storm had killed Xiks on several worlds, seen some of their atrocities, and still what he'd found in his dreams had nauseated him. Somewhere the killers had found prey, hunted, paralyzed, then feasted. Something of both sides had come through to Storm: the blood-mad hunger of the hunters; the sudden burning pain in the throat, which subdued the prey; then the avid joy in gulping hot blood, quivering live flesh. That would have been bad enough. But it was the terror, then the awful agony of the prey that had jolted him awake.

The second time his mind had known what was to come and he'd felt only the terror of the prey before he woke. That had been bad enough. In the fleeting touch Storm had known the first to die had been animal, the second a person. Nor could those who died have been far away. Storm's normal gifts linked him and his team at a maximum of four or five miles. His abilities under extreme stress had tested out to some ten miles. Further than that he could not drive a mental link to his team even under drugs. He sat drinking a cup of hot swankee and considering. It was possible the killers were broadcasting while he was receiving. In which case he could be picking up their broadcast from a much greater distance.

He sat by the fire until the sky lightened to dawn. Then he rose to saddle the horse. He'd move slowly in the direction from which he'd felt the killers. He'd move with everything on alert, although so far the enemy only hunted at night. But there was always a first time for change. If he could find the skeletons of the prey he could gain some idea of his range for picking up their hunt. The person who died had seemed the closer. He nudged the pony into a steady walk. Surra ranged out ahead and to either side as she searched the rough land. Above, Baku's eyes were watching. If there were skeletons to be found, one or the other would find them.

At midday he camped to spell the pony and allow Hing to rest. She vanished with happy squeaks to return just as

Storm was finishing his meal. With her she dragged an arrow. Not merely an arrowhead, and not a damaged missile. This arrow was intact, so Storm took it from her gently. He examined it. New, not weathered from lying outside more than a few hours. Unbroken, with markings he did not know other than that they were native. It was likely Hing had found a body with weapons intact. That made it unlikely the warrior had fallen in battle. A victorious Norbie or Nitra enemy would have taken spoils.

But the killers did not. Unless blood was spilled on the quiver they would have left it alone. He turned to the meerkat, who waited patiently for her treasure to be returned.

"Where, where did you find it, Hing?" He reinforced the words with a mental question. A series of pictures. Of Hing as she poked into holes and corners of rocks, and found the arrow—where? She gave a small trill and scurried off. Storm followed. The meerkat dived through a tunnel in the grass and ended up in a pile of boulders. There around the side of one large slab was an opening. An old Djimbut warren, the entrance broken larger. He nodded, Djimbut were a native Arzoran animal like a large wombat. They were diggers, preferring to live in a large burrow. Often they enlarged a burrow over several generations and whole families lived in it. Deserted burrows were sometimes used in turn by travelers in the dry country as night shelters, since even a smallish one would take a rider and his mount. Hing scampered inside and returned with a second arrow. Storm let her keep it. Right now he had other things on his mind. A way to light this burrow was one of them.

He'd left his flashlight behind, but downslope there were puff bushes. The fat cotton-wool blossoms made excellent emergency torches under the right conditions, as the settlers had found. Storm picked an armful and gathered several long thick sticks. These he split lengthways, packing the fluffy blossoms into the length of the split. With half a dozen sticks prepared he tucked them into his belt, readied one last stick and lit it. The blossoms burned, each in turn lighting those below. Holding the light in front of him he stepped, stooping slightly, through the entrance and raised the light stick to see what the burrow held.

Before him, laid out on the floor, was the native skeleton he'd half expected, half feared. Beside the victim lay his gear. Bow, quiver of arrows, and his travel pouch. Underneath him—Storm moved, bending over to see, yes. Patterned cloth. The blanket woven by a warrior's closest female relative. It brought good fortune to a warrior, helped to balance bad medicine with good. Parts of it that must have been stained with the victim's blood had been eaten away. Storm didn't know the pattern. Not Shosonna, anyhow. Logan might know.

He dug a couple of the light sticks into the packed earth and swiftly sketched the pattern, listing the colors as well. For now he'd give the native a temporary burial. His tribe, once identified and informed, could give proper rites. Next Storm turned to collect the bow and quiver. That would help identify . . . he looked more closely at the arrowheads. Amongst the hunting arrows were others with wickedly barbed heads, war arrows. Once before he'd seen arrowheads like these. Nitra!

But what was a Nitra warrior doing within Shosonna lands and so close to the Basin? From outside came a quick flash of warning as Surra gave the alarm. Riders approached against the wind, they were close to the burrow already. Storm stamped one of the light sticks into darkness. The other he left on the far side of the skeleton. Let that distract those outside for a moment as they entered. Then he slipped along the wall by the entrance to where the shadows were darkest. He waited.

Chapter Six

At the Quade ranch Tani was bored. Everyone had been treating her like an invalid and she was becoming tired of it. She'd firmly repressed the memories of her nightmare. So firmly indeed that she remembered nothing but a vague unpleasantness. She was sick of bed and staying inside, being pampered and fussed over. Outside were new things, horses to ride, Logan to keep her company. Her team longed to run the slopes and small gullies of the Basin lands. But it was Mandy whose needs became imperative. The paraowl wanted space to stretch her wings. She wanted to fly. Then, too, the mixture she fed on was as boring as Tani's captivity. She demanded live prey, a tasty Arzoran rock mouse, perhaps. Tani grinned.

Slowly she sat up and listened. Almost everyone had left the main house. Brad and his riders were out working. Brion and Kady were busy in the laboratory. Only the cook was inside still. Quietly Tani dressed in riding clothes, adding the special pad that clipped to her shirt. It covered the length of her shoulder and upper arm and was a favorite perch for the paraowl. With claws such as Mandy had padding was needed despite the bird's gentleness with her friend.

Tani quieted the delight of her team, then examined the window. It was made to open outward, although there were strong bars. In the early days the settlers had built ranch homes as small fortresses. Not against the natives so much as against the lawless men of their own kind in the days of First Settlement and little law.

Tani investigated to find that the bars were on a metal frame that also could be opened. Moving carefully she opened both frame and window. The window was small but a slender girl could squeeze through. She did so, enjoying the faint feeling of childlike naughtiness. Behind her came the coyotes, rejoicing in the new smells as they sniffed the slight breeze. Tani reached back in to lift Mandy out. The large bird fluffed her feathers in delight. Tani giggled quietly. There was no danger. The natives were all friendly. Tani had even learned the finger-talk, just for fun.

The young meerkats squeaked imploringly so that Tani paused. She looked at them. She didn't have the right to let them come with her. If anything happened Storm would be furious after the way she'd told him off before. Not that anything would happen. But just in case, they'd have to stay here. She made her decision known and ignored hopeful noises and small cries of protest.

It was moving from Big Dry to Big Wet. Temperatures were cooler. Occasional light showers were falling, which would in another three months become steady sheets of rain. But for now she would not have to fear flash floods. The yoris were the only danger. The big lizards mated during these periods between major seasons. At such times the males carried a lethal poison, but the team would know about them.

She knelt beside the building wall, calling her friends. She passed to them the pictures she'd seen in the tapes. She felt their understanding. They would watch.

She hesitated. Perhaps she should take a stunner. Then she shrugged, why bother. And to obtain one she would have to enter the main part of the building. She might be seen and her small expedition prevented. The team would be alert for yoris, she had only to circle any they found. Instead she climbed back in the window. She reached for a keypad and left a short message for her aunt and uncle. She was going for a ride, the team would be with her and she'd be back sometime. She picked up her belt. In many compartments along the inside were useful small items. She added her knife, just in case. It rode in a fringed sheath her father had made for her shortly before he died and she cherished it. The knife itself was of top-grade steel, over a foot in length, honed and sharpened to a razor edge.

To it she added her travel pouch. It held dry rations, a small bowl, eating utensils, and a lidded pot with insulated handles at both sides and over the lid. It also contained a sewing kit, and a small medicine kit, which was more important as far as Tani was concerned. She stood a moment, then gathered up two canteens. Logan had been very dogmatic on the subject of always having water. She could fill them by the corrals.

Tani peered around the corner of the house. The door of the mobile laboratory was shut and from the half-open window came the sounds of voices in consultation. She knew the pattern of sounds. Her aunt and uncle were working, discussing the possibilities of their experiments as they worked.

They'd be oblivious to anything short of loud explosions. The ranch kitchen faced the other way and unless the cook came to the side door Tani would be unnoticed.

She pattered quietly along to the corral. Once out of sight she filled both the canteens and hooked one to her belt. Then she peered through the high corral rails. There were several horses there brought in by Put Larkin late the previous day. One caught her eye and she gasped. She'd heard some of the evening's discussion. She'd been in bed eating dinner and trying hard to wipe nightmares from her mind. With her dinner finished she had felt like eating some of the fruit usually kept in a bowl on the table near the dining room door. She'd got up, found the fruit, and was just about to return to her bed when she heard Brad speak.

"Those young horses of Put Larkin's arrived this afternoon."

Storm was interested. "What are they like?"

"Good animals, all but one."

"What's wrong with it?" Logan queried.

Brad laughed. "Nothing on looks. I think we need a witch or a princess from a fairy tale to ride her." He chuckled again. Then his face went sad. "Your mother would have adored it. Raquel always loved beautiful things."

"Is it beautiful?"

Brad nodded. "Larkin brought Astran duocorn crosses into Arzor about a year and a half ago. You'd remember, Storm. It was soon after you arrived here. There'd been a mix-up with two of the mares and they were already in foal when they were shipped. They foaled right after they arrived and Larkin kept the foals."

Storm spoke slowly as he recalled the event. "Yes. The

mares escaped for a couple of days. Someone left a gate open. They got them back and shipped them anyhow but they'd bred while they were out. To a duocorn stallion, Put thought, judging by the foals."

Logan grinned. "They wouldn't be so easy to handle."

"They weren't. One foal was a colt, the other's a filly. Duocorns grow faster than horses. At a year they're old enough and strong enough to take a rider and this pair are three-quarter-breds. They tried breaking the colt and he went crazy. Put's decided to keep him as a stallion for crossing back over the Arzor mares. The filly's the prettiest thing you've ever seen. They've had a saddle on her and she's been lunged and mouthed. She's been taught manners for someone on the ground, as much as she's willing to learn. But no one can stay aboard longer than she wants them to. Put sent her over to see if Storm can handle her. She's for sale to the ranch if we can manage her."

In the hallway Tani had stiffened. A filly, gray as mist and unridden. She yearned to try. Cautiously she bit into her fruit, listening to the conversation.

"Is she that bad?" Logan was asking.

"She isn't good. Being three-quarter-bred she's horned and knows how to use them. She bites as well and she can buck so none of Put's boys can stay on. She's powerful and she's going to be bigger. Foals from her will be a wonderful addition to the ranch if Storm can tame her."

Storm spoke thoughtfully. "Duocorn mixes usually bond with a rider."

Logan laughed. "Then you bond with her, Beast Master. I bet Rain would like a nice mare all to himself."

The talk drifted to other things, and Tani left silently.

Now she was outside in the first light of a new day, looking at the horse they'd talked of. She stood there transfixed. She'd seen many horses before. She'd been riding as soon as she could walk. Bright Sky was Cheyenne and to him there was nothing more essential than that his child be a rider. Tani had taken to it like Mandy to the skies. It had been one of the things she had not lost with her father. Alisha, too, was a lover of horses and had seen to it that Tani had continued chances to spend time with the big beasts. In some of the places her mother worked there'd been times when Tani hadn't been able to ride for months. Always she returned to it with renewed enthusiasm. To her, the amount of available mounts to ride was one of the best things about Arzor.

Now the girl walked to the high railings and her eyes feasted. The filly was just over fifteen hands in height. Her hide glowed a gray so pale it was almost silver in the sunlight. She was single colored, unlike most of the horses Tani had known on the Quade ranch. The mane and tail flowed in a long cascade of bright silver. Conscious of admiration the filly posed. The horns that gave her ancestors the name of duocorn stood out sharply. They were almost black, shading to gray at the tips. The filly's body was a solid ball of muscle, as if a far bigger horse had been condensed down to the filly who stood there. Tani spoke softly.

"Daughter of the wind. Child of the silver lightning." The filly's ears pricked forward. "Sister in pride. We are two, we are one. Share strength with me." The filly took a step closer to the human. Other humans had tried to master her. Their voices had been rough, harsh with demand. None had hurt her but she'd resisted the orders. This one's voice was quiet. She asked, not ordered. Without thought Tani was applying the same mental touch as she used with her team. She stroked with words, soothed and coaxed with emotions. She allowed the admiration she felt to flow over the argent filly.

"We are two, we are one. Share speed, share joy as we race the wind."

Tani was inside the corral now and the filly dropped her head to nibble inquiringly at a long black plait. Here there was no fear scent, no scent of anger and demand. No emotion that required domination to be content. The girl pushed the head away, gently stroking the soft muzzle. "Out there are better things to eat. Let us find them together?"

The filly nuzzled into Tani's shirt. Teeth that could strip a hand to the bone lipped slender fingers. The horns curved out in a slight upward curve and were wickedly sharp at the points. Tani scratched around them as the filly all but purred. She studied the filly's hooves. Like the horn bases, they were black. She ran a hand down the slender iron-muscled leg and a hoof lifted obediently.

"Good hooves," Tani told her approvingly as she rapped them. She pictured the joys of being free. "We can go for miles." In turn she received a rebellious flash. The filly hadn't liked the large heavy saddles the Larkin hands had tried on her. Nor had she approved the metal bit. Tani nodded. "No need for that, girl. Storm uses the type of bridle that doesn't have a bit, and a light saddle. He's got spares here, I know. We can use those."

She pictured the lighter gear, the feel of it. The pleasure of riding together, sharing abilities. Unconsciously she also allowed her wistful desire for the filly to be felt. The horses she'd ridden to date could never measure up to this one. A soft nose thrust into her hands. The filly was conquered. Not by brute power but by admiration and something that could be the beginnings of love.

Tani ran to fetch the pad-saddle and light leather-braided bitless bridle. Piece by piece she held them up to be sniffed: the saddle, bridle, and the soft woven saddle blanket. The filly graciously accepted them. Tani opened the gate a little, holding the reins, and the filly trotted out to join her, flicking the earth disdainfully under her hooves. In her was the yearning to run as she'd run with her mother. Tani reached the filly's back in a light leap. The horse whirled but the rider stayed firm, moving with the heaving body beneath her as if one with it.

Lifting her head the filly danced a few steps, testing. Her rider swayed bonelessly and the filly was satisfied. She raised her head as Tani reached out for the mental bond with her team. She gathered the filly in as the coyotes approached. The filly should not fear; the filly did not. These things were small, she could stamp them underfoot if she wished. But her rider said they were friends. The filly lowered her nose to find it licked by each coyote in turn. It tickled and sensations both physical and emotional were pleasant.

Tani signaled and Mandy, waiting patiently on the fence, flew silently in to land on Tani's padded shoulder. The filly screwed her head around to look. Her rider indicated no danger; the filly accepted. They moved out and no one noticed their going. Beyond the buildings the light wind brought fascinating scents to them all. It teased the filly's mane and Tani's neck. It ruffled the fur of the coyotes and Mandy's feathers. They walked into it, their speed increasing until with a small whoop Tani leaned over the neck of her mount and urged her to run.

The answering surge of speed left her breathless, her pleasure meeting and mingling with that of the filly. The indignant paraowl was able to stay with them but Minou and Ferarre were left behind as the filly hurtled onward. They slowed by common consent once she had shaken the kinks of confinement from her legs. Tani did not realize how far they had come in that one long burst of speed. The coyotes caught up and they moved on at a swinging, ground-covering trot. It was wonderful to be out on their own. No Logan, nice as he was, to worry about how far they were going. No Storm, eyeing the mount she brought back as if he expected it to develop saddle sores overnight. No Brad fussing as if she were delicate china.

They were free to explore, to travel to the very edge of the Basin if they wished. Maybe they'd meet some of the Norbies. She'd been here days now and never met one. Tireless, the filly moved in her long, smooth trot. After two hours, Tani glanced back and was startled.

"We've come a long way. I guess we should think about going back in another hour or two." The filly's flash of protest merged with those of the team. It had been too long since they'd been free of ship confines and alone with their human friend. They could camp and have a night away? A half-memory of her nightmare drifted across the girl's mind and was met by reassurance from the paraowl. No bad dreams. Mandy would hunt them from her.

Tani looked across the land wistfully. It would be a shame to go back so early. She might not be able to get away on her own again. Even if her aunt and uncle accepted that she could care for herself, the Quades had been firm that she was not to ride alone. It was nonsense, Tani decided. They just fussed because she was new to the planet. She'd watched the education tapes about Arzor. Apart from the yoris lizards there wasn't much danger in the lower lands. In the Big Blue's mountains there were predators like the Mountain Flyer, but she didn't plan to ride that far. Her aunt and uncle would scold a little if she were away too long, but they wouldn't really worry. She'd left a message so that they'd know nothing had happened to her.

But she wouldn't stay out for the night. It would be unfair to upset everyone. She would ride a few hours, enjoy the time with her team and the filly. She sighed softly. Then she'd come back to the ranch again. She rode on, at a walk but occasionally breaking into a canter at rider or mount's whim. By midday she was ascending the last slope of the Basin. She should turn back now but the wild land beyond drew her. Something out there called, and Tani ached to answer it. The team agreed. They wanted to hunt the desert, so like that their ancestors had known. The filly's ancestral lands had been green. But she enjoyed the strangeness of this desert land and the freedom. She walked on down the rim and her rider did nothing to halt her direction.

Just one hour into the desert, Tani thought. She could give everyone a rest and something to eat, then she could ride for home. She was hungry and the team reinforced that, telling her they were hungry as well. Tani had taken ration bars, but they would do only if nothing else appeared. She'd read about grass hens in the tapes and down here she could see places where they might be found. If she brought back a couple of the plump grass hens, Mr. Quade would be more likely to forgive her long absence. She dismounted and searched for stones, gathering a dozen or so that fitted her hand. Then she walked ahead, the filly following. In a patch of long sun-seared grass Minou circled, relaying the scent: edible and interesting. Tani waited until both coyotes were in position, then she signaled. The coyotes advanced delicately. A covey of grass hens exploded from the tangled grass and Tani threw as the coyotes leaped high.

Ferarre had a hen, Tani's stones had brought down two more. The second was still fluttering until Minou seized it. She crunched once and the flapping ceased. Mandy sideslipped in for a landing on Tani's shoulder. In her mind was the picture of rocks only a small distance ahead. They curved and a tree and other debris had collected over them. They'd make a suitable shelter to build a fire. One hen; just one to eat? They rounded the boulders and Tani approved. She dug out the tiny waterproof box from her belt and lit quickly gathered dry sticks.

With the fire lit she unsaddled and rubbed down the filly. It would not be fair to leave her mount saddled while Tani ate. But they must go back as soon as the grass hen had been shared. It was light late into the evening, but once everyone had eaten and rested, they'd have to race to make it home before it was completely dark. Tani hurriedly collected larger branches to stack by the flames.

With the coyotes contentedly eating their prey and the filly grazing the tough grass nearby, Tani could turn her attention to herself and Mandy. She half filled the pot and placed it to boil, then she plucked the grass hen and spitted it over the flames. Food for the paraowl was easy to find. It was still light enough to hunt and the girl could act as a beater. She moved quietly to the grass and stamped through it suddenly. Mandy floated silently in on the small movements. Seconds later she held a small plump rodent in her claws. She bit once, then waited. Tani stamped some more and a second rock-mouse was seized. That, Tani informed her paraowl, would do. If Mandy was still hungry after them, there was some of her food-mix.

The girl returned to the fire to find the water in her lidded pot boiling nicely. She added swankee powder, stirring it with her spoon. She seemed to have made rather a lot, but if she didn't drink it she could clip the lid down hard and take it back with her. The grass hen was roasting delectably over the fire. It dripped fat, which sizzled and smelled wonderful. Tani waited as her dinner cooked. In the small circle by the boulders all was peaceful.

Well fed, tired by the hours of riding, Tani leaned back against the fire-warmed boulders. Her eyes closed slowly. The light was fading from the sky when she woke again with a jump. She looked upward.

"Damn!" The explosive word made her team turn to look at her. "Yes, you may well stare. It's too late to go back now." She glanced over to where the filly grazed. "I can't risk your legs on rough ground after dark. I guess we're all here for the night."

The girl ate again. Then with the filly's saddle blanket wrapped around her, travel pouch under her head, she lay down and fell quickly asleep. The team would be alert. They would wake her if there were danger. But danger must be recognized. Tani had told the team that the natives were friendly. Logan had not mentioned the Nitra. The wild tribes normally lived many days' travel away. And if of late they'd begun to press closer to human-held lands, the Basin had not seen them. Neither Storm nor his stepfather and halfbrother had expected Tani to go far enough to encounter them. Tani knew nothing of the Nitra; the information tapes had not spoken clearly of the distinction between the Nitra and the more friendly Norbie clans.

She slept quietly. Once she began to dream but the linked team woke her at once. She sighed, turned over in her blanket, and fell back into sleep. With the interruption she did not rejoin a linkage that would have held her to the death of another. Through her the team sensed the death but did nothing. It was not relevant and it was far away. Nearer was a camp of not-people. But Tani had said there was no danger. The team drowsed. If danger appeared they would act.

Tani slept the dark hours away, waking finally just as the sky paled to lavender light. The fire had died to coals. Working quickly she added wood, placed the swankee pot over the flames, and kicked up a couple of rock-mice for Mandy. Grass hens would do again. After that she must head back to the ranch. She hadn't really meant to be out all night. Kady would scold and Brion would be annoyed. Tani picked up her unused stones and shifted her focus to a fresh patch of grass. The covey exploded again as she advanced, and she brought down two of the grass hens. More walking and two more were coyote prey, a third hers. She could cook a hen and eat it. She would take the other two back. It might help her in placating irritated adults.

She plucked all of the birds quickly, spitted one, then tucked the others in her travel pack. Tani placed the swankee pot on the coals, inhaling the aroma with pleasure. There was a sort of sweet chocolaty scent to good swankee. She'd enjoyed the taste from the first cup of it offered to her. Brad had laughed and said she must be born for Arzor. Here the humans drank gallons of it. They'd learned the habit from the natives, who loved it and with whom it was a valuable trade item.

Minou yapped sharply. Tani stiffened, sliding back further into the boulders and unsheathing her knife. From a different point Ferarre yapped. Riders were incoming. Nothumans. Be alert. Tani smiled then. She shifted back to the fire and added enough water and swankee powder to fill the small pot. The grass hen was spluttering juicily. The girl pulled the others from her pack, adding them to the spit. She sat back to wait eagerly. She was about to see natives. She'd show them she knew the way to behave when they visited.

A short distance from her shelter four Nitra warriors conferred. They'd been sent to find someone. The medicine woman hadn't said whom. They'd just been told they would know the right person when they were found. Once they found this person they were to bring them back alive and undamaged to the main camp two days' hard-riding away. They were warriors, not fools. They knew that humans fought like a yoris at mating time. They'd find one alone. It was a difficult and dangerous task, since the Norbies were out as well.

One of the Nitra out scouting at daybreak had cut tracks. Very strange ones. There was a ridden horse, but also the tracks of two animals unlike any he'd ever seen. The tracks were recent and the rider would have camped for the night. The Nitra had eaten and broken camp to follow. Now they conferred just before the heap of boulders they knew sheltered their target. Their soft twittering speech was growing agitated. Finally the senior of the four spoke. They would go openly to the camp, following custom. It would be their quarry's response that would tell them if it were the one sought.

Anyone other than Tani who saw them approaching would have reacted violently. The Nitra were enemy to the Norbies and to humans. Mostly they were enemy to any other Nitra tribe as well. The usual response was to take cover and start shooting. Tani merely looked up as they rode toward her camp. Well short of her boulders all four warriors dismounted. They selected smooth sticks from quivers and at a signal fired each into the air. A Nitra did not waste a real arrow in ceremony as did the Norbies.

Tani beamed at them. They'd followed custom, just as the tapes said. She raised her hands, signing slowly and carefully. "The fire is waiting. Share food, drink. A knife is sheathed before friends."

Four Nitra stared at her. They saw a small slender human female, unafraid and offering hospitality. In their savage desert females were scarce and respected. A young female was unprotected once only in her life. When, before she mated, she went alone into the desert for eight days and nights. She went without food or weapons save a knife. Without shelter save a blanket. She could take no more of her gear than she could bear on foot, although she might take a mount if her family had one to spare.

No one would accompany her; she must go and survive alone. If she returned she would be counted as a member of the tribe. The land had taken her to itself in acceptance. If she did not return her body would be found and burned where it lay, returning to the heart of the land that had claimed it. For the living female the Thunder-Drummer would listen to her adventures and from them chose her true name. From that day of her return she would never be unprotected again. Male warriors of the Nitra fought and died. Females were rarely harmed, and even then it was almost always by accident.

The warriors sat on the other side of the fire, accepted cups of the brew they loved, tore at well-cooked grass hen with strong teeth. Tani was discussed in the sounds no human could speak. This human female must be on her name journey. They studied the single blanket, the sheathed knife. She carried no bow or stunner. It was allowable to take drink—if one's family could provide. But the grass hen was fresh. As they approached by the grass patches, they had seen the marks where she had taken it.

Tani admired them. She studied the height and the slenderness. The oldest native must be over seven feet tall. Their skin was of a similar color to Arzoran soil, a sort of reddish-yellow. She saw the small curving horns on the hairless, well-shaped skulls and hid a giggle. They could almost be related to the filly. The warriors wore wide bands of yoris hide from armpit to just below the crotch, with splits over the narrow hips to allow movement. High boots covered their legs, and like her they had belts that carried a number of pouches and a knife each.

The latter caught her attention. Each knife rode in a fringed and decorated sheath similar to hers. She loved the colorful designs in red, gold, and blue beads. Perhaps they'd let her look more closely once they knew her. The senior of the four knew the finger-talk. He signed slowly in case she needed the slower movement to catch his meaning.

"Others travel with you, who?"

From behind him a coyote yapped softly. The warriors turned to see the coyotes watching. Minou and Ferarre faded back into cover and the Nitra were amused. The female had warrior sense. From above them came the vibration of great wings, more felt than heard. Tani stood as the paraowl dropped lightly to the girl's padded shoulder. Tani's fingers wove slow signs.

"Friends travel with me. Gifted by the spirits to be my companions." She signaled and Mandy rose quietly into cover again. It did no harm to be cautious. The natives might shoot if they were frightened by the animals.

The Nitra nodded to each other. This was the one; they were sure of it. The Thunder-Drummer would be pleased at their success. They must take her to the camp. The oldest warrior spoke firmly. The female must be persuaded without violence. To drag one unwillingly from her name-trial would bring great ill fortune upon the clan. The others agreed hastily. On the other side of the fire Tani drank and smiled happily at her guests. It was all just like the tapes. She wished Storm could see her now.

Chapter Seven

Storm had troubles of his own.
The first to enter the cave where the dead Nitra lay was
also Nitra: an older warrior who turned to glance at
Storm almost casually. Storm froze. Fight? No, better to
wait. They didn't seem hostile as yet. Something very
unusual. Three other Nitra entered and fanned out,
watching him, as the oldest of their number examined
the body slowly and carefully. Then he stood, signing to
Storm.

"You find, how?"

Storm signaled and Hing ran to him, swarming up
his breeches to the crook of his arm.

"This small one. She is always curious. She seeks
pretty things to play with. She finds the arrows and
brings one to me. I go in search of the owner."

"Why search?"

Storm's swiftly moving fingers explained his reason-
ing and the warrior nodded. The Nitra reached out, moving slowly and gently with one hand while he signed
with the other.

"She is like horse? She is spirit friend to you?"

"Yes."

The long slender fingers touched Hing's coarse fur,

stroked her back cautiously. Hing rolled over in Storm's arms so that her belly could be tickled and the Nitra gave a small grunting chuckle. From those watching came similar sounds. The Nitra dropped to a squat. Storm followed suit, Hing swarming up to sit on his shoulder.

"Our Thunder-Drummer sent us. She says we must find one whom spirits have chosen. We are to bring that one back to our camp. She will speak to that one of great danger that walks the land."

"Danger?" Storm's fingers queried.

"Death comes out of the desert lands. Many die. More are found dead each time. They not cry to their clan for aid. There is no sign they fought to live. They seem to die in their sleep. Only bones are left. At first only those far from camp died. Herders, hunters. Females on name-trial. Then those who sleep alone in camps. Now all fear to sleep alone. Even those who sleep by a campfire die. We leave the desert, forsake our own clan lands, when one of our warriors wakes at first light. He celebrated a good hunt with food and zerel beer. He is a warrior, he slept well but would have woken at a cry. He finds his mate is stripped bones beside him. It is horror past bearing and the clan flees."

Storm bowed his head. He could taste the horror that must have been. "What did that warrior do?"

"He prayed to the Thunder the next night, then killed himself to lie with his mate." The slit-eyed pupils widened as they studied Storm. "You know of this Death-Which-Comes?"

"We know. We seek ways to destroy it. Our wise ones say we must know its spirit before it can be destroyed."

The warriors around him nodded approval. "Your wise

ones are truly wise. So say those amongst us Who-Drum-Thunder. Our Thunder-Drummer says to bring you to talk with her. You will come with us?"

Storm considered that. It was what he'd been hoping for a week ago when he thought of taking the Carraldos to talk with Nitra under peace poles. No one at the ranch expected him back for days. He'd stay on the alert, write a note quietly and give it to Baku. If anything happened to him he'd order her return to Brad. There was also the thought that right now the Nitra were asking him politely. If he refused they might insist—not so politely.

Normally the Nitra fought anything that wasn't Nitra. This time they'd approached him almost as someone who could be a friend. They were warriors and not fools. Nor were their medicine men and women, Those-Who-Drum-Thunder. If they wanted him to talk with them it was possible he'd be allowed to depart again in one piece. He asked. Fingers flicked agreement.

"You come and talk, then go in peace. That is our Thunder-Drummer's word."

Storm stood slowly, letting them see he intended no attack. "I ride with warriors. We talk of Death-Which-Comes-in-the-Night. Maybe we learn from each other. To learn is good."

The leader nodded, signing, "To learn is good. We ride. Call your spirit friends. They will come with us."

Storm signed back, "The bird flies, the large furred one follows on foot, the small one rides with me. Is that good?"

"It is good."

The oldest warrior mounted, then leaned down to give orders to his comrades. He led off and Storm followed, Hing nestled against his chest as they rode. Surra padded along quietly as Baku swung on leisurely wings overhead. Behind them three warriors made sure that the pitiful bones were sent to the Spirits, as was custom. They mourned briefly according to ritual before they, too, followed. They caught up with their leader and the human close to midday, when they made a brief camp.

At another camp, Tani had heard the same request. She looked around at the earnest faces. They were alien but she could feel the sorrow for their dead, the fear of their own lands turned against them. She lifted her hands to sign.

"My kin will worry. I should return to them today. But I can send my bird to tell my kin not to fear. I will tell them I ride with warriors who will protect me."

The Nitra leader breathed out. Praise be to the Thunder. The female's name-trial had ended this morning. Their offense in asking her to ride with them was that much less and—he had an idea.

"You ride with us in safety, I swear. Our Thunder-Drummer will listen to you, give you a new name for the clan. All shall be well."

Tani grinned happily. That was great. Her father had told her of such naming customs when she was small. Her own ancestor, Wolf Sister, had received that name because of courage in raids upon the Kiowa. Tani's father had always been very proud of his bloodline. Her fingers moved.

"I shall be proud to take a new clan name from your Thunder-Drummer. Wait a very short time. I will speak to my bird. She flies to my clan to tell them I am safe. I return soon?"

"Maybeso five days."

Tani laughed. "I say six," her fingers said. "Maybeso I spend a little time with friends."

Around her the Nitra's eyes met. This one was surely the one they'd been sent to find. She was fearless, naming them as friends who were warriors feared by the settlers and Norbie tribes alike. She was like no other human they had ever known in their lifetimes. They sat in silence as Tani gave the message. Mandy drifted into the sky and was gone. The leader watched her out of sight, then turned to the girl.

"Will the bird find you if we ride?"

"She will find me. We ride now?"

A nod was the reply and Tani stood, reaching for her gear. The Nitra noted her movements as she packed swiftly. They saw experience in the way she tucked the items away without hesitation, each in the correct place. Tani hefted the pad-saddle and bridle, then walked to where she knew her mount was grazing out of sight. The warriors had not sought out the female's horse. One horse was like another. They followed Tani now, to gape incredulously as the filly answered the girl's call. What was this? No horse they had ever seen wore horns such as this. Nor had they ever seen one of silver with eyes that turned, lavender as the sky, to study them in turn.

They saw the horned head lower to nuzzle the girl. Tani hugged the thick, powerful neck, whispering to the filly. "I'm going to call you Destiny. Look what's happened and all because we went riding together."

The filly snorted softly. Then she stamped a warning at the gaping Nitra warriors. No one rode her whom she did not approve. It had been so with humans, it would be so with these not-people. The Nitra leader backed a pace obediently. The female had strong protectors. No wonder she could wander without fear.

Tani read the warning. She turned as she mounted, signing to the Nitra leader. "My horse is also a warrior. I ride her who is my spirit friend. Those who are not spirit friends to her cannot so ride."

The leader nodded. It was seen. Nor did he wish to lose a man to the strange beast. He'd read her attitude; unlike horses, which rarely attacked, this mount would kill happily. He had no knowledge of Astra, the world from which the duocorns came. It was lush and fertile in most places, but it hosted many very formidable predators, and the duocorns had evolved as herbivores but also as fighters, eager to protect their own lives and those of their foals. The warrior spoke firmly to his subordinates as they fetched his and their own ponies. They should leave the female's horse alone. Let her care for it, let her ride the beast. The Thunder had sent her to them, let them not anger the Thunder. Behind his back the youngest warrior scowled angrily. He had killed his enemy. He was not to be ordered like a child.

On the back of her Destiny Tani looked down, waiting. The leader swung up and led them slantwise down the long slope heading toward the Peaks, where the clan now had their camp. They had no time to waste; he shifted his mount to a rocking canter with a nudge of his heels. Five riders accompanied by two coyotes headed toward the mountains. One-Who-Drummed-Thunder waited.

A short time later a paraowl planed in to a landing by an agitated Kady. "Mandy!" She called her husband. "Brion, come quickly. Mandy's just flown in. She must have a message."

Her husband appeared running. Logan and his father arrived at the call. They'd been almost as worried as the Carraldos. Logan had ridden to the Zamle clan of the Shosonna tribe and even now his friends were scouring the edge of the Basin for signs of the missing girl. Both Quades knew of the filly's ferocity. They feared for Tani despite Kady's assurances that with her Beast Master gifts Tani would have taken the filly only if the mount had accepted her. Kady waited until they were standing by her, then turned to the paraowl.

"Give message to Kady."

Mandy spoke in a voice in which the inflections and manner of speech were all Tani's.

"Aunt Kady. I'm sorry but I just had to go for a ride. I met four of the natives and they've asked me to their camp. I think they want to talk about that killer thing. I'll be back in six days. Don't worry, they've said they'll take good care of me, and they're really nice. Oh, and I took the silver filly from the corral. I hope that's all right with Mr. Quade. She's behaving very well and she's wonderful to ride. I love you both and I'll be back soon."

The paraowl eyed the stunned people before rising quickly into the air. She ignored cries to wait. She'd delivered her message, now she'd find Tani again. This world was providing Mandy with more interest than there'd been for her in many months of ship traveling. The live food she was finding here was far better than the mix she was given aboard ship, too. If she stayed with her human's family they'd only have her speak her message over and over. She knew about humans. She was gone, leaving four people to stare at each other.

Mandy caught up with her human just as the small group rested at midday. Destiny wasn't tired, but the Nitra mounts had been worked hard for several days before Tani's tracks had appeared; they must be rested. To the Nitra, horses were almost as precious as the secret water holes of the desert tribes. The Norbies who lived in the more fertile land and often worked for the settlers could obtain horses by trading or as payment for herding work. The wild tribes had nothing to do with humans and preferred it that way. The only drawback was that they thus had far fewer chances to obtain horses.

Most of those they did get were stolen—from the more civilized tribes or the settlers. Life in the Big Blue was ferociously hard. Nitra died, and so did their mounts all too often. The four warriors traveling with Tani eyed the silver filly with awe and envy. Tani was aware of both emotions, and through her filly also knew the feelings. She showed off while the other mounts rested, standing hipshot in meager shade. The youngest warrior stood first once they were ready to ride on.

He moved to one side toward the coveted mount. Then, acting as if he were just about to stroke her, he reached out. His hand closed about the bridle rein. This was only a young mare, even though she was beautiful. He was a horseman from the moment he'd been born. But on Astra the duocorns contended with predatory birds similar to giant eagles, they were also preyed upon by huge fast-moving lizards and cat-like animals. They had developed the reflexes, muscles, and fighting spirit as well as the weapons to handle them. They ate grass as herbivores but their attitudes were those of predators.

On the Terra now gone there'd been other herbivores that it was unsafe to anger. But the young Nitra had never heard of elephants, nor would he have believed the warnings. The filly was young and smaller than most of her purebred kin, but there was no lack of speed, power, or will to fight. The warrior ignored her readiness. He'd ride her a little, show the human female that the Nitra were warriors.

He had no chance to show Tani anything except how he could die. As he leaped for the filly's back, Destiny struck with savage speed and lethal intent. Her head dropped, then swept upward as her horns slashed open his chest. She seized his shoulder in razor teeth and flung him down, and as he fell her hooves drummed a death tattoo. Then she stood in feral alert, waiting to see which of the natives would approach her next.

Tani had sprung to her feet as the filly struck. She reached her first and spun to stand before Destiny. Her hands stumbled through frantic signs.

"Do not harm her."

From the brush Minou and Ferarre snarled a soft warning. One wrong move and they too would fight. From the skies Mandy saw her human below and dropped to join her, only to shear upward again as she read the danger. She hovered above them, her deep sweet piercing cry also a threat to any who would hurt her human friend. Destiny stamped in warning. Then she spat. The taste of not-people blood in her mouth was disgusting. The action was so Nitra-like and so unexpected that the leader jumped. Then, slowly, he began to smile.

Mentally he was assessing the situation. If that stupid one had not been killed by the filly, he might have had to slay him anyhow. No leader could afford a warrior in his group who directly defied him. The boy had been overproud and too quick to act. Sooner or later he'd have died, or gotten one of the others killed. It was better he was the dead one. They'd take the body back, that they owed the boy and their clan. As for the female and her mount . . . His fingers twisted as he admired the ready stance of Destiny, Tani, and her team. They were warriors, and the Nitra admired none more than a true warrior. He signed, speaking the words at the same time.

"We do not hurt the horse." His words were warning to his comrades as much as reassurance to Tani. "The horse did right. I ordered that foolish one not to touch her. He chose to disobey me, who was his leader. He paid the price for his stupidity and disobedience. The horse's spirit is strong. You stay with us? We ride again for clan camp?"

Tani sighed in relief. Somehow she was sure that was all the truth. She signed agreement and followed as the leader walked his mount off down a winding animal trail. Behind them the body was bundled into its blanket and tied to the pony. Then they trotted in pursuit of the two ahead.

That night the native mounts were leg-weary and hungry. They camped early so that they might graze. Minou found them all a small supply of water, cupped in a large, half-hollowed stone. They drank sparingly while admiring the coyote's abilities. After the day's ride they were out into the desert fringes. Any water found was a blessing from the Thunder. The Nitra leader marked the spot in his mind.

Another day's ride and they would be in the new valley the tribe had taken for their own.

Tani unsaddled Destiny and went hunting grass hens. With the coyotes' aid she found enough to feed the three of them. She looked at the bodies, hung them in a nearby Erlan bush, and gave the signal to continue. Mandy was swooping happily on rock-mice and had fed well. She ignored further hunting, drifting off to sit on a bush and digest her dinner. The coyotes looked up, then spread out again. Tani gathered more stones and finally added two more grass hens to her bag. She returned to lay them down by the warrior's supplies.

"Share this food. Save our dried food until it's needed."

The grass hens were accepted with enthusiasm. Dusk was approaching but something was making Tani nervous. She moved and moved again, looking around and behind her. The Nitra saw and queried her discomfort.

"I don't know," Tani signed back. "There's a strange feeling in the air. Some sort of danger. We should go from this place." They eyed her. "Perhaps the thing that kills in the night comes. I only know death is close to us."

She'd been reluctant to speak in case they thought her silly. But her father had often said it was better to be wary than careless. Better to have the living laugh than the family weep over their dead. The Nitra leader seemed to be taking her seriously.

"From which way do you feel death comes?"

Tani stood and looked around, trying to feel the answer. At first she could not be sure, then it was as if a signal strengthened. Her hand rose to point. "From out of the desert, I feel it from that way."

There was no discussion. The leader twittered several words to the other Nitra and the camp was packed again. The indignant horses were saddled and riders and beasts departed, heading briskly away from the perceived danger. The new camp was less comfortable, but they slept unharmed. Soon after dawn Tani woke to see one of the Nitra warriors slipping from the camp. He returned just as the swankee was ready. The leader waited, listening to the report. Then he turned to look at Tani. It was a long slow considering look with a hint of awe.

He did not need to tell the female how many other Nitra rode in search for one marked by the Thunder. But one such four-group had found the old camp and taken it as their own. The warrior who had returned had seen them. They lay, heaps of fresh bones around the ashes of the fire. Taken by that which kills in the night. Taken in place of the three who had listened to the female. They owed her three lives of the clan. A blood-debt must always be paid. Moving deliberately, he drank from his mug until every drop of the precious drink was gone. Then he squatted and waited until her attention was focused on him.

He made a sign with his fingers. Tani followed the motions. They were new to her and her fingers said so. There was a moment's stillness, then the leader signed again, slowly.

"You shared your food and drink with us. You saved our lives with wisdom given you by the Thunder. Those who came to the camp we left, they lie dead. One to whom the Thunder speaks warning is an honored warrior. We are warriors. I lead. It is proper I share my small-name with you. I—" Again his fingers twisted. "In clan I am known as Mafiikyy. It means one who jumps high."

Tani was interested. "Why did you jump?"

The other warriors who did not know the finger-talk so well had been following the signs as best they could. They saw from Tani's face what the question had been and for the first time she heard native laughter. It was a soft spluttering sound and her happy gurgle mixed with it.

The signs flickered again. "I was young. I killed a bird, the mountain flyer. It is no easy prey even for a warrior, and this one was large of its kind. I took the claws for a necklace. I thought myself a great hunter. I showed the claws around our clan fire. I stood up that night and tell everyone of how I killed the flyer. It is true it is a strong fighter, but perhaps I boast too much. I sit down again on my blanket. Rock-mouse has crawled into a fold for warmth. I sit on the rock-mouse. He is angry and bites me very hard. I jump very high, yell very loud in surprise. So I am given that as a small-name. You understand, do your people have small-names?"

Tani managed to stop giggling. She could just see all that. Her hands signed. "I have small-name, yes. I am," this time she spoke the length of her name aloud. Then her hands moved again. "It means Sunset. I am the daughter to Bright Sky. After the Bright Sky of a fine day comes the Sunset."

"Your father is here?"

"My father was killed by enemies many years ago. My mother was killed by the same enemies. The enemies destroyed my home. I live in the home of my mother's brother now."

There was a soft hiss of commiseration from around the camp. They knew how that could be. Jumps High considered swiftly. With her name-trial completed, this one was free to choose. Sometimes a female without immediate family chose to change clans. It would be a big advantage to have in their clan one who could warn when the Death was coming. And the clan already owed her three lives. He signed again.

"You share our clan home. We are people of the Djimbut clan. I will speak to the One-Who-Drums-Thunder. My mate will name you our cousin. You will be a woman of the Djimbut clan if you wish. Stay with us, not stay with us. Still you will be kin. Is it good?"

Tani felt a tear trickle down her cheek. She reached over to clasp Jumps High's hands. She could only nod as the tears came faster. He gave an almost human-sounding sigh and patted her shoulder.

"Make your choice later. Now eat and drink with us. Rest a little. Then we must ride. We will be with the clan by sunset. Sunset will be with the clan."

Tani began to laugh and their own laughter rose with hers. But as she ate and drank she realized something. Partly because of the finger-talk, which limited them to simple discussion to some extent, she had assumed the natives to be not stupid exactly, but maybe not that clever. But Jumps High had made a pun by using an alien name in the signing. That was anything but dumb. She was still thinking about it as they rode, so that she persuaded Jumps High and his warriors into telling her more about their way of life.

It was akin in many ways to that of her father's own race in the days before the white-skins had come. Gradually as she watched the quick signs she came to understand what they had first believed about her. They were wrong, Tani thought. But not so wrong. Many of the tribes including the Cheyenne had once had the custom of fasting alone in the wilderness or desert for many days to learn their true name.

In recent generations as many had returned to some of the old ways, this was done again. She had never done so. She had been too young at first, and then there was no more Earth and the few of the blood who survived had spread far and wide across a number of worlds.

She'd learned from Logan that the Quades were a mixture. Storm was wholly Navaho by a different father, while Brad, his stepfather, was part Cheyenne. And Logan, Storm's halfbrother, was a mixture of Navaho, Cheyenne, and white. No doubt some of their customs differed, yet she had felt very at home with them. All but Storm. The Beast Master who sought out a war to fight and allowed his beasts to die. Storm was leaving to talk to native friends, Logan had told her. She was talking to native friends, too, now. She went back to teasing Jumps High into telling more of the old tales told around their clan fires.

Chapter Eight

Storm's party had ridden most
of the day. For much of the ride one or another of the
Nitra had been absent. Scouting ahead, Storm believed.
It had been an odd ride. He was with the group but not
of it. None had spoken further to him and it was as if
he were almost unnoticed. Not that this was more than
an illusion, he knew. If he'd tried to leave they'd have
noticed him very quickly. Toward dark they'd come to
a camp. Nothing elaborate, merely several puff bushes
clumped around and to one side of a rock spire. But it
would provide shelter for the night.

The one who knew the sign-talk had indicated Surra.
"The big animal will hunt?"

"She will hunt now. She will bring back meat for us.
You will not shoot when she returns?" Storm added.

The warrior eyed him with the air of a grandmother
being told how to suck eggs. "We will not shoot. We
are hunters, we will know when she returns."

Nothing more was said. Surra hunted successfully
and returned to share the small deer she had killed. Baku
had flown and returned to sit on one foot using the other
and her beak to pluck the fat grass hen she'd taken. One
of the warriors walked slowly to stoop beneath her busy

claws and retrieve some of the undamaged feathers. He plucked grass and some of the puffs from the puff bushes. From these he twisted an odd shape, which Storm studied with interest.

The thin grass cord had become a net that imprisoned several of the puffs, and below on a further length of cord hung a tiny swirl of soft breast feathers. The warrior looked up to see Storm's gaze fixed on him. He spoke to the one who knew how to sign. Storm waited. The oldest warrior turned to look at him, then his fingers spoke.

"We pray to the Thunder which lives in the sky. This is our prayer sent up to the Thunder. All birds belong to the Thunder. That tree is a sacred tree." His hand pointed to a lone falwood tree. "We send the feathers of a bird and sacred-tree leaves to speak for us. You understand?"

Storm nodded. The puffs were lighter than air, since at the right time of the year they would detach from their bush and float away to seed a new bush in some other location. He also understood the idea, it was not so different from many he'd known as a small boy on Earth. He watched as the warrior holding the odd construction walked toward a solitary falwood tree. He collected several of the dry leaves and wove the pieces through the puffs. Then he returned to the fire and in turn each warrior touched the small ball of grass and puffs. Then it was carried to the edge of the camp.

The warrior who had made it raised it up into the air. The wind came in a greater gust and it sailed from his fingers out across the land below the small rise on which they had camped. Storm watched. The floating symbol rose and fell in the air, dipping and swaying with the small feathers below swinging on the thin grass cord. It did not touch ground again for so long as he could see. The Nitra about him twittered approval. The oldest turned to Storm and signed.

"That is good. The Thunder has heard and listens to us. Our prayer is accepted. Now we make camp and sleep. Tomorrow the ride will be long, but the next night we sleep with clan."

Storm nodded. He shared Surra's gift with the Nitra, who roasted it over the campfire. Everyone ate quickly, before Storm rolled into his blanket and slept. He was alert enough to mark the guard change as each Nitra in turn took watch, but other than that awareness he slept well. He woke to saddle his mount with the others of the group.

"Which way do we ride?"

"Toward the mountains. It will be a long ride. Will the big animal be able to keep up?"

That was a problem, Storm thought. Surra had been tired enough by last night and they'd only ridden half a day. She'd be unable to stay with them in a complete day of hard riding. Nor was it practical to take her with him on his mount. He could let her ride behind the saddle briefly, for a short lift across a wide shallow stream or over some other obstacle the big cat did not approve, yes. But not as a second rider for many hours. He looked up.

"She cannot run so long. Maybeso we can ride slower, take a while longer to reach the camp?"

There was a twittering of discussion. It became heated, then died as the oldest Nitra spoke in tones of decision. Then he signed,

"We can take an extra day. Ride more slowly. But that

is not so safe. Death-Which-Comes-in-the-Night hunts here in these lands. We wish to leave swiftly from this place. We listen to your wisdom."

Surra came to rub against Storm's knee and he stroked her. More than once she had ridden on supply carts. She'd been carried on a packhorse that was only lightly loaded, apart from Surra. The ranch horses, which were used to her, would accept carrying her at need and at Storm's command. It would be uncomfortable for her to ride and they had no spare mount, anyhow.

He worried that what he said might bring trouble. If Surra couldn't keep up, they could decide to see that she stayed behind—permanently. Although, their Thunder-Drummer had said to bring him and they seemed to count the team as part of that order. He dropped to squat on his heels, his fingers flicking through the signs.

"I do not wish to make danger for you. But where I go the big animal goes too. Maybeso you ride on ahead, leave me signs for the trail. I can follow more slowly with the spirit friend."

"We do not leave you alone."

That was one idea that he could discard. Storm signed again. "Anyplace you know that may keep away thing that kills in night?"

"There is noplace we know where that is sure."

That was another idea he could forget. "Any road shorter? Maybeso with help of spirit friends there is a shorter road I could take? I take that with them, I go ahead and you catch up to me later?"

That produced a vigorous twittering from one of the warriors. His fingers pointed and his hands waved as Storm struggled to understand. It appeared the Nitra did know of a shortcut that might be taken if . . . the finger-talker returned to Storm.

"That warrior hunted here once many seasons ago before we moved camp. He say there may be a shorter road but it is not easy."

Sometime later Storm was agreeing heartily with that. Still, he was fascinated by the path they were traveling. It hadn't been made by the natives; that was certain. Instead it was akin to the steps he had once used that were cut into the cliff near the sealed caves. This was another cliff, but it led down into a deep canyon. On the far side the shallow niche steps led upward again.

Three of the Nitra had taken all of the mounts and were riding hard to reach the far side by passing around the canyon head. At that end the rush of water over generations had flattened out the end of the rocks, so a ridden horse could climb down and back up the shallower slope. Storm and the youngest member of the Nitra quartet were on foot with Surra. Hing clung to Storm's shoulder as they trotted along the animal track. Something used this path, but what he couldn't say. The earth was beaten hard and the light rains had not yet penetrated this far into the desert.

They reached the other side of the canyon and Hing leaped down to begin the scramble upward. The steps had never been deep, Storm believed. After years of erosion they were even shallower now and there were places where it was hard to climb. By the time they reached the top both were breathing hard and pleased to rest a while before the mounts and riders came in sight again. Only Surra had found the way short and easy and she was always happy to relax in the sun. But the canyon climb had taken many miles from the journey.

Now they had no need to hurry. Those who had ridden had changed mounts back and forth, making more speed than usual. They could ride steadily but quietly, allowing their mounts time to cool down, and still reach the camp before nightfall. Yet there was agitation amongst the riders as they came up with Storm and his companion. They said nothing until both were mounted again and they had turned onto the trail. Then the oldest warrior nudged his mount to ride beside that of Storm. His hands began to weave the story.

"Many groups from the clan have gone out at the command of our Thunder-Drummer. Our scout found signs left on this trail that another group rides with success." Storm wondered what unfortunate had been seized, and what attributes had made the Nitra believe this other one to be special, but the fingers continued to flash signs. He concentrated.

"It is ill fortune for a group that went before us, on the same trail into your lands. The scout saw no sign they had returned. He rode back along the trail to seek them out. He found only death. He thinks they found no one who was as our Thunder-Drummer described. So they begin to ride back again. They camped that night in a shelter by rocks. Death came in the night for them."

"Ill fortune for warriors," Storm signed back. "All were dead? No one escaped the Death-Which-Comes-in-the-Night?"

"No one."

"How did this happen? Did none guard, watch over sleep of friends?"

The signs seemed to take on an exasperated tone. "They were all young. Young warriors fear nothing, believing themselves invincible. They slept without guard by the fire. They died where they lay."

So four young and careless Nitra had been killed. What had happened to their mounts, then? There had been none brought along by the riders of this group. Storm asked.

"That is strange. The other group who finds one to bring for the Thunder-Drummer, they camped at that shelter first. Our scout says the signs are clear. They camped there only a little time, then they packed and left the camp. They took a site further away down the trail. At first light one of them went back to the first camp, found what had happened. They gave the dead the clan rites, then they took the horses and rode for the clan."

Storm mulled over the information. It seemed that someone in that first group must have felt danger. The horses were the interesting thing. The killer had taken four Nitra, smaller prey, when they could have had four horses.

"Your other group took the dead warriors' horses? Why did the horses not run when Death-in-the-Night came?"

The oldest Nitra made it clear he understood the implications.

"The horses were tied very tight and could not get free easily. They were a small way from the camp. There was much sign, the horses fought hard to be free but could not escape. Yet Death-Which-Comes-in-the-Night did not take horses. It chose Nitra. Frawns died before Nitra. Horses died before Nitra. But now Death-Which-Comes has tasted Nitra blood, it takes Nitra only if it can find us."

Damn. If that was right, whatever these things were, they

were targeting people. They'd take animals if they found nothing else to hunt and eat. But if there were people around they'd take them in preference. Were people easier prey, or did they taste better?

"I found a young warrior of our people dead by that death," Storm signed, thinking as his hands moved. "His blankets where he'd bled on them were eaten, the wood of his bed chewed, too, where his blood was on it. You find horses dead. Is it so with them? Is the ground where blood was spilled eaten away?"

"Not so. But so where the Nitra die. Death feasts on our blood. It seeks out every drop and leaves nothing."

That must be at least a part of it. There was something in the blood of the natives and humans that attracted the killers.

"Your people are great hunters. You travel far trails in the desert. You even know trails across the Big Blue. Have any of your clan ever known death like this before?"

"We have never seen it. In all clan history our Thunder-Drummer says there is no knowledge of this."

"Humans and Nitra die. Horses and frawns die. Have you seen the bones of other kills? What else does this thing kill?"

"We see the bones of feefaw birds. There are more than usual. Not so very many more, but more than die most seasons. We think that is not the death itself. With less frawn in these lands, the feefaw have less frawn hair for nests. The nestlings die more easily from the cold at night. The parents use the nests later. They too die from winter cold if the hair is not there for lining. We do not see other bones."

Storm rode in silence the rest of the day. Already this

killer thing was causing subsidiary deaths. That wasn't good at all, and it was like a puzzle. What did humans, Nitra, and Norbies have in common with horses and frawns, apart from life itself? Hing rode happily, squeaking now and again as she saw something that interested her. Storm refused to put her down and by the time they reached the camp she was indignant about it. However, he continued to grip her gently. If she vanished into one of the Nitra shelters she could be mistaken for a danger. He had no desire to have her injured or killed.

Her complaints came louder and he was vaguely aware of someone approaching him.

"I'll take her."

It took a breath before he realized that the words had been spoken. His gaze jerked downward to meet that of Tani. "What are you doing here?" he gritted through his horror.

"Jumps High asked for my help. He said the medicine woman wanted to talk to me." Mistaking the reason for his agitation, Tani was reassuring. "It's okay. I sent Mandy to tell the ranch about it. They know I'm with Norbie friends."

Norbies! Friends! Storm opened his mouth and shut it again abruptly. How could she know? It seemed no one had thought to tell her about the Nitra. That they were the wild tribes in contrast to the Norbies' more civilized ones. That they hung the hacked-off bow hands of enemies in their shelter smoke-holes to cure. Or that they warred with humans, Norbie, and even other Nitra tribes on occasions. That they . . . he held himself motionless as one of the Nitra warriors walked up to the girl. She turned to face him and their hands flashed. So, she'd learned the finger-talk somewhere. Probably from tapes, her signs were the more formal versions. Not fast but quite fluent. He read the signs and blinked.

Tani was addressed as a clan-friend and cousin to the warrior who spoke. His gaze was caught by a movement and he saw the girl's coyote pair slipping through the crowd to rejoin her. The Nitra appeared to accept them. His gaze shifted to scan the camp. There, on the branch of a dead tree. The paraowl. He looked back at Tani in time to see the warrior finish signing, then pat her shoulder as he left. Storm said nothing but his eyes widened, then narrowed slightly.

That had been something about a new name. He remembered Nitra customs and half guessed at some of the reasons she might be safe. He dismounted slowly and handed Hing to the girl.

"She wants to explore. Can you tell your friends that she won't hurt anybody and if she takes anything she shouldn't, I'll give it back."

Tani nodded, her hands moving as she faced the crowd, smiling happily. To Storm's amazement some of the Nitra smiled back at her. He waited until she had finished and released Hing, who scurried off at once.

"Tani, how long have you been here in the camp?"

"We got here last night. I'm staying with Jumps High's family. His mate is so nice. And they have two daughters. We've had a wonderful time."

Storm wondered for a few startled moments if he was hallucinating. It had to be almost the first time any human had ever described time in Nitra hands as wonderful. He was even more startled when two Nitra girls appeared, each seizing Tani by a hand to draw her away with them. In all his time on Arzor he'd never seen Nitra women. They were guarded and protected like the precious water holes. He allowed his gaze to slide unobtrusively over the camp as he unsaddled his mount.

There weren't as many females to be seen as males, but they looked much the same as the Norbie women of Krotag's Shosonna. They were handsome, the small curving ivory-white horns on the hairless heads only adding an exotic touch. They were a little shorter than the Norbies. The males would have averaged no more than seven feet of extremely slender height, although they all gave the impression of wiry strength and endurance. The women averaged perhaps six inches shorter, their slenderness giving an elegant grace to the adults and a gawky charm to the girls.

The women wore the yoris skin corselet slit over the hips, but spreading from beneath it they added light frawn fabric bloused trousers that tucked into calf-high laced boots of yoris skin. They also wore jewelry. Some of it was rough-polished semiprecious stones only. Some had claws and teeth interspersed between the stones. One old woman wore a collar that covered her from shoulder point to shoulder point and dipped down almost to waist level. The Norbie males often wore such items, but only the males. This one was not of claws or teeth but composed of exquisitely carved plaques; it looked both ancient and very valuable and Storm looked away quickly. It would not be good if the clan thought him to be too interested in a valuable item.

Storm could see no other woman, and few of the males, wearing such a collar at all, and those others were all of the usual type. The oldest warrior from the group that had taken him came from the crowd as they watched Storm without speaking.

"You come now to the tent of our Thunder-Drummer. She speak to you and Sunset."

Storm was four paces in his wake when the last words registered. He stopped, signing a question. "You say 'and Sunset.' You mean at sunset, yes?"

The warrior was impatient. "I speak 'and Sunset.' The female of your people who came with Jumps High. She is friend to clan. You come now!"

Storm followed with apparent meekness as he mulled over that startling information. The "Sunset" must be Tani, but how had the girl become accepted as a friend to a Nitra clan? Whatever she had done it must have been unusual and effective. Settler women had often been left unharmed in the old days after Nitra attacks. But the Nitra didn't rush out to claim them as friends of the clan. Even if they had taken Tani's status to be that of a female on her name-trial, they wouldn't have accepted her casually. She must have proved herself a valuable friend in some way.

From what he'd understood, the clan's Thunder-Drummer, their medicine woman, had sent groups of warriors out on a search. They were to find one or more people who were different. Exactly what difference they'd looked for, Storm was uncertain. They'd taken him, he thought, for his team. Maybe that was why they'd taken Tani, too. Except that on the trip back she had somehow impressed them mightily and was now accepted as clan-friend. He stooped to enter the dwelling. It was large, being both home and Wizard House for One-Who-Drums-Thunder.

Within its walls a circle of Nitra sat waiting. Tani was there, too, sitting by the male who had spoken to her earlier. The old female with the magnificent necklace was there as well. Her face, now painted in the significant patterns of a Thunder-Drummer, was almost unrecognizable. Storm sat hiding his surprise. The settlers had been on Arzor six generations, and the only Nitra contact until that time was with warriors.

In Norbie society women were the keepers of the campfire. The ones who held the tribe's memories and lineages. Males were the warriors and hunters. It looked as if women were even more amongst the Nitra. He had not realized the Thunder-Drummer was a woman, the sign for that was sexless. It meant simply One-Who-Drums-Thunder. Sitting to the right of the One-Who-Drums-Thunder was a young male with a badly scarred and twisted leg. Normally the Nitra would have quietly encouraged one with those injuries to die. Their land was harsh. The clan could not afford to feed useless mouths, which meant the boy must have a valuable function. Storm waited and saw.

The oldest warrior from his group entered and sat. The woman nodded. He began. In his own soft twittering speech he explained how they had searched and found one who had animal and bird spirits to accompany him. As he began to talk the boy raised his hands and signed. He kept pace with the story in the fastest and most fluent finger-talk Storm had ever seen. Apparently that was for their benefit, because the old woman lifted a hand. She spoke and the boy signed.

"You speak this talk, he signs not too fast for you to understand?"

Storm nodded, he could follow the boy's signs even if he could not have signed that quickly himself. "The female of your kind. She does not understand such swift talk. You will tell her anything she must know?"

His hands signed agreement.

"That is well."

Around the other side of the circle Tani had understood more of the signs than either expected. She smiled slightly. It had only been for her amusement that she'd learned, but she had used both the learning from the cortex impresser and then the visual tapes. With a week of teasing Logan into helping her and then several days' continuous practice with Jumps High's group and his family, she could now understand the talk at a faster rate than her unpracticed hands could make the signs. It was the slowness of her fingers they had mistaken for slow understanding. She would watch hard now and see how much Storm told her.

She guarded herself. She'd read of other cultures and visited over a dozen planets in her life. She knew misunderstandings were common enough and once in the clan camp had begun to see what the Nitra's initial mistake had been. She'd noted the bow-hands drying in the smoke outlet of the shelter. A warrior had died for each of those hands. It neither surprised nor disgusted her, contrary to what Storm would have expected. Tani had grown up with the stories of Cheyenne conquest from her father. The past of Ireland, too, had been long and bloody, as were its stories. Alisha and later Aunt Kady and Uncle Brion had told her those.

Tani had hunted with her team. She knew that all things die in their time and that to draw back in horror at the native trophies would give offense. She'd made a quick signed comment about being in the home of true warriors and thereafter ignored both trophies and the subject. But she had noted the quick reaction of pleasure and pride. She'd done the right thing. She watched the story of Storm's capture unfold. It took little time and then Jumps High started his tale.

This took far longer as time and time again one in the circle would wish a part of the story retold. The part where she had warned them of Death-Which-Comes-in-the-Night. How Jumps High had chosen to believe her and moved the camp. And how the other group had taken the camp later and died for it had to be told over several times. Until every nuance was sucked dry. As the story continued past that point she noticed even Storm was regarding her with interest. Tani grinned to herself. He should see that you didn't have to be a team-wasting, war-trained Beast Master to know things, too.

She was right. Storm *was* interested. Her story explained for a start just why the Nitra were accepting the girl as a clan-friend. He, too, hid a smile. She hadn't known they were Nitra, that was the base of everything. Logan hadn't told her that beyond the Norbie tribes lived the Nitra. It appeared that Logan had simply assumed Tani would never be in a position where she would meet Nitra, and had refrained from possibly scaring her. So when four warriors came out of the dawn, Tani had met them as friends. She'd offered food, drink, and the shelter of the fire.

To the surprised warriors, that had marked her as a female of high status to begin with. Finding she had animal spirits who traveled with her had underlined it. Then, she had saved their lives, they had believed that she heard the Voice of the Thunder. It made her, not quite a Thunder-Drummer, but one similar to an apprentice and to be honored. Her happy acceptance of them and the return offer of her own small-name had sealed their decision. Around the circle the tale was continuing.

Storm had not known until then that Tani had taken the filly. He listened as Jumps High related how the young mare had attacked and killed the warrior who tried to ride her. He was more than fair in the telling, Storm thought. The Thunder-Drummer wished to see this warrior horse. Solemnly the circle trooped out to the horse herd. Tani called the filly and they stared at her. The medicine woman turned to Storm and her aide's fingers flew.

"Our clan-friend rides this one. Can you do so as well?"

Storm shook his head, signing a negative, then he expanded on that.

"Maybeso I stay on this one's back. That is not riding. Her heart is given to Sunset alone. This horse would hate me if I force her to carry me. To ride her when she is unwilling is as if I forced a warrior to be slave to me. The horse accepts only Sunset. No other rider, not ever again."

From the corner of his eye he saw the sudden distressed look on Tani's face. She hadn't understood the depth of the bond a duocorn could form. The filly would never be any good now as a mount. Not for anyone but Tani. When the girl departed from Arzor she must leave the filly, but only as breeding stock. The silver horse would never again share the joy of two as one, feel the delight in her own speed amplified by the emotions of her rider. Storm wished he hadn't made that so clear, but the girl had to know sometime.

Tani hadn't known. All she could do now was walk up to hug Destiny's warm neck. The medicine woman observed and, being wise, said no more. They returned to the shelter and the story was concluded. Then they sat in silence. It was some five minutes later when the Thunder-Drummer stirred. Her voice and the signing began as she turned to Storm.

"Your people seek an end to the Death-Which-Comes-in-the-Night. Sunset can hear it if it is close and she listens. Can you also do this?"

"I don't know," Storm told her honestly. "I've never tried while I was awake, although I've dreamed of it. But Sunset heard the death while she was with your warriors and awake. She may be more sensitive to it."

The woman pondered. "Amongst the clans there are few who can drum Thunder. But sometimes in times of danger those who do are able to link power. Such a time was when a false Thunder-Drummer came against us, saying do my bidding, I am Lord of the Thunder. You saw this thing?"

Storm nodded. "I was there. I saw the power of those who drum truly. I saw the false one overthrown."

"Then, don't you think, man whom spirits follow? The girl can hear the death, maybe you can link with her to hear more strongly."

Across Tani's face flashed a look of disgust. Both the medicine woman and Storm saw it. The Thunder-Drummer shook her head.

"I do not force. I only suggest. But if something is not done I fear this death will eat up the world. Against that who would not fight? Who would not risk anything to save their clan?" She stood slowly. "I will rest. Let you rest also and think." Her eyes turned to gaze at Storm. "You are free of the camp, but do not stray past the borders lest our warriors think you are leaving us without farewell."

She reached out to touch Tani's arm. "Come, eat with me, little sister. Tell me of your family. Jumps High says your parents are dead and your home gone, at the hands of an enemy. I would hear of how that happened."

Storm watched them leave until only he remained sitting with Hing in his lap, and Surra, who had found him by the horses, leaning against his leg. His mind was dark. If it would save Arzor he'd link with Tani, but it would not be pleasant. For some reason the girl disliked him, or at the very least distrusted him. Once or twice in training he had linked with other Beast Masters. The linkage was minor, just a sensing of emotions, and in those cases the emotions had been more curiosity and interest.

Through any link with Tani would come much stronger feelings. Even if she agreed. But then he thought with relief that she would have to agree for a link to be forged, and she'd made it plain she would never do that. He relaxed a little. Once the Nitra understood they'd let them leave. Maybe back at the ranch he could persuade her to think about it. She liked Arzor. He could play on the possible death or destruction of the planet. He had time, he could wait for understanding to come.

Chapter Nine

The next day the camp was active. Tani crawled out of her blanket to find that she was summoned.

"I go on scout," Jumps High signed. "I and my group. If you wish to ride with us, we will go as soon as we have eaten and the horses are made ready."

Above, the lavender sky was brightening toward a day of sunshine. Tani stretched and grinned. Destiny would enjoy a day out and so would the others of the team.

"No one will mind if I bring my spirit friends?"

"That is good."

Laughing, she ran to wash, then return to where Jumps High's mate prepared food. Small Bird turned to hug the girl.

"You sleep well, Sunset, now eat. I make fritters. You have had them before?" Tani shook her head. "You will like them." Small Bird was positive.

Tani enjoyed the horva fritters. Now that she'd eaten one of Small Bird's fritters, she remembered she'd had them once before at the Quade's ranch. They were made from a native Arzoran grain, although the Nitra ones seemed to have been made from a wild variety of the grain and tasted slightly different. There was lorg berry jam to ladle over them and Tani ate greedily. When she rose to leave she hugged Small Bird. She'd discovered that the Nitra within a clan were an affectionately tactile people. They liked to hug friends and family, and touching was a part of their clan life. The girl liked that. Her parents had both been openly fond of each other. Within their tiny family, Bright Sky, Alisha, and Tani had hugged each other often. Her parents had kissed regularly in passing, both their small daughter and each other. Affection had been a constant underlay of their lives.

Kady and Brion were loving but were less open about hugs and casual pats. Tani had not known it until now, but she'd missed the feeling of contact. Her first introduction to Small Bird had been when the woman swept her into a warm embrace of welcome. The girls had hugged her in turn after that. Tani had been surprised at first, then pleased. After two days she hugged back matter-of-factly. It was the way one behaved and she liked it, the touch filled some gap in her heart that had been empty until she was brought to the clan. Now she scrambled her gear together and carried it out to the horse herd, in search of the filly. She didn't have far to go.

Destiny pranced up from the edge of the herd. She made a mock pass at her friend with her horns slicing air in a wicked upthrust movement, then she turned to dance sideways.

Tani laughed. "Yes, we're going out. A lovely long ride with friends."

From behind her there was the soft sound Nitra made when they wished to draw attention. The girl turned to find the Thunder-Drummer behind her, interpreter at her shoulder.

"You ride with Jumps High. Ride carefully, little sister. Word came to me at dawn from another clan. The death struck at them last night. A family lie dead."

Tani stared in horror. "How many?" her hands asked.

"Three. A warrior, his mate, and a small son. We do not have so many children we can spare any. And the loss of a family is a great loss to a clan. The clan grieves greatly for them. It seems to me that the death grows larger and more hungry each time it slays. Their Thunder-Drummer goes now to a sacred place to ask of the Thunder what they should do. Such a place I sought many days ago. There I prayed to the Thunder. Answers I was given to questions, but not all."

"What did you learn?"

"That I should send out warriors to find those who will battle the death."

Tani knew about oracles. Sometimes the message was obscure, and at other times it could be easily misinterpreted. Often those receiving it read more into it than was there.

"Did it say we'd win?"

The Thunder-Drummer shook her head. "It said I should seek and find. I asked other questions. That one was not answered. Others were. It seemed to me that this was meant." The hands paused to give weight to what followed. "If those we found cannot win, then no one can, but the battle is not for them alone but for many. Those we found shall be as the arrowhead. Those who aid them are as the shaft and the feathers that aid the arrowhead to fly straight and to strike a killing blow. I have seen the stars wheel about you, Sunset. I have seen you raise up our world in your hands and hold it as a mother holds her child. And behind you I have seen another stand whose face I could not see. In the smoke of the sacred falwood I have seen dreams. Ride safely, clan-friend."

She turned on her heel and was gone, the interpreter following. Tani stared after her. Then she shrugged. If it was, it was. She returned to the filly, saddling and bridling her swiftly as Destiny danced. Then she swung up into the saddle and headed for where she could see Jumps High and his group waiting for them.

It was a peaceful day. They returned toward evening with all pleasantly tired and hungry. The coyotes had demonstrated that they could find and drive game, so that over the saddles of two of the warriors hung merin deer. Both were yearling bucks. They'd make a very welcome addition to the clan's cooking pots and would be meticulously shared. From Destiny's saddle rings hung a string of grass hens. Tani would take those to share with the family who sheltered her.

She was smiling gently as she swayed to the filly's pace. It had been a wonderful day. She must give Mandy another message for the ranch and send her there. She could let them know where Storm was as well. She looked over the camp happily as they slowed to circle toward the horse herd. Arzor was so lovely. It looked just the way her father's own lands must have looked once. She sighed. If only he and Alisha were here with her, how they'd have enjoyed today.

Her face was still wistful as Storm approached. He slowed. She seemed to be in a half-dream and somehow he didn't want to disturb her. She looked so sad, as if something were missing that she had lost a long time ago. She had lost as much as he had. And she was Terran, young, afraid of losing more. She was of his kind twice over and he'd only reacted angrily to her. The small sad face moved him strongly.

Impulsively he stepped forward and drew her into a gentle hug. He too had been influenced by the tactile habits of the Nitra. Amongst them warriors hugged; touched, stroked arms in friendship. Storm had found he did not mind it.

With his team he had always been affectionate. Brad rarely touched. Logan was different. From their first meeting had come an acknowledgment that half-brothers they might be in blood, they were full brothers in feeling. After that Logan had casually laid an arm often over Storm's shoulders. Or thumped him gently in rough affection. Now, seeing the wistful memories in Tani's gaze, he did as Logan or any of the Nitra would have done.

Tani had been hugged so often since she arrived in the camp that she reacted automatically, hugging back. For a moment it filled her heart. There was no desire in the warmth, simply kinship and understanding. In her long loneliness she could momentarily accept the solace. Then she realized who it was. As he released her she leapt away. Her eyes were startled and wary. For a moment she stood poised for flight, looking at him. Then she was gone running toward the shelter of Jumps High, where his mate would be preparing food. She slowed after twenty paces. There was nothing that said danger.

Ahead Mandy perched on her branch, studying the girl. She looked at her friend, then very slowly revolved her head until she was surveying the girl from upside down. Tani giggled. It was a silly trick but Mandy knew it always made her feel better.

"You're a daft bird and now I want you to find Aunt

Kady. Give her a message." Her voice shifted as she linked, impressing the words. "I'm fine and Storm is here with the clan, too. We'll be back in a few more days, I think. Don't worry about us. I love you both." She eyed the paraowl. "Repeat!" Mandy did so flawlessly. "Good, now fly carefully."

The paraowl lifted off into the warm air. In direct flight she'd be to the ranch and back before Tani slept. She'd fly the return in the dark, but that wouldn't bother Mandy. She was an owl with an owl's night vision when it was required. Tani looked after the fading speck.

She could still feel Storm's arms around her. It had felt odd, and what was annoying her was that it had also felt right. She snorted and shook her head like the filly, to clear it. One hug didn't make him a friend. He was still a Beast Master, one who wasted the lives of his team to save himself. But he did seem to love his team. Tani was confused by that. He had Hing with him in the camp and Tani had found the small beast charming. She'd also realized both that Storm's team loved and trusted him, and that Hing was lonely without Ho, her longtime mate who'd been killed.

Brion Carraldo had looked over the Arzoran ecology reports and agreed that meerkats could fill the place left by the rinces. Tani had spent a good amount of her time soon after arrival on building embryos for that purpose. It had been her way of doing it that had caused the problems with Jarro on the ship. By now, and with forced growth, many of those would already have been born. As well, she'd created a clone from the male adult meerkat they had in the stasis tanks. More of the meerkats could be added to the tiny population here once the scientists had made further studies. Indeed, by the time Tani returned to the Ark, that first batch should be old enough to join Hing's offspring. The older male would be perfect for Hing herself. Tani decided to mention the meerkats to Storm. Her dislike of him had melted at the hug and in a hitherto unrecognized knowledge that perhaps Storm was as lonely as Tani was herself, at times. He wasn't as welcome here as she was. The meerkats would give him something pleasant to think about. She ate with her clan friends, then departed again in search of the only other human here. It was almost dusk.

Storm met her with the bland, smooth face of one who was embarrassed at his own actions. Tani didn't notice. She was too pleased with the good news she was bringing. She burst out with it as soon as she saw Hing was there, too, cradled gently in Storm's arms as he scratched her paler stomach fur, his mouth curving in a small half-smile as the meerkat churred her pleasure.

"I don't know if Uncle Brion told you, but Hing will love it. I built a bunch more meerkats from the material in the Ark and if nothing went wrong there should be six at the half-grown stage. They're in incubators and they should be ready to join Hing and her family in a couple of weeks. The Ark's staying longer than that so I can see that they all get on together. One of them is in the forced-growth tank so Hing can have a full adult mate once we get back to the ranch. Maybe I can even do a couple more to widen the genetic pool. I had to tell you so you didn't keep on worrying about Hing."

For the first couple of sentences Storm hadn't understood, but then the message penetrated. He looked down at the meerkat where she lay happily in his arms.

"Seven," he said, softly marveling. "She'll have a whole

clan, too." "Yes. With her and her four kits there'll be twelve." Tani reached over to stroke Hing. "Of course she'll breed. That will help teach the young ones how to look after kits. Once they are old enough the clan will probably split into two groups. You should look for a suitable burrow far enough away so they don't feel one group threatens the other."

Storm sat down on a log. He'd seen the sudden sadness in the girl's eyes when she'd assured him that Hing would have a clan again. He lifted the drowsy meerkat.

"You hold her for a while. She likes her stomach stroked." The corners of his mouth turned up again in a slight grin as Tani obeyed. Then he looked at her.

"Your uncle said that your father was Cheyenne, and a Beast Master. I met him once. Tell me about him."

Tani eyed him a little shyly. "Why?"

"I liked him. He was a good man. A good fighter too. He had a dune cat on his team, like Surra, only male. The time we met we talked of letting them mate once the war was over. Did your mother ever tell you how he died?"

"She never wanted to talk about it. I'd like to hear."

Storm sighed. "About halfway through the war the Xiks invaded Trastor. Trastor's only been settled two generations and the population then was no more than fifty thousand, scattered all over the main continent. But it's a rich world and they had warehouses dotted around, holding valuables for off-world shipment. Your father was caught on-planet by their destruction of the space port. He tried to send his team to safety out of the port area, but they wouldn't leave him. The Xiks had a number of hostages they were torturing for information, so Bright Sky went in to free them. He succeeded, but after that the Xiks had him targeted. He set up groups of people to raid Xik supply depots. He made contact with off-planet command finally and when they attacked, he led his guerrillas to attack the Xiks on-planet, near the port.

"He was killed trying to get one of his group to safety after she'd been badly injured. His team went berserk. They died still killing the enemy. With Bright Sky gone no one could call them back." He glanced at her as she mechanically stroked Hing. "Understand. He tried to save his team. Their loyalty to him wouldn't let him send them away. And Command didn't make him fight the way he did. Your father was Cheyenne. In the end he saw that all humans were his clan and Xiks were their enemy.

"The people on Trastor buried him and his team together. I was on the planet the year after. They'd covered the grave with plascrete and engraved it as a memorial."

Tani looked up, her eyes filled with tears. "What does it say?"

"There was his name and then the names of the team. And underneath the names there were two lines." Storm fell silent a moment as he remembered. He'd stood there reading the words and wishing that one day he'd merit such a tribute.

"They say, 'Nothing is won without sacrifice.' Then under that it says, 'Their deaths bought Trastor's freedom.' I talked to one of their people. She said that it was true. The original Xik attack had been so unexpected that they'd taken many of the Trastor Command prisoner. Bright Sky freed them. Then he taught farmers and miners guerrilla tactics and coordinated counterattacks against the Xiks. He brought hope to people devastated by what had happened. He showed them they could fight back—and they did, with his example to lead them. Bright Sky and his team are greatly honored there."

Tani sat in silence. This was not the picture her mother had painted. Alisha had claimed Bright Sky's life had been thrown away almost casually by the Terran High Command. Now Storm was saying that this wasn't the way things had happened. She didn't want to believe her mother had lied, but Storm's tale fitted with too many other things she'd heard. Aunt Kady hadn't tried to belittle her sister-in-law, but she'd told Tani more than once not to believe all Alisha had said in her grief.

But if Alisha had been so wrong about that, if she had twisted what she knew and told her daughter, what of her other teachings? Tani remembered her mother talking about Beast Masters. Saying they threw away the lives of their teams to preserve themselves. Over and over Alisha had pointed to Beast Masters returning to add new trained animals to depleted teams. After her father's death Tani had grown up believing that others of his kind spent team lives as if they had no value. Over the past few days, though, she'd seen how much Storm cared about his beasts.

She'd opened her mouth to tell him of her confusion when there was an outcry in the camp. Natives were running toward the place. From where they converged Minou was yapping for her to come swiftly. Tani bolted to her feet and ran. Storm passed her as they reached the edge of the crowd and she followed in his wake as he forged past the agitated clan. There was a yoris. It was the season for mating and the big male would have full poison sacs. He must have strayed near the camp and found himself cornered by several of the playing children.

Four had fled past him to freedom. The fifth, barely past being a toddler, was trapped, shivering in fear where he crouched on top of a small rock. He was still within reach of the big lizard who was making aggressive gestures toward the child, showing its poison fangs in openmouthed anger. To interfere and anger the lizard further was to risk an attack by the yoris on the child. The lizards weren't bright. If enraged they often tended to attack whatever already held their attention. Storm almost tossed Hing to Jumps High and gave the rallying cry for the team.

Tani had slipped from his side and circled the yoris. Minou and Ferarre had joined her. They knew this game. From Tani's mind they understood that it was serious, they must hold the lizard's attention. It must not turn back to the child. They struck, first one, then the other, sliding, flickering shadows in the soft dusk. Each slash of sharp teeth opened another smarting scratch in the yoris's softer underhide. The upper hide was steel tough. But they played the yoris, one coyote teasing it to stretch out its neck, turning its head far around toward the irritating creature as it tried to bite, the other coyote slipping in unnoticed from the opposite side to slash at the lower belly or chest, where the hide was thinner.

Surra arrived and Storm signaled her to wait. The coyotes were holding the lizards attention well. He whistled again. Baku disliked flying at night but she would obey. She answered him from above: she was ready. The Nitra had brought torches. Many of the warriors now held these aloft so that all could see. The light danced and shifted but it was sufficient. Storm reached Tani in swift strides.

"Be ready. When I tell you, call your team back." He saw

her quick sidelong glance. "It's all right. Baku is waiting to strike. We've done this before." She nodded understanding and agreement. "Good."

His will spun out, reaching the eagle where she soared. "Now!" She dropped wing over and stooped, her claws out to strike. She was plummeting downward. His hands closed over the girl's shoulders. "Be ready . . . ready . . . call them back now!"

Tani did so. Minou and Ferarre slipped back, one to either side of the furious lizard. They bounced and yapped as they withdrew, keeping the lizards eyes fixed on them. They halted just out of reach and from above, from out of the dark the terrible strike of a raptor came. Baku had dropped two hundred feet at full speed. Her wings snapped out to lift her again as she reached nearly to the earth. At the lowest point her claws made contact with the yoris's head. It staggered. Big as it was the impact of the strike left it half stunned. Then it flung its head back in rage, reaching for the thing that had hurt it even as Baku soared up again.

Storm had been waiting for that second. His stunner was out and he fired once, discharging the entire clip in that burst. It took the lizard in the throat. The yoris fell sideways, twitched convulsively, then straightened out in death. From beside Storm, Surra padded over to check the body. Then she turned away. She had no interest in dead lizards, which smelled bad and tasted worse. A woman ran past Storm to lift the child from the rock. She hugged him and was joined by others of her family, all hugging the rescued one.

Storm backed quietly out of the rejoicing. He didn't like crowds and had a feeling he could be the center of this one shortly. His mouth quirked into a half-smile as he saw Tani doing the same thing.

"Your team fights well."

Tani reddened a little. "So does yours. Baku was wonderful."

Storm grinned more openly. He whistled and braced as the eagle dropped from the sky to his shoulder. "She's a hunter. She enjoys that sort of work. So does Surra. She's quite annoyed with me that I didn't let her join in."

"Why didn't you?"

"There was no need. Your team had the yoris under control." The coyotes came out of the night to look up at him. "Yes, we're talking about you two. Nice teamwork." Their mouths opened, showing tongues in identical grins. Storm laughed, turning to smile at Tani. "If Mandy had been here and you'd had a stunner, you could have done the whole job yourselves. You can next time now that you've seen how it's done."

She dug a toe into the earth. "I guess I could." Her mother had disapproved of killing. But then, if Storm hadn't killed the yoris there would have been a small boy dead. The yoris had been a clean kill. The child would have spent fifteen agony-filled minutes before he died. She looked up at the stars, brilliant in the sky. Somewhere out there were the ruins of Earth. The humanoid Xiks had killed and killed. For love of killing as much as to win a war they'd begun.

She'd always wondered about the start of that war. Had it been that both races liked the same sort of world to colonize? Had it been that being so similar, they'd each expected the other to be more understanding and struck out when that belief failed? No one seemed to know. Already books were starting to appear: long analyses of the root causes of the war, memoirs, and fictional novels of occupied planets. None of the serious works agreed on much, and the fiction was still less helpful.

Why had they destroyed Earth and Ishan? It was believed that the flamed planets had been destroyed to break Terran wills. A sort of look what we can do. We'll do it to other worlds if you don't surrender. It hadn't worked. Instead humans had fought with a greater ferocity, and in the end the Xiks had been driven from all worlds but their own home world. Knowing how the Xiks appeared to think, it was quite possible that if they built up their strength again, they would start another war one day. Rumors continued about their holdout groups, and talk was that their Xik command had never truly surrendered. This war was over but nothing could replace what so many had lost. Tani had lost her parents, her world, and the feeling of belonging.

Her gaze ranged over the sky, recognizing some of the stars. Something was blotting out a portion of the sky. Without thinking she clenched her fists. If that was the enemy, she'd fight. Her father had died fighting, she would do no less. A soft call made her relax. Mandy was returning from the Quade ranch after delivering her message. Tani called the paraowl in. Then she stood stroking the soft mottled feathers as she considered everything she was learning.

Her mind shifted, moved, and settled into a decision. Alisha had felt that all fighting was wrong, only saving people was right. Her mother had lost half of her life when Bright Sky died. Because of that she'd damned everything that had conspired to take him. She'd been wrong. There were times when you had to fight. The trick was to know when that time was. To have allowed the Xiks free rein to do whatever they wanted wouldn't have been right. She remembered something she had read once. That for evil to triumph it was only necessary for good people to do nothing.

Beside her Storm had sensed the turmoil of her thoughts. He remained, standing in silence, waiting until she should be ready to either talk or leave him alone. Her thoughts had taken only moments, now a movement from the girl indicated she had decided. Tani cleared her throat.

"You wanted to hear about my father?"

He moved toward the log. "I'd like to. Why don't you sit down and tell me."

He waited. Tani slowly took a step toward the log, then another step, until she could sit. She wasn't sure where to begin, but Alisha hadn't wanted to talk about Bright Sky much after he'd been killed. Tani had tried. Alisha had finally told her daughter that talking of the man she'd loved deeply hurt her too much. They would never forget him, but it wasn't necessary to remember him in words all the time. Tani hadn't felt that way, but she'd been not quite six. She had obeyed.

Now Storm wanted to hear and she couldn't find the words to begin. She remembered how her father had shared his team with her. How proud he'd been when Tani had started school. She'd made him a tiny dream catcher for his last birthday. Not the pretty commercial things that appeared in the shops and were worn by everyone. This had been a real one. She'd taken a willow withe, bound it in the teardrop shape and netted it with fine strands of her hair that she'd plaited into cords.

One of the little hawks in the breeding center had provided two small feathers to hang below the willow loop on a short length of hair cord. After that the child had a problem. Only the best was good enough for her father. The stone in the center of the web must be the best she could find. She had found it at last. Not turquoise but an amethyst. A good one, dumped in a bowl of small junk and broken discarded jewelry. She'd added it in triumph.

Then she'd wrapped the dream catcher and given it to her father for his birthday.

She found that she was telling the story aloud. "I said I'd made it so he wouldn't have bad dreams. The dream catcher would keep him safe forever and ever. He said he'd carry it always. He had to go the next day. He did come back once before he died, and he opened his shirt pocket to show me he still had it. He said, 'See, sweetling. I always carry it, right next to my heart.' Then he went away and never came back." She made a tiny choking sound. "I guess it didn't work against Xik bad dreams."

She wept without a sound. Her team crowded around her, Surra pushing in gently to lick Tani's hand. Hing chittered indignantly. Storm should do something. He felt again the surge of protectiveness he'd felt when he saw her asleep after her own nightmare. He reached out and gathered her to his chest. Her tears dampened his shirt as his arms closed about her. He spoke softly when at last her grief eased.

"Weep for a warrior, then take up his bow to fight. Out there is an enemy. Bright Sky would not let a world fall when he could save it. Face the nightmare, Sunset Which Follows the Bright Sky of Day. Follow in the tracks of a monster-slayer."

He felt her move back against his arms and he released her. Tani sniffed unromantically, then bit back a slightly hysterical giggle. She felt the support of her team, the strong warmth of the man beside her. Fragments of the nightmare she'd had floated up into her mind. An enemy. An enemy here. She nodded once in the darkness. That was what she should fight. She cleared her throat and spoke huskily.

"I will. My father was from the line of Wolf Sister of the Cheyenne. He was always proud of that, and he was a warrior. We'll talk about it tomorrow."

His voice came out of the dark. "Good. And maybe before we start, you'll make me a dream catcher too, daughter of warriors. I've never had one."

He heard her footsteps patter away, but before she was quite out of earshot she paused and her voice drifted back to him.

"If I make one for you, where will you carry it, Beast Master?" She was gone while he still sought a reply. He sat, Baku balanced on his shoulder, Hing sprawled on his lap, Surra leaning against his legs. It was as well she hadn't waited for a reply. He had no idea of what his answer might be. Maybe if she made the dream catcher he'd discover it.

Chapter Ten

Tani slept late, exhausted by her remembered grief. She found when she woke that she felt better than she had felt in a long time. Alisha's own grief had not allowed her daughter to weep. She'd been too afraid of the way her mother was acting. Too busy comforting and distracting the woman sunk in an abyss of sorrow. Tani had learned to suppress even her father's name, and by the time her mother died it had become a habit. Last night the ancient wound had broken open and drained.

She hugged Minou and Ferarre, who had come to her. "I'm fine, really. I guess . . ." Her voice trailed off as she followed the alien thought in her mind. "I guess if my father was a Beast Master and good man even if he was war trained, then there could be other good Beast Masters. Alisha always said there weren't. But she never told me about Father saving Trastor, either."

Minou whined softly, licking her face. "Hey, that tickles." Her voice became introspective again. "You know, Alisha lied, really. She always told me that Father died because Terran Command sent him to his death. That isn't the way it was." Her eyes stared at the shelter wall, but in its place she saw a simple plascrete slab engraved with her father's name. "I'd like to go there one day. Meet some of the people who knew him last. I'd like to see that inscription on his grave." Ferarre jumped on her and began to play a chasing game with his mate. "I get it, all this is too serious. All right, then, let's eat."

She threw on her outer clothes and ran to check Destiny. The filly came to meet her, nuzzling affectionately into Tani's shirt. The girl scratched around the sharp curved horns before carefully looking the part-bred duocorn over. Destiny was still growing. She mustn't be overworked, but there were no signs of that. Tani was a lightweight and Destiny was immensely strong. Even the long ride to the camp hadn't made the filly more than pleasantly tired. Yesterday's ride hadn't even done that.

The girl walked back to where the cooking lean-to was exuding wonderful smells. Small Bird smiled a welcome, offering scrambled grass-hen eggs with fried thin strips of their meat. Tani took the plate, thanked her, and ate heartily.

Small Bird's hands danced at her. "The food is good?"

"The food is wonderful." She saw the pleasure in her friend's face. "Where are your daughters?"

"They bring a gift for you. From One-Who-Drums-Thunder."

Tani squealed, "A present?"

Small Bird guessed at the alien words and nodded. From behind Tani Storm spoke. "Who is receiving a present?"

Tani looked around. "Me. Small Bird just said her daughters had gone to get me one. It's from the Thunder-Drummer." She looked at the bow Storm carried. "Were you looking for me?"

"I wondered if you'd like to go hunting. Surra was away

last night. She came back with *half* a young merin deer." His face was a parody of indignation.

Tani laughed. "And you're looking for the other half."

"No. I know where that is. I'm greedy. I'm looking for a whole one. Surra knows where several are grazing. She'll take us there."

"When do we go? Do we ride?"

"We can go anytime today. Merins don't change feeding grounds until after dark. They were there by first light, they'll be there until dusk tonight. We will have to ride, though. Just a few miles." He looked at her, his face becoming serious. "Tani, have you seen one of the clan watching you?"

She glanced up at him in surprise. "They all watch us. We're new."

"No, this one is different. I've seen her looking at you and there is hatred in her eyes. Surra says she smells of it when she is near you."

Tani shrugged. "I haven't noticed anyone. I'll watch out, surely the coyotes would have smelled her if Surra's right."

"Did you ever ask them?"

She shook her head. Minou was nearby and Tani linked to do so now. To Tani's surprised interest Minou was certain. There had indeed been a female of the not-people who lingered by Tani. She had smelled of hate and grief. The coyotes had watched the female but she had done nothing as yet. Ferarre trotted up and endorsed that. Tani was starting to feel worried as she told Storm of the team's agreement.

He was glancing about as he apparently concentrated on whittling a stick and talking to her. "She is not a young woman. She is dressed in the usual clothing, but this one wears a necklace of Rock-Flyer claws. The pendant is polished quartz with a pair of yoris fangs flanking it. She is here now." With an effort Tani kept herself from turning around to stare. "Good girl. Yes, she slips to the left of you. She is half hidden behind a shelter but she watches. Does your team play games?"

For a moment she was puzzled, but she caught at the idea. A quick signal and Minou was returning with a short, thick stick. Tani tossed it high and both coyotes leaped to catch it. Jumping, tossing the stick, humans and coyotes worked their way to circle the watcher. She realized their intent too late. Storm confronted her, his hands signing questions.

"You watch the girl, why?"

She stood there stolidly, making no attempt to respond. He tried several more questions without reply. Then the Thunder-Drummer pushed through the small crowd growing about them. She turned to Tani.

"What happens?"

Tani's fingers flickered. "Storm said there is one who watches me. His spirit beast smelled anger against me on this watcher. I ask my own spirit-friends. They say it is so. Storm says this woman spies upon me. Our spirit-friends say this one grieves greatly and smells of hate when her gaze falls upon me. Storm said she was watching us as he spoke. I played a game with my friends. We trapped her while she thought we were not noticing her. I asked her now what is it she wants of me, why she watches? She says nothing. She will not speak to either of us."

The medicine woman smiled gently at the girl. "There

is no need to ask of Walks Quickly what she wants of you. I know. Her son was the foolish one who was slain by the spirit-friend you ride."

Storm's eyes narrowed. "Does this Walks Quickly mean to harm Sunset?"

There was a quick twittering between watcher and medicine woman. "She says she watched the new clan-friend only."

Storm's hand lifted in slow emphatic signs. "That is not the report of my spirit-friend. Nor does a friend lurk watching a friend from the shadows. Sunset is my kin by our common blood. Your clan has named her clan-friend. The one you rightly name foolish was warned by Sunset and by his war leader. He chose to close his ears to their words. One life was taken by Sunset's spirit-friend. Yet Sunset's wise warning saved the clan three lives in exchange."

From the crowd a tall Nitra warrior stood forward, his mate with him. The interpreter translated with his hands. "My son was behind the fangs of the yoris. The clan-friend and those who follow her held the yoris at bay. Then came the other ones, they made the kill and my son was unharmed. Four lives has she given the clan in exchange for the one her beast killed."

His mate twittered softly. "I also witnessed. It is so. I owe the clan-friend a life."

Jumps High joined them. "I was war leader. I warned Tall Grass most strongly to leave Sunset's mount alone. She spoke so, too. Yet he disobeyed me, his leader on the trail. For that I had the right to kill him. The mare slew him first but let Walks Quickly hear me. If the mare had not killed I would have done so. The clan is held together by obedience when there is danger. Thus we are not as the grass hens, scattering each for himself."

The Nitra woman ceased her passive pose abruptly. Her voice rose in a furious chirping shrillness that hurt human ears. The interpreter's fingers raced. "Her evil spirit killed my son and you crawl at her feet. You name her clan-friend and set these other lives against my son's life. What are they to me? She killed him. Drive her from the camp. I call on the Thunder to judge her." About her there was indrawn breath from the listeners.

The Thunder-Drummer moved. In that stirring she seemed to gather majesty to her. She took a pace forward, no longer the quiet woman Tani had liked. This was power. Her voice lifted, deepening with strength. Her hands drew a quiet faraway sound from the small drum at her waist. It continued as a soft undercurrent as she spoke.

"I have heard. We do not bargain with life against life. Yet Sunset made no bargain. She met our warriors as friends. She shared with them food and drink, fire and wisdom. She gave, asking nothing. She followed when they said she was needed, asking not where she was led. When a child of the clan was in danger she acted. She did not stay to bargain with his mother. What was given freely was returned freely. She is of the clan."

Thunder snarled softly. "The Thunder hears, let it answer, judging as Walks Quickly demands." Above them, there was a flare of lightning, slashing to the earth. Sparks flew, purple in the air; the power drained harmlessly into the earth and was gone. The drum rumbled thunder, echoed again by the sky. The Thunder-Drummer nodded, as if in acknowledgment of a decision shared with her.

"This is clan law! None in the clan may make war on another within the clan, save that they are given such a right by the Thunder." The eyes she turned on the defiant woman seemed to glow. "Hear me. This right is not granted you. Lightning came and did not strike the clan-friend; Thunder speaks against you. If you move against Sunset the clan turns from you. You shall be as a girl on her name-trial. You shall walk away from the clan to live or die by your own hand. This is the will of the Thunder. Hear it." The small drum gave one long rumble and fell silent.

Walks Quickly stood staring, hatred now openly on her face. "I hear." Her voice was raised in a shriek. "I do not accept!"

As she spoke and the interpreter's hands matched her words, Storm reacted. He was experienced in war. It was no surprise to him what came next. Even as the woman produced a knife and leapt, his arm went out to sweep Tani to safety. Surra, raging at the threat, leaped also and the Nitra went down under snarling fangs. Others had moved as well. Jumps High had the screaming woman by the arms as he dragged her from beneath Surra. The dune cat slunk back at Storm's order. A thread of scarlet trickled from a scratch on one furred shoulder.

Overhead thunder roared abruptly. The Thunder-Drummer looked at the writhing screaming woman of her clan. "Release her."

Walks Quickly staggered forward as her arms were freed. She looked around the half-circle almost snarling as eyes turned aside. No Nitra would aid one who had defied the Thunder. It had not been simple defiance. Walks Quickly had asked for a judgment, then refused to accept it. Worse still, she had then attacked one who had been named as in-clan by the Thunder. Jumps High walked to her shelter, then returned some minutes later, bearing a rolled blanket. He placed it on the ground, squatting to unroll it as he displayed what lay within.

Tani saw a thin-bladed knife, a coil of grass string. Dried meat and a water-skin. A pouch lay there. From the dusting of flakes on the draw-strung opening she suspected that it contained herbs of some sort. Whether they were spices or medicine she did not know.

The Thunder-Drummer pointed toward it. "Take up the trail, Walks Quickly."

"I have the right to take more. I can carry it. And my son's horse is mine. I take that also."

The medicine woman shook her head. "You have heard the leader on your son's trail. He says that if Sunset's mount had not slain your son he would have done so for his diso-bedience. The horse belongs to the clan. But you have the right to take all you can carry. One of you go with her. See she takes nothing that is not lawful." She watched with ap-proval as the two who had spoken for Sunset flanked Walks Quickly. That was well. They owed the life of their child to the clan-friend. They would watch well what an enemy chose to take.

Tani was on her knees, examining Surra's shoulder. Storm eyed her with amusement. The knife had barely cut the skin. If the cat had shed more than half a dozen drops of blood he'd be surprised. But Surra was playing shamelessly to the praise and petting. Storm caught the medicine woman's gaze and she, too, smiled. She lifted her hands to sign.

"Take Sunset away. You wished to hunt. Do so. It will distress her when her enemy returns to cast more abuse at her as Walks Quickly will, if Sunset is still here when the outcast one departs."

Storm nodded. It took tact, but within minutes Tani was walking with Surra to find Storm's shelter, where, he assured her, he had a tube of antiseptic salve that would ensure the wound would not infect. Once there, he left her practicing medicine without a license and went in search of Jumps High. Fingers wove and twisted and the swift talk ended with both warriors in agreement. Storm returned to find Tani satisfied that Surra would be well. He eyed the big cat as she rolled smugly on her back, the girl's hands massaging along her belly.

Surra had loved every minute of the fussing. With her scratch cleaned and salved it was as he'd thought. The skin had been barely broken. He sent a picture of the merin and the big cat was back on her feet in expectation. Tani looked up.

"What . . . ?"

"We did plan to hunt. Surra expects us to keep our promise."

That was the right way to put it. The beginnings of protest in Tani's face cleared. "Of course. My father used to say you should never break a promise to child or beast. Neither understand. I'll get my things." She ran to her shelter to emerge almost at once carrying Destiny's tack, and with Minou and Ferarre at her heels.

"Will Surra mind if they come with us? They'd like to hunt too."

Surra answered that for herself by going to meet the coyotes. She touched noses politely, then turned to pad off down the trail from the camp. Storm grinned.

"That's your answer." Inwardly he was surprised. Surra was a queen. She liked to hunt alone. That she was happily allowing the coyotes to join with her was interesting. He'd known she was fond of Tani, approving of the girl as one who understood her. That this approval extended to the girl's team he had not fully realized before.

Tani was readying Destiny. The filly danced wildly in excitement. Tani swung up, laughing, her slender body swaying to the gyrations of her powerful mount.

"If we don't go this minute I think Destiny is going to turn completely inside out."

Storm adjusted his quiver and bow, then nudged his mount to follow Surra. Destiny danced after them. Where the trail dropped from valley end to the desert below, Jumps High was waiting. He too carried a powerful bow and a full quiver of arrows. Behind him his mount bore a rolled blanket. A quiet pack pony trailed his mount. He said nothing but fell in with the small hunting party. Tani beamed at him. She liked the quiet, sensible Nitra.

Surra padded on. They left the valley behind and moved toward the desert fringe where it met the true desert of the Big Blue. The cat swung east, then down a long gully and back to where in the shadow of the foothills she had found the merin feeding on a sheltered patch of the long tough desert grasses. Then she halted, waiting. Storm read her suggestion and relayed it to his companions.

"The merin are about half a mile away. Leave the horses here. Surra will circle. The merin will run this way and we can take them from the brush as they pass."

Tani looked at him in disgust as they dismounted. "That's all right for you. What am I supposed to do. Jump on one with my teeth?"

"You've killed grass hens," Storm said teasingly.

"Sure. With a stone. It'll take more than a small stone to bring down a merin." The deerlike creatures were only about waist high to a Nitra but they moved at great speed and their outward-circling curving horns protected the sides of their head.

Jumps High intervened. He patted Tani on the arm, then as she turned to watch he removed the blanket roll from his saddle. This he handed to the girl, making the sign for her to open it. She did so cautiously, to find a beautifully made bow within the first circle of woven frawn wool. She held it up, admiring the carving and sinew bowstring. Then it occurred to her that a bow without arrows was useless. Eagerly she unrolled the rest of the parcel.

She gasped. Within were quiver and arrows as she'd hoped, and the quiver was a masterpiece. It was made from yoris hide, but the skin had been cut and fitted so that the scale colors formed clan patterns. She was speechless as she stood there, her fingers tracing the small figures of the Djimbut, the Lightning, and the tiny knife, which was the sign of the warrior.

The arrows were works of art. The heads of four were a white glittering quartz while the remainder glowed an almost lambent soft green. Tani held one up. "They're too beautiful to shoot. I want to make them into a necklace and wear them." Storm signed that behind her back. Jumps High's face lit with pleasure. His fingers moved.

"There is no need to waste the arrows. You have other

gifts from the clan. The bow and the hunting arrows are from the three warriors you saved with your warning. My mate, Small Bird, made the quiver for you." He grinned widely. "She says she is used to me, she does not wish to train another mate. The green war arrows Stream Song and Swift Killer give to you. It was their son you saved. The Thunder-Drummer sees this one . . ." His finger pointed to Storm. "He wears things of power. The clan talks together. We say that you too hear the Thunder and should have things of power to wear."

Tani looked questioningly at Storm. "Things of power?"

He reached for his shirt to pull free the Navaho necklace he wore. The work was old, showing the dull sheen of silver and the warm blue-green of the turquoise. Then he pushed up his sleeve, displaying the ketoh, the bracelet, now ornamental, which had once been the old practical bow-guard. Tani gaped at it.

"It's wonderful, is that all?"

Storm shook his head. "No, there's a belt. One of the links required mending. I left it at the ranch." He looked at Jumps High. "What makes you say they are things of power?"

The Nitra warrior smiled. "Thunder-Drummer so-says. She says the things may come from very far away but their power calls to hers. She agrees it is proper Sunset also wears such. Women—" His hands flicked in an explanation, which Storm translated for Tani.

"He says the women thought you should have a set that matched mine. They're made for Those-Who-Drum-Thunder. Usually from the same stone as the arrowheads. They show the thunder-flowers, which are both sacred and good fortune. The women make the plaques during the leisure times in spring and fall, when the hunting is so good they need do little work. Each family who owes a life has given a number of the separate pieces. To make a gift someone gathers the pieces that are already made, so they have only to be linked or strung. None but a Thunder-Drummer or one they approve may wear such things." Thoughtfully he added, "I suspect that's very few."

Jumps High was unwrapping the final package within the blanket. It was parceled in a square of frawn-wool fabric and he unwrapped it carefully. Then with gentle hands he straightened it, displaying the pieces on the natural blue-gray background. Tani gasped. Her fingers reached out to touch in wonder. Storm could only stare. For their clan-friend those who owed a debt had wrought a marvel.

The work was in the white quartz and the warm green of the arrowhead stone. On the fabric glowed a bracelet. It was of six small green and white flowers linked together by fine metal chains. The belt was similar but the buckle was carved in the rare veined quartz, and flat metal circles came between each flower. He recognized them. They were the trade pieces used by Nitra clans. Many were works of art in themselves and used only for ceremonial trades. But the masterpiece was the necklace. It deviated from his in that it was not the flat engraved plaques.

Instead, this was a multitude of beads made from the green or white stone. It was patterned in such a way, however, that the beads produced the flower motif. The pendant below was a single large flower. In the center glowed an eye-stone. They were rare on Arzor. It glowed like a drop of dark honey. Through the middle was a slitted line like the half-closed pupil of some nocturnal beast. Most were red, a few a warm lavender or white. But rarest of all was the one that showed green. The eye stone inset on Tani's pendant glowed green.

Jumps High lifted the necklace and placed it about her neck. She stretched out her wrist and watched as he fastened the bracelet. Storm took up the Nitra belt and threaded it through her trousers, coiling the shabby discarded belt to stow in her saddlebag. The Nitra warrior signed.

"The flowers are the thunder-flowers. They blossom when the Thunder drums above, when rain falls. These will bring good fortune to one who wears them as a gift." He turned to Storm and his fingers flashed faster. "I do not say things of power will protect her from Death-Which-Comes. Thing-Which-Slays-in-Night has own power. But other clan see this they know she has power. Not be so quick to kill clan one, maybeso."

Storm explained. Tani grinned. "In other words, it brings luck, but don't rely on that too heavily." She signed slowly. "I understand the words of Jumps High. These are the most beautiful things I have ever owned. Please tell those who have given them to me that I'll treasure them all my life. When I die, my body will wear them so the Thunder knows I am clan friend to the Djimbut."

Storm saw she was almost in tears and signaled Surra. The cat padded up to thrust an impatient head against the girl. Hunting. They'd come to hunt. They should stop wasting time on things that could not be eaten. Tani staggered, laughing at a second hard nudge.

"It looks as if we should hunt before Surra gets mad at us." She looked shyly at Storm. "You do think Jumps High knows how much this means to me?"

"He knows. Now, as you say. Let's hunt."

They returned near to dusk, the overloaded pack pony complaining with a slowed pace. Three plump yearling buck merin was too much in the pony's opinion. Tani was absorbed at once into the chattering knot of women who greeted the hunters' arrival. They patted her, hugged her, and admired her ornaments. The children admired the bow Tani had used with a skill that had slightly surprised Storm. But then Bright Sky had been a warrior. No doubt she'd learned from him at first and continued to practice the skill in honor of his memory. The Ark would have an exercise area; a ship that size probably had a very large gymnasium, with room for an archery range. He leaned against the weary pony as he helped unload the meat. Later he'd ask what had happened to Talks Quickly. For now he was starving.

Chapter Eleven

At the Quade ranch Mandy had planed in for a landing by the mobile laboratory. She opened her beak and gave a sweet piercing call. Kady came running. She caught up a mini-recorder, and a couple of lastree nuts on the way, showing the nuts as she ordered.

"Give Kady message."

Mandy obliged, then sat happily cracking a nut while Kady replayed the message on the mini-recorder. Brion joined her to listen. He looked puzzled as he heard.

"She keeps saying she's with the natives. I thought Brad checked."

Brad had arrived. "Is that another message from Tani?"

In reply Kady played the message again. It was Brad's turn to look baffled.

"She says Hosteen is with her, but where? Logan asked around. The Shosonna saw him last a number of days ago. He went out to check the line cabins and ask the Norbies to move the stock further in from the edge of the Basin. Gorgol says he never told them and they haven't seen him. Let me hear the message once more, Kady." Again Tani's voice spoke through the paraowl.

"I'm fine and Storm is here with the clan, too. We'll be back in a few more days, I think. Don't worry about us. I love you both."

Brad had listened intently. "She says the clan, but we know they aren't with the Shosonna. Which means they're with another clan. But Logan has passed the word through all the Norbie clans. None have admitted to seeing them."

"Which means what?" Brion asked.

Brad's face was sober. "Which means either they are with a Norbie clan who for some reason are denying it, or . . ." He hesitated.

"Or?" Kady demanded.

"The Shosonna saw signs several days ago that Nitra scouts were around. It is just possible that Tani was taken by them and Storm went with her."

Kady shivered. She'd heard enough from Logan and Brad to know of the Nitra. They weren't fond of humans at any time, although because of clan custom they rarely harmed a female. But with the killers driving them from their lands and the stress of clan deaths, they might be more inclined to hurt a human female they caught wandering. Brion shook his head. Kady relaxed a little as she listened. He was right and she should have known better.

"No, Quade." Brion Carraldo's voice was serious but not distressed. "I don't think so. I'm not saying she isn't with them but firstly I know my niece. There's been no fear in her messages. She links to Mandy. If she was being made to say what Mandy relayed, then the bird would have let us know that the message was a fake. It isn't. In the first message she didn't mention Storm. In this one she says he's with her. I think he arrived later. Again, if she thought he was in danger she'd have tried to indicate that to us."

Brad knew more of the Nitra than this out-worlder, but he wanted to believe. His face must have shown the struggle, because suddenly Kady gave a chuckle.

"Of course they're both happy and unharmed. Look at Mandy." She pointed to where the paraowl was cracking a second lastree nut. "She's part of Tani. Do you think Mandy would be so unworried if Tani were afraid or in any danger? That message was only hours old. Unless something terrible happened after Mandy left, Tani and Storm are fine. The message said Tani thought they'd be back in a few more days." She started to move back toward the laboratory. "I, for one, hope to have something to tell them when they return."

Brion joined her and they were soon at work again. Brad Quade headed for the kitchen. He always thought better with a mug of swankee in his fist. He believed the Carraldos. At the time of the message Tani and Hosteen were unhurt, and the girl at least was unafraid. That meant there'd been no threats against her and she'd seen nothing that scared her. If she was in a Nitra clan camp, that was almost unbelievable. The Nitra were trophy takers. They collected the enemy bow hands to dry in their shelters.

It was because of that that the more civilized tribes feared them. Surely Tani would see the bow hands drying in the smoke-holes of the clan shelters and be terrified. Logan arrived just as Brad was finishing his drink. Storm's younger half-brother had liked the girl from the Ark and his first words were a question.

"Any word from Tani?"

Brad repeated the message. He followed that with his conclusions.

Logan stared from the door out over the ranch lands. "You think she was picked up by Nitra scouts?"

"I think it possible. Logan, what did you tell her about the Nitra?"

"Nothing. I talked about the Shosonna and our friends in the Zamle clan. I told her about some of the customs. The way to greet those who approached your fire, the way to behave. I told her that any natives she met were probably friendly." He grinned. "Do you know; she'd seen the finger-talk on one of her tapes. They have a cortex educator at the Ark and she'd used that and the tapes to learn the signing."

Brad turned sharply. "How good was she?"

"Good enough. She'd manage to talk to any native who could finger-talk reasonably. She made me practice with her when we were riding."

His father went silent, sitting at the table, his face blank, eyes staring absently at the door. Logan waited. Finally Brad looked up.

"Think of this. She goes riding, taking that filly. No Nitra would ever have seen a horse like that before. Then there's the coyotes and the paraowl. You told her camp etiquette. If Nitra scouts came riding in she'd have followed that, not knowing about them and believing any natives would be friendly. I checked, she took trail bars, canteens, but most important, she took a can of swankee. So if she had that as a drink and offered it . . . Logan, how would Nitra react if they were only scouting and not on a war trail?"

Logan scowled as he thought. He'd grown up with the

Norbie clans, and in many ways the wild Nitra tribes would not be so different. His words came slowly.

"Much is ritual and custom. If she greeted them as friends, offered food, drink, and fire, they might accept before they thought. If they had done that, then by law they could not harm her within her camp. Once they had talked with her they would have been intrigued."

"Intrigued enough to invite her with them back to the clan?"

"Yes. It seems clear from her messages they did. Maybe at first it was to have their Thunder-Drummer make the decision. There's something you don't realize." Brad waited. "Dad, we think of her as a kid who's ignorant of the Nitra and the danger. You're scared she'll see trophies in the camp and react the wrong way."

"Yes?"

"I don't think she will. We were talking once about the natives on Ermaine. They eat the heart of a respected enemy or a powerful predator to gain his strength. Tani was there with the Ark after the war finished. The three of them were invited to a feast and saw that happening. Tani said it was just as well they didn't offer it to her. I asked what she'd have done if they had and she looked a bit surprised. She said to each their own customs. She would have refused if she could do it without giving great offense. If not, she'd have pretended to eat and hidden the offering in her sleeve or something. It didn't bother her. It was just something another race did."

"And you think she's likely to think that way about the Nitra?"

"Yes. Dad? Did she take any weapons?"

"Only her knife," Brad said absently.

"No stunner, no bow?"

"No stunner, at least we haven't found one missing. Bow? She can't shoot, can she?"

"Yes, she pulls a light bow but she's a good shot. She learned it from her father to begin with, and then from her aunt. Tani says Kady took up archery years ago as a hobby and they often shoot together. They have an archery range in the ship's gymnasium."

"Well, there isn't a bow missing from the house, so Tani didn't take one unless she took her own."

Logan nodded and dived for the door. He was back in a few minutes. "They say she didn't bring her bow from the Ark. It needs a new bowstring and she left it."

Brad eyed him with narrowed gaze. "That weapons business means something to you?"

"Maybe. I heard something years back from Krotag. There's an old custom of name-trial the Norbies don't continue any longer, but the Nitra do. I don't know too much about it but it may be relevant. Look, I'm going to ride out to see the Shosonna again. I want to talk to Ukurti and see what he knows."

"What will the Thunder-Drummer tell you?"

"Nothing, perhaps. I'll be home tomorrow sometime." He paused by the door. "Oh, and the Norbie tribes closer to the deserts say the death is killing more often and more at a time. The Nitra are moving out into areas not taken or leaning hard on Norbie clans to move up."

Brad looked worried. "I know. Dumaroy is raising hell

with Kelson. The Native Protection League is starting to talk tough, and if this isn't cleared up soon we could have the Patrol itself becoming involved here. Get going, boy."

He was still watching as Logan vanished in the distance. The Carraldos had not yet managed to get samples from the killer. Until they did, no one could identify the possibilities. Was the thing an escapee from the sealed caves? Or something that bred in the mountains behind the desert portion of the Big Blue and swept out every hundred years or so before dying back again? That was unlikely unless the intervals were much greater. None of the tribes seemed to have any oral records of the death. The Shosonna Thunder-Drummer alone could recite significant events for several hundred years.

It could even be a mutation, something that had escaped from the sealed caves, bred with something on Arzor, eaten strange foods, lived near the wrong mineral—and changed. He sighed. Every time a man thought he had no problems, every time things were peaceful, something always went wrong. He only hoped Storm and the girl were managing. The messages indicated they were unhurt, but with the Nitra that might change at any moment. Maybe Logan could find good news to bring back. Brad knew the Carraldos were a little worried, despite Brion's words, but they kept on working. He'd better do the same. There was always work on a ranch.

Tani was up early and helping Small Bird with the breakfast. After that she went to practice with her new bow. Storm had gone apart to talk with Jumps High. He wanted to know just how Tani's enemy had left. The Nitra was clear about that.

"I talked to my friends. Walks Quickly left only a small time after us. She carried a large pack so she was bowed down by it. She took many, many things, grass cord and wooden pegs for snares, fire-maker, two blankets, a bridle . . ."

Storm's hands interrupted the recital. "Why would she take a bridle? The Thunder-Drummer said Walks Quickly could not take her son's horse. And weapons? Did she take weapons?"

"She had no horse, but maybeso she might find a stray." Storm understood that. Jumps High was delicately suggesting the banished woman might either sneak back to steal a mount or try to do so from another clan. "She took weapons also," the Nitra continued. "She took knives, her good bow, many arrows. Warrior arrows as well as hunting arrows. Stream Song watched, all this she saw."

"Stream Song?" Storm questioned.

"It was her child Sunset saved. She watched Walks Quickly very closely. See everything she took. She advised I warn you both that Walks Quickly is full of hatred. She could circle in the night. Return to find where Sunset sleeps and kill her. Then steal a horse, ride fast and far away. Maybe she could find other clan to join."

"I thought another clan would not take in one the Thunder-Drummer sent away?"

Jumps High snorted. "She tells a very good story, and maybeso they take her in. More likely they do that if she comes with a good mare to ride. We have good mares in the Djimbut clan. If she kills Sunset, steals a mare, then rides far, another clan may not know. Watch over Sunset, tell the spirit-friends to watch also. If Walks Quickly harms Sunset, the Thunder-Drummer will send warriors to find Walks Quickly. For the killer of a clan-friend we would hang their bow hand to dry. Good trophy, but not good if Sunset is dead."

Storm hid a shudder at the information. But it did emphasize how the clan felt about Tani. Or was it the way they felt about their clan member?

"Walks Quickly is popular in the clan, they like her?"

A head was shaken slowly. "She quarrels often, with too many. None like her, she had no friends. She is greedy, sharing nothing without orders. She cared only about her son. His father, her mate, is long dead. He died fighting the Merrin clan. He was rich, a fine hunter, a good warrior. Walks Quickly gained it all when he was killed. If she comes back to hurt Sunset, you may kill her. No one in the clan will speak against you. The Thunder-Drummer said Walks Quickly is cast out, she is not of the clan anymore. Sunset is clan-friend."

That was clear enough, Storm considered. The woman's banishment had declared her no longer of the clan. Until or unless she joined another clan she was outlaw. An enemy to any clan. If even Storm, who was with but not of the clan, killed her, it was permissible. Particularly if he did so to save a clan-friend or to prevent theft from the clan. He rose from where he had squatted on his heels. Even so, it might be safer if he passed this on to the team.

He noticed Mandy was back, and after alerting Surra and Baku he drifted over to the paraowl. It wasn't so easy to make contact with the large bird. Paraowls had been used in a few teams near to the end of the war. Bright Sky had one of the first as a team member when he died. The first ones had been too conspicuous with their ghostly white feathering. It wasn't until Kady had isolated the gene for the brown shades that they'd begun to be used for Beast Masters. Storm had heard a little about them, but not a great deal.

He did know they were predators and omnivores. They ate fruit, nuts, and seeds. They could also kill and eat small animals, and on occasion larger prey. On Ishan the paraowls had hunted a medium-sized herbivore called a lanour. The female paraowls would seek out the yearling lanour. The vaguely goatlike animals had hard heads. A paraowl female hunting to feed babies would kill in a fashion similar to the way Baku had struck the yoris: in a blazing stoop from a great height using clenched claws to break open the skull on impact.

A trained paraowl would also strike sideways, breaking the neck of an enemy. Storm strove to make Mandy understand the danger to Tani. At last he believed she accepted his information. Then he went in search of the girl. He'd alert her and make sure she would be wary. He found the coyotes first. They were easier to alert. Both had watched Walks Quickly and both considered her a danger. They would guard. If the not-human came as an enemy, Minou and Ferarre would be ready.

And after all that, Storm thought in exasperation, Tani was missing. Off setting snares with Small Bird's daughters. He grinned unwillingly. She fitted into Arzor like a frawn come home. They should ask if it was permitted to leave the clan soon, though. The Carraldos must be quite frantic by now and Brad would be worried. They'd know from the messages Mandy was carrying that Storm and Tani were alive and unhurt.

All the same, the Thunder-Drummer had brought them here for a purpose. What, he didn't know and had not been told. Tani seemed to have simply accepted that she would know when the time was right. She was having too much fun with the clan to mind. He wandered off to join the cook fire and eat. After that he chose to enter his shelter and sleep. A warrior should eat, drink, and sleep when he could. Storm planned to stay awake for the next few nights and be alert for enemies. One enemy in particular.

No Nitra clan slept heavily. But that night it was still Storm who was first to know there was trouble. Surra slid out of the dark and touched him with her muzzle. From her he received the impression of enemies. No, not one, several. Coming this way, here soon. His mind reached out to Baku at once. The eagle heartily disliked night flying but she would cooperate. He heard the faint rush of wings as she lifted aloft over the sleeping camp. Surra had vanished again.

He threw on his outer clothing, seized stunner and knife, and like Surra vanished into the shadows. He reached the Thunder-Drummer's shelter first. She would know who to wake. She was already watching the entrance as he slipped inside. She reached out a stick and stirred the coals to give just enough light to show his hands as he signed.

"My spirit-friend gave me a warning. Enemies are coming. Maybe four or five. Maybe more follow."

That would tell her it was not Walks Quickly, or not the outlaw woman alone. The medicine woman gave a low call.

Her interpreter appeared and was instructed in their own tongue. Storm waited patiently. She turned back to him as her servant departed.

"I think the enemies seek horses. But maybe I am wrong. You will fight with us?"

"Sunset is of my clan. You are her clan-friends. I will fight. Our spirit-friends will fight too. Tell me what you want me to do."

She smiled brief approval. "Watch the horses. Stop the enemy if any try to steal our herd. If they attack the camp, you protect Sunset."

Storm bowed slightly and trotted silently away. Surra had circled and was nearby. Tani would be awake by now. The coyotes had probably been awake even longer. They'd see no one had sneaked up on Small Bird's shelter. A stab of warning cut into his mind. He hissed softly. He'd learned that as a danger signal from the Shosonna and it seemed to be accepted that way here. In the dark horses moved restlessly. He could hear one of them stamping angrily.

Then the night broke open. There was a high wavering whistle of agony from some Nitra. The horses exploded outward from their mob, squealing in panic. In what had been the herd center a filly was busily murdering one of the not-people foolish enough to lay hands on her. Around the camp fires blazed up. A warrior pulling himself astride a bucking pony was dragged from it by Surra. Storm's knife took her prey as he turned on the big cat. It would do no enemy any favors to use a stunner tonight. The clan would have a slow and unpleasant way with a captive.

A sound behind sent him dropping to the ground, to rise slashing backward with his knife. A body folded over it and dropped limply away. Baku screamed attack from near a fire. Storm had the brief impression of a warrior running with the eagle riding, claws sunk into the back of the warrior's shoulders, beak stabbing at the unprotected neck. Stream Song's mate rose up and struck home and the warrior fell with Baku disengaging neatly. She waddled a few quick paces, then lifted into the air again.

From above a running enemy came the vibration of wings. He slowed to glance up, just in time to receive the paraowl's strike. His head jerked sideways as he collapsed, his neck snapped by the impact. It seemed as if the enemy were retreating. From the west of the camp came the harsh snarling yapping of an attacking coyote. Storm spun, running for the shelter. It was rare for a Nitra clan to harm women and children, but Minou wouldn't be making a sound unless she were in battle. The herd was well away on the far side of the camp. By the time he reached Jumps High's home the fight could be over. Still he ran. Surra raced with him.

The sound of fighting was already dying down. Storm flung himself into the dark by the shelter and listened. He wasn't going to run onto a knife. Surra crouched for a moment, then stood leisurely to stretch. The enemy not-people gave no more trouble. Storm took his cue from her. He hailed the shelter softly.

"Tani?"

"Come ahead, Storm."

He entered to find Tani busily rolling a bandage around Small Bird's arm. Possessions lay scattered, some broken or otherwise damaged by trampling feet. She glanced up to nod a greeting before splitting the end of the bandage, then fastening it with a neat bow. To one side of her a body lay with

Minou sitting smugly beside it. Her mate sat by the entrance. Surra padded in and touched noses with the coyotes, her emotions those of approval. It seemed that neither of them had been needed.

He indicated the bandage. "Is that bad?"

"No, a gash. I cleaned it and pulled the edges together with clamp thorns. The bandage is just to keep it clean for a few days while it starts to heal." Her eyes turned to the body. "It would be nice if you could get that out."

Storm blinked at the matter-of-fact tone. Then he saw beneath the surface. Tani was holding in her urge to be sick or to start shaking. She was sure her friend here needed her, and so long as that was so she would be strong. He reached for the body's shoulders and, half lifting it, dragged the corpse out to where fires blazed high in the camp center. Laying it with the others, he looked down at the wounds.

A real cooperative effort. The warrior had half a dozen deep bites along arms and legs. There were three long shallow cuts down his calves and thighs. On one side of his neck was a ragged tear. A shoulder had bled heavily from a knife wound while a second thrust had reached his heart. Storm suspected the young warrior had blundered into the shelter and struck at Small Bird before realizing she was a female. Or it might be that in the heat of battle and the excitement he had not cared.

From the damage to the shelter's items the warrior might just as well have stepped in a fire-bees' nest. He'd been attacked in retaliation by the coyotes, Tani, Small Bird, and even perhaps her two young daughters. The young warrior had blundered about, trying to strike back while being distracted from any of them by the next attack from a different direction. He'd been dragged down and killed as wolves on a deer. If his spirit was still around it must be cursing the impulse that had made it choose that particular shelter.

Jumps High came out of the dark to look down at the body. "Who kill?" Storm shared his finding and his amusement, which was echoed in the Nitra's dark eyes.

"I counted. None of our clan died, one only is badly hurt. The enemy lost many." His fingers indicated the number.

"Twelve," Storm said, and whistled softly. "Did any of them escape?"

"I do not think so. When daylight come we shall go on a hunt. We must find the clan horses, but if the Thunder is kind, they will not be far. Maybeso we will find enemy horses. That would be very good."

It took several hours for the camp to settle again. Guards watched while those who could slept. With first light Tani was out to find Destiny. She called as she walked; the filly trotted out of the brush and lowered her head. Tani saw the ugly stains that sheathed the horns from tip to hilt. But the filly was waiting for praise. So far as she was concerned she had acted rightly. Tani supplied both praise and cleansing. She didn't blame Destiny for protecting herself but she didn't have to look at the stains, either.

Storm was out with the warriors. They found only one more enemy. He'd dragged himself far enough away from the camp to die in peace. The enemy horses were further. The medicine woman's interpreter had come with the group. He studied the horses, then the ground. His fingers flew.

"We have missed an enemy. See, there are fourteen horses. We counted thirteen enemy dead with the one Sunset's spirit-friend killed. Somewhere one waits. Let us return and circle the camp. We search for a trail. Your spirit-friends will help?"

Storm nodded, sending out both Baku and Surra in reply. Surra found a trail and followed, the Nitra trotting lightly along on foot behind her. The trail wound off to the west. The warrior seemed to have been one of the younger ones who'd attacked from that direction. The Nitra trotted tirelessly. Baku soared higher. She could see no movement below. Almost ten winding miles away, the trail ceased by a jumble of rock and brush. Storm and a tracker looked it over.

"He came here before dawn. He was very weary. To travel this far in the dark is not easy." Surra was checking about with interest. Storm received a flickering picture from her mind.

"We spread out and look all around this place. My spirit-friend says one she knows from the clan came here also."

They found the second set of tracks leading in from a different direction. Storm recognized them as did the tracker, who gave a grunt and signed briefly.

"Walks Quickly."

Storm had a premonition. It was almost noon. It was unlikely that either of those tracked here would have remained in hiding that far into the day. Of course, they might have fought and mortally injured each other. But somehow he didn't think so. He went in silence to a puff bush and prepared torches. Then, with one lit and held before him he entered the cave another warrior had spied.

The light fell on two skeletons. From their positions, Walks Quickly had died in her blankets. The warrior had entered before the killers had finished feeding. His bones lay jumbled barely within the entrance. Storm stepped out from the cave and looked up toward the Peaks. The death was moving closer. As the feefaw flew the cave was only five miles from the clan camp. Of course the camp was also out of the desert and several hundred feet higher up. He wondered how much difference that might make. Beside him the warriors were preparing to perform the funeral rites. When they completed that, they gathered up the dead's possessions and departed.

Storm halted on a rise to look back. From the desert death came in the night. He'd taken samples from around the skeletons and now carried these in his shirt pockets. He must return and give the information to the Carraldos. If he could return quickly they might be able to tell something from them. He'd talk to the Thunder-Drummer as soon as he could.

Chapter Twelve

It took the remainder of the day for the camp to quiet again. The enemy bodies were removed and given the rites to quiet their spirits. Many new bow hands hung in the smoke-holes of the various shelters. Storm had refused his. Instead he had gifted them to the Thunder-Drummer. The offering had met with nods and quick twitters of approval from the Nitra. Bow hands gave power.

The enemy possessions were shared out with care. Tani had at her disposal the possessions and mounts of the warriors that Mandy and the filly had killed. The two warriors Storm had killed had been well-endowed by clan standards. This time Storm drew approval by handing over all they owned to Tani.

"Clan-sister," he said formally with both hands and voice. "You are clan-friend here. Let you gift where you will."

Tani turned to Small Bird and there was a quick flurry of signs. Tani nodded slowly. She stepped to the pile of possessions and studied them and the mounts standing beside the heap. Then she moved with deliberation, taking from the quivers a dozen of the hunting arrows and adding them to her own. The man-slayers arrows she shared between Jumps High and the interpreter.

To the latter she said, "That you might protect the heart of the clan."

It was a delicate compliment both to the interpreter as a warrior and to the clan's Thunder-Drummer. Storm hid a grin. Then Tani called Stream Song, handing her a bow, quiver, and the remainder of the hunting arrows she had withheld.

"For your son. May he be a warrior as his parents are." Another bow and filled quiver went to a young boy on the edge of being accepted as a hunter. His face glowed with joy and pride. Little by little all that the enemy had brought was shared out. Occasionally Tani turned to Small Bird for information but Storm was interested to see that the girl understood the system of clan-sharing. By the time she was done most families had received some small item.

Finally only the horses remained. One was lame, an elderly mare, but able still to give a foal or two. This went to Stream Song, whose face showed her pleasure. Two were geldings, good animals but nothing special. Tani took their reins and led them to Small Bird. To the tall Nitra woman she handed the horses and signed.

"For she who is my cousin in the clan, that she may ride."

She returned to take the reins of the other mount. This was a prize. A mare, no more than five and of real quality. Storm suspected the animal had been stolen from a Norbie clan or even a settler's ranch. He watched. There was no hesitation, the mare was led to the Thunder-Drummer and the reins given into her hand. Storm noticed that before Tani handed over the reins she had made sure all saw her knotting them. The action appeared to have some ritual significance.

The medicine woman turned, speaking to her interpreter. His hands flashed.

"You give me a great prize?"

"A prize for the clan. Let her breed foals for the strength of the clan to grow."

The Thunder-Drummer made the sign of acceptance. "For the clan, then. It is well done. Go now, Sunset; eat, rest. Tomorrow you return to your people."

Tani stared, "I have to go home?"

"We do not cast you out, but it is time." Her eyes turned to eye Storm with amusement. "Before your clan-kin steals you away to them." There was a twittering of laughter at that and the Thunder-Drummer smiled. She reached out to pat the girl's arm. "You are clan-friend to the Djimbut. We do not forget. But those of your blood surely worry. At noon we will say farewell to the Sunset. Come to me and speak alone before that time."

She led the mare away. Storm stared after her. He wasn't sure what the past days had brought, but it was clear the medicine woman was working to a plan of her own. He shrugged. Medicine took its own paths. It was better not to get in the way. Tani had gone off with Small Bird and Jumps High. Her arrival and their acceptance of her as cousin had done Small Bird and Jumps High no harm, he mused. On the contrary. The warrior had originally owned his personal mount and shared a pack horse with another warrior.

The enemy killed in the shelter had owned a poor mount and meager possessions, but all had gone to Jumps High's family. Tani had refused anything from that victory. On top of that Small Bird now owned two horses herself. She could ride when the clan moved and use the second gelding as another pack animal. Better still, she now had a spare horse she could offer to her daughters when they came to their name-trials. A girl on name-trial had a higher chance of survival with a pony to do the work, and with the speed for her to escape danger. It was no wonder Small Bird had looked so happily at the gifted animals.

Storm saw to Baku. She'd be molting soon. She still would be able to fly if he imped her flight feathers to repair any that were broken, but she would be lazy and reluctant to take to the air unless she hungered badly. Paraowls molted as well. He hoped Mandy's molt cycle wasn't the same, or they'd have no eyes in the sky. Storm hadn't forgotten the death even if Tani had. He'd said nothing to her of the pair they'd found as skeletons. Their possessions had been quietly shared among the party who'd found them. Walks Quickly certainly had taken enough, Storm had thought. Maybe she'd planned to live in the cave she knew of for some time. Waiting for an opportunity to steal from the clan that had cast her out.

He'd mentioned to Tani that they had found the woman, and a missing warrior from the raiding party, dead. He'd spoken in such a way that she had believed them to have murdered each other. He finished caring for the eagle and stood admiring the sky. It was deepening toward late afternoon and the clouds swirled with shades of purple and lavender. Storm yawned widely. Gods, he was tired.

He plodded wearily to the small shelter that he had been given to inhabit alone. Surra was already there lying comfortably on his blankets. He hugged her, running his fingers down her spine until she purred and seized his hand in velvet jaws. From her nest in the corner of a blanket Hing squeaked at him. He beckoned and she sprang into his lap. For long minutes he sat, feeling the life, the affection of his team. Was this how it was for Tani? Yet a portion of his love was tempered in fire. Together he and the team had fought, killed, survived.

There was trust as well as love there. He knew that when danger struck he could count on them as they could count on him in turn. Surra purred, nudging him. He received a picture of Tani standing over the warrior she and her team and friends had killed. The coyotes flanked her, snarling at the fallen enemy. Storm understood. Here too was trust. Tani's team had fought beside her. An enemy lay dead at their hands. He'd been thinking of her as an inferior. Not because she was a woman, but because she was young and untrained.

Yet she had done well. She'd become a clan-friend here, where in previous generations many settlers had died at Nitra hands. Even the Norbies feared Nitra. Tani came and went, rode and hunted, shared fire and food and laughter with the clan. The Djimbut clan claimed her as their own and Storm knew enough about the Nitra to know it was no light or casual claim. If Tani were to die on Arzor it had better be a very clear accident. Only one other had ever been a clan-friend. It had occurred in the days of First Ship. Patterson had been a medic. He'd found a clan dying of neomeasles and been fortunate enough to carry a small supply of vaccine.

Like Tani, Patterson had been in some ways an innocent abroad, a restless man with a liking for new places and the habit of trusting those he met. He'd trusted the clan and been right. They'd named him clan-friend. Patterson had come and gone for years in the clan lands, prospecting for the then virtually unknown and hence very valuable eye-stones. He'd finally found a tiny pocket of them and taken out a dozen of the rarest green. He'd been murdered for them and the lawless gang at the port had celebrated their good fortune.

Word had taken almost two years to seep back to Patterson's clan. After that it had been a murderous mess. Clan warriors had ridden for the port. They'd taken a man at night and wrung from him the names of the clan-friend's killers. It had been a night of blood and death after that. For the clan it was a matter of honor. One of the killers had survived and a badly wounded Nitra warrior had returned alone to his clan to report. He had remained, but more had ridden out to complete the killing.

They'd succeeded. Of the eight men who'd murdered Patterson, seven had been killed by the clan. The eighth, trapped, had killed himself rather than fall into Nitra hands. The clan had lost half of its warriors, but Patterson was avenged. It had been those events that had led first to a Native Protection Force and then to strictly enforced laws. Of course, the laws in the end protected humans as much as the natives. No government wanted a clan-hunting vengeance across the port and towns.

The Djimbut clan had named Tani as clan-friend. If she were ever murdered they'd tear the planet apart in search of her killers. He knew he'd better com Kelson and let him know about that, once he returned to the ranch. Storm stirred the coals of his fire. There was a little heat there. He added twigs and once the flames leaped up he reached for the swan-kee pot. Just as well they were going back. He had enough left to drink a mug tonight, but tomorrow there'd be none. He shared cold meat with Hing and broke one of the small flat rounds of bread in half.

He built up the fire and lay down. Hing snuggled in on one side, Surra on the other. The big cat had refused his offering of food, clearly she'd gone hunting before he returned to the shelter. They slept, but Storm woke in the early hours of the morning from a dream of running and hunting. The blood had been hot in his throat as he fed, the warm quivering flesh a delight that had thrilled through his entire body. Feeding was ecstasy. He sat up, reaching for water. He drank, then craned forward. From where he sat he could see the entrance to the shelter of Jumps High and his family. Light flickered there, too.

No doubt the dream had come to Tani as well. It no longer surprised him that she didn't want to think about it. That had been one of the most unpleasant experiences Storm had ever known. The gloating ecstasy in the pain the killers caused left an acrid taste like old blood in his mouth. He spat to clear it. Then he lay down again. It opened up possibilities. He'd felt nothing the previous night when Walks Quickly and the enemy warrior had died. Tonight he had felt the death hunt and kill, but only while he slept.

The death must have taken its victims the previous night while the clan was still awake. Tani had felt nothing, or had she? He must speak to her. He felt sleep drifting closer and again surrendered himself to it. His last thought was that they must ride out in the morning and find the victims' skeletons. He needed to know where the kill was so that he knew from how far away he and Tani could read it. The samples he'd taken were older. He'd take fresh ones for the scientists. He slept as across the desert death feasted, savoring each agony-spiced mouthful.

With dawn Tani was awake and donning her outer clothing. Minou and Ferarre had gone off earlier to hunt grass hens. The plump birds were more easily taken if one was in place when the sun rose. The girl went in search of the Thunder-Drummer. She arrived in time to be offered food. Tani accepted and sat. The interpreter was absent but that did not matter. The Drummer could sign well enough. And anyhow, Tani would rather speak in private. For a time they ate in peace, then the girl's hands rose.

"You say it is time we returned to our own place. You asked our help. You sent warriors to search for us. What have we done to help? Nothing I know."

The medicine woman added a branch to the fire. She did not wish to speak hastily. Much of what she had done was because of her falwood visions. In the smoke of dreaming she had seen . . . much. But to speak of some of it could be to send paths twisting in other directions. At length she began.

"I dreamed. The Thunder said in my dream that I should search for strange ones who would aid the clan." Her hands slowed, the girl must understand clearly. "Beyond clan there is the land itself. That-Which-Hates is not from the land. I dreamed you would learn the trail death takes to us, to the land."

Tani drew in a breath but remained silent. The Nitra knew little of science, but with the samples Storm had, Kady and Brion might indeed be able to do as the Thunder-Drummer hoped. If that much of the medicine woman's dream was right, then more could be, too. She leaned forward a little to indicate attention.

Slender hands moved in patterns. "I dreamed. A part of my dream I may not tell. It was a medicine dream. This I may say to you. Two be as one. Many together may be as an arrow in the heart of an enemy. You are the arrowhead to strike home. Fear must not bind you, little sister, daughter of warriors, clan-friend to the people of Djimbut clan, clan-sister to a warrior of your own kind. Trust him, he dreams also. Blood calls to blood. Hear what it says."

She reached out to take one of Tani's smaller hands in her own. With the hand remaining she signed emphatically.

"I see death on all roads, only one where it is not. In a place where death crosses other trails you will stand with your spirit-friends. Beside you stands another. Together you ride. Blood on your trail and I cannot see the end of it. This I think, Sunset. In two is strength. With two, maybeso the trail will be smoother. Ride well, live or die as a warrior."

She sat back. Tani was absorbing the words. How much was merely good advice and how much was true dreaming she was uncertain, but she'd remember it all. A memory crossed her mind and she smiled.

"That reminds me," Tani said as she signed. "Jumps High said you'd give me a small-name."

The Thunder-Drummer eyed her with amusement twinkling in the black eyes. She knew the misunderstanding that had arisen when her warriors had found the girl. Still, her warrior had so-said. The part of the dream she had not told Tani had covered this. She had dreamed of the Thunder. In the rumble of power she had heard the dream. She should bind the girl to the land. The chains should be of love, unbreakable and willingly worn. Anything that would help that was good.

She smiled and her smile was warm with genuine affection. "Your kin named you Sunset. In the Thunder I hear another name. The clan see you, I see you, as Sunrise. What is more beautiful than the sun as it lights the sky with all the shades of daybreak? What is sweeter than a new beginning? You shall be Sunrise of the Djimbut clan. Wearer of thunder-flowers. Traveler with strange ones. Rider of the spirit-mare. Clan-friend, little sister to one who is named in ceremony and in this life as Speaker of Dreams. Is it well?"

Tani caught her breath. "It is well, elder sister."

"Go then. Tell your name to the clan and make ready. At sun-high you ride." She watched as Tani rose to her feet and left the shelter. The other one would be here shortly. She'd seen the questions in his eyes. She was right. Her interpreter rejoined her as Storm slipped in and sat cross-legged before the fire. Storm waited in silence.

"You would hear why you were brought here and why I now send you away." He nodded. "To you I can say more. I dreamed. Because of the dream I brought you to the clan. I will not weary you with all I dreamed, I tell only what I believe to be the meaning. There are two. Apart they have little power and Death-Which-Comes-in-the-Night can slay them. Together their power is greater. One is a warrior. He would fight an enemy as he trained to do. The other is young, untried and unaccustomed to war. Yet her heart is strong and her power would be greater if it were sharpened as a knife. What is needed to sharpen a knife?"

"Oil, a whetstone, and hands to use them," Storm replied.

It was a riddle similar to others he had heard.

"So! You shall be the hands. The oil, that has been her time here. We have named her clan-friend. Shown her kindness and the ways of the clan. She is one who is truly bound where there is love. We have bound her to clan and land. When the time comes that she sees we will die, then she will fight for us."

"And the stone, Thunder-Drummer?"

"That shall be bloodshed. No," as Storm stiffened to attention. "I have seen no death for either of you. But blood poured upon the land. That I have seen. Ride well, warrior. Bind her power to you that together you may conquer." She clapped her hands in the signal that the audience was ended.

Storm went first to Baku. He'd use the team to find whoever had died last night. He found Tani already there with Mandy.

"Storm, I had another nightmare last night. I'm certain it was a native who died. Mandy thinks she got the direction from me. She's going to fly out to see if she can see any loose horses or an empty camp. Will you send Baku out as well?"

He nodded, turning to impress the search on the eagle's mind. The birds lifted aloft almost in unison. Tani sat down beneath the dead tree to wait. Storm sat with her. It was a comfortable wait. Neither spoke but both felt as if they waited with a friend. Surra and Hing joined them, followed by the coyotes. Clan members glanced at the small group as they passed but did not approach. It took half an hour before Mandy floated down to land on Tani's shoulder. She drew the powerful beak along the girl's cheek in a caress, transmitting a picture as she did so.

"Mandy's found something."

Storm stared up as an eagle screamed above them. "So has Baku. In a different direction." His face went hard with worry. He said nothing of his fear. He'd wait to be sure. The team apart from the birds and horses would stay in camp. There would be a long ride during the next two days as they made for the ranch. Let Surra, Hing, and the coyotes rest now. Tani had Destiny waiting and Storm's mount also had been saddled and tethered. They rode out with Baku leading the way overhead.

The pitiful remains were those of a girl from a different Nitra tribe. Storm stood after he'd examined the skeleton.

"On her name-trial. From a poor tribe."

"How do you know?"

"No horse, few possessions, and those here are old and worn. Look," he indicated. "And I think she was younger than most. The tribe needs all the women it has so they send out their girls young."

"That doesn't make sense," Tani objected. "Small Bird told me that the older a girl, the better chance she has to survive. If they send out younger girls more would die."

"Normally, yes. Which makes me think she must have come from a tribe that's been hit hard by the death." He looked over the land. "She died about four miles from the camp. We'll follow Mandy now. Leave the girl's body here. I'll tell Jumps High when we return. They can collect her gear and give her the death rites."

Tani mounted, signaling the paraowl to fly. Keeping contact she rocked at a slow canter, off in a circle to the east. They were in the true desert after several miles. Storm estimated they were nearly ten miles in a direct line from the camp when Mandy dropped lower to hover over a clump of brush. Storm dismounted and approached cautiously. The brush clump must have been often used as a temporary camp. It was hollow in the center, with a circle of stones and the ashes of many fires. To one side a stack of gathered wood lay unused.

He waved the girl in. There was no danger here. Not now. Destiny came in dancing, her nostrils crinkled in disgust. Tani leaned over to look at the reason.

"Ugh. How many, Storm?"

"Five warriors. One was sleeping apart under the edge of cover. May have been the guard." He looked up. "Notice something? All the people are skeletons and so are four of the horses. The other horse is just dead. I think our walking death may have killed more than it could eat this time. Or maybe the meal took so long it didn't have time to finish. Either way I can take samples, and I think I see just where to take them from."

Tani had dismounted and was peering at the horse's throat. "Yes, I see it too. Like a small bite but a whole tiny scoop of flesh has gone."

"Right. I'll cut out a chunk of the flesh all around that. Tani, have you any idea how long any DNA on this might last?"

"That depends. We don't have any way to seal it. But if there was an exchange of material we could get something off it if we make it to the ranch by tomorrow night."

"But the fresher the better?"

"Of course."

"What if we sent a message by Mandy, and the sample by Baku. They'd be there in a couple of hours."

Tani looked as if she'd like to jump up and down clapping hands. "That's brilliant! You wrap the sample right now. Give it to Baku and tell her to go. I know what to say to Brion and Kady. Mandy will be there just as fast. She isn't carrying anything."

Storm unfastened his canteen and gave both birds a generous drink. Then he sent Baku off, the wrapped horse flesh tied to one leg with a strip of soft cloth. Minutes later Mandy rose into the air in pursuit. Storm and Tani rode back quietly to the camp. Jumps High was there and Storm took him to one side at once. It wasn't long before warriors left hastily, heading in two directions. They'd collect the abandoned items and give the dead the spirit rites.

Storm went to finish gathering his own gear. Finding two death places had confirmed his fears—and his hopes. The death had split. From the tracks and signs he'd read the victims had died several miles apart but around the same time. As for hopes, Tani had "heard" the killer at almost twice the distance Storm had read it. Not only that, she'd been able to read the direction, whereas he had to rely on Baku to find the victim.

The Thunder-Drummer was right. Inexperienced or not, Tani had the stronger abilities. Somehow he must convince the girl to help him seek out the lair of the killer. But that would mean purposely reaching out to them. It was nightmare enough for Tani that she unwillingly shared their hunt at times. To do so deliberately was something he feared she would not accept. He sighed. The medicine woman had given him a key. If he persuaded Tani that her friends were in danger she might agree.

With his gear packed, Surra at his mount's heels, and Hing resting happily in the front of his shirt, he walked his horse over to where Tani was just swinging onto Destiny. The coyotes gamboled around Small Bird and her daughters. Tani leaned over to hug her friends.

"Take care. I'll come back, visit you all when I can."

Jumps High twittered as his companions rode up. Seven warriors Storm noticed. The clan intended their guests to return safely and to show them honor at the same time. The trip was tiring, particularly for Surra and the coyotes who must run. But at last they neared the Basin rim. Their Nitra leader halted the small group. Jumps High signed rapidly.

"We leave you here. Thunder-Drummer says we may provoke no fight," his hands said. "Ride well, Sunrise." The girl hugged him and the other two warriors from his original four-group.

Storm signed a farewell and headed his mount for the Basin rim. They were over and dropping quickly past where they could see the Nitra. Tani looked back. She said nothing but her face was wistful. Then she turned to look ahead. Brion and Kady must have been mad at her staying away so long, but the sample sent by Baku would have left them too busy and involved. She'd escape with a mild scolding now, if they even remembered that. Destiny's pace picked up and Tani nodded. Home soon.

Chapter Thirteen

They rode down the final stretch of land, the ranch buildings looking larger and closer with each stride. Mandy had remained, waiting for Tani at the ranch after the bird's flight. Now she flew to Tani's shoulder with a flurry of wings. They saw Logan step past the corrals and stare. He yelled, his voice tinny in the distance. Tani flinched.

Storm smiled at her. "Brave up, Sunrise. Now we find just how angry your family is with you."

"They won't be," Tani told him. "They'll probably be too busy with the sample you sent to say much." There was a kind of soft sadness in the words. "With a puzzle like that to unravel they'll be in the laboratory day and night until it gives up its secrets."

The words gave Storm a further insight into her life. She'd lost parents who loved her and had spent all the spare time they had with their child. Brion had been Alisha's older brother by years. He and Kady must have been set in their ways when Tani arrived. They cared for her, that Storm had seen. But it still wasn't the family love she'd known. Her own words had said that she knew she was less important than a good scientific puzzle. She was used to it, accepted that was the way. But underneath the acceptance was a sense of loss for what she'd once had.

Had he talked to Logan he'd have already known that. Logan had often been indignant in that first week as he rode with Tani. Her aunt and uncle weren't unkind. They seemed to care. But they never had time for her. If they weren't in the laboratory working they were talking about their work. The only time they really talked to the girl was when she'd worked with them and they discussed further tests. Now and again they did remember to ask how her day had been, or what she would do that morning. But mostly they assumed she was happy and busy. If she wasn't, they expected she'd say so.

Logan liked Tani as a friend, but there was no great attraction between them apart from friendship. He preferred girls who were quite different, but he'd come to like Tani a lot, as herself, as a friend he could talk to. In a way she felt like a little sister. On her behalf he sometimes found himself angry at the way she was ignored.

Since Tani wasn't unhappy, she never complained to Brion and Kady. But Logan wasn't the only one who had noticed her isolation. Brad Quade also had seen it. Sometimes he'd quietly prompted her aunt and uncle to ask after her day. Each time he'd seen the pleasure that small bit of attention had given her. He'd encouraged Logan to keep the girl company, listening to her accounts of the things she'd seen on their rides. She lit up when she was interested in something. Brad heard Logan's call now and smiled.

"Hey, Hey! Everyone. They're back."

He hurried to where he could see the two riders walking their horses wearily down the slope. His heart lifted and he ran. Logan trotted with him and together they arrived beside the riders several hundred yards out from the buildings. Storm slid down. Brad's hands closed about his shoulders.

"You are okay, son?"

"I'm well, Asizi. So is Tani."

Logan had gone to sweep the girl from her mount and been warned off firmly by Destiny's lowered horns. He laughed up at Tani.

"Come down before this savage beast of yours eats me." She dismounted, laughing back happily. Logan hugged her hard. "Thank the Thunder you're okay. We worried about you. How did you manage to tame that horse? Where did you get to? What clan did you stay with? How did you . . ."

Tani giggled. "Whoa. Wait until we get home and we can tell it all together then. Where are Aunt Kady and Uncle Brion?"

Logan shrugged. "Working. When aren't they?"

Tani looked at him and her voice chided. "Logan, if they can find out what the killer is, then that's far more important than me getting back from a few days with friends."

Storm glanced over as they met, noticed the hug, and looked away quickly. They were the same age. They enjoyed each other's company. What else could he expect? But a shiver of sadness went over him. He blinked. What was he thinking about? Logan could hardly do better, and Tani loved Arzor. He switched his attention back to his stepfather as Brad continued.

"The Carraldos have been working on that sample you sent ever since it arrived. They could tell us almost at once that it didn't come from Arzor. It isn't native."

He began to walk back toward the ranch buildings.

Storm walked with him as they talked, Tani and Logan still chattering as they followed.

"What did they find? What sort of material?"

"Poison, and they believe from the size of the bite mark that the killer is a group of insects in some form. Like a swarm of bees or an ant nest. The jaw radius is small. They believe that the swarm specializes. The front-runners are the ones that carry poison to paralyze the prey, then the rest of the swarm feeds. It's all theory as yet. They're running just about every DNA test known to them. They say the more they learn, the more they can then run other tests against outside material. With a full range completed, if anything agrees they should have a match."

Storm had listened closely. "So they are trying for a total reading on the killer? With that completed they'd check it against everything on databases they can access. If the original information is complete and there's a match anywhere, they will find it." Brad agreed.

"How far along are they?" Storm queried.

"Another couple of days and they can start running comparisons."

Storm blew out a breath. "That's a good start. I just hope they find something. Have they any idea how long it could take on that?"

Brad shook his head. "Nope. I talked to them about it. There was a lot of science but it all boils down to anytime. They think that straight comparison checks could take another three days. They can leave the work mostly to the computers in the Ark. It's the other stuff. There's a number of planets that have information that isn't linked in. They started Jarro, the guy you tangled with, contacting these other places. He's uploading information from any of those who'll cooperate. That takes longer, as a lot of it isn't in standard format, I'm told. They can set the receiving computer to interface so the programs will be rewritten to match, but again, it all takes time."

Storm looked out across the ranch. "And what do we do if there's no match?" he asked softly.

Brad sighed. "We lose the ranch, maybe Arzor for humans. Maybe the natives lose everything including the planet, too. What's it like out there?"

"Bad. Tani and I found some evidence to suggest some of the tribes are losing heavily. What about the settlers. Has anyone else been killed?"

"No, thanks be. Even Dumaroy is staying quiet. A sort of lull-before-the-storm quiet, mind you." His face crinkled in wry amusement. "You know Dumaroy. But show him something he can fight and he's a good man to have at your back."

"I know. Look, Tani will be starving and we've the animals to see as well. Can we eat while we talk, or even before?"

Brad laughed. "You underestimate me, son. I gave orders the minute Logan starting yelling he could see you. The cook has food and hot swankee ready. Miller is waiting to take your horses. All you have to do is take care of your teams and come inside."

Tani was dubious but even Destiny was tired. The filly went meekly off in the care of a hand. Another hand produced an uncooked frawn haunch and the coyotes settled to eat. With her team seen to, the girl headed for the table. She sat, accepted swankee, and drank eagerly. Then she sighed and relaxed back in her chair.

"That's so good." She looked at Storm. "Do you think it could be addictive?"

Brad smiled at her. She was tired and browner, but she looked lean and fit rather than ill treated. "No, swankee has some caffeine but no great amount. I daresay if you took to drinking fifty cups a day it might not be good, but if you keep it to twenty-five I'm sure you'll be fine."

Tani grinned. She was tired and feeling a bit light-headed at being back. "If I drank that much no one would ever see me. I'd always be in the bathroom." She drank the rest of the mug, refilled it, then reached for bread. "Ummm. That's something I missed."

"The clan didn't have bread?" Logan inquired.

Storm answered. "They have a sort of flat campbread type, it doesn't rise. They make it from wild grain that is ground and baked, sometimes with flour made from nuts added. They cut a hole in that and fill it with berries. It's pleasant and probably satisfies their need for something sweet, too, but it isn't real bread. Not as we get it here. There's no butter, either."

He helped himself liberally to the bread, buttering it thickly as a demonstration. Logan grinned.

"Want me to bring the berry jam?"

His half-brother nodded. "Yes, please."

Logan passed over the lorg-berry jam, which had been on the table in front of him. Then, moving quietly, he added pot after pot of the other kinds until even Brad was laughing. Storm eyed his half-brother over a virtual barricade of jam.

"Of course I won't be able to tell you about our adventures until I've eaten all of this."

"Oh, in that case . . ." Logan began removing the pots

again. Storm held on to a couple, passing one to Tani.

"Try this. I think you'll like it. It's made from those little blue berries you picked with Small Bird."

She took it silently, her mouth full. She hadn't realized how hungry she'd been. Today, once they'd had breakfast with the Djimbut clan, they'd ridden without pausing to eat. Storm had been eager to get back and so had she. The Nitra wanted to return to the clan camp. By unspoken agreement they'd kept going. She felt grubby too. Just as soon as she'd eaten and they'd answered all the questions, she was going to fill her bath as full as it could manage, allowing room for her. Then she'd lie in that until all the dirt soaked off. After that she'd sleep.

She spread jam and bit into the still warm bread. The jam was as good as Storm had claimed. Across the table he was starting to tell his story. How he'd found another victim of the killer and how the Nitra had found him. He ended the story with his arrival in camp and his first sight of her. Then they all turned to look at Tani. She swallowed her last mouthful of bread and jam and began her own tale.

It took a long time to tell it all. There were times when she saw she was surprising both Brad and Logan, but she was at a loss to understand why. They were Arzor born. Surely there was nothing she'd have found out they didn't already know. She plowed on to the point where she'd first seen Storm. After that they told the stories in turns, Tani adding bits about Small Bird and Jumps High and their family. She also talked about Speaker of Dreams and saw the surprise on their faces more strongly this time. She stopped.

"Is something wrong?"

It was Storm who replied. "Tani, she gave you her medicine name. That wasn't a small-name. She does have one, but her people mostly address her by title. But I heard the other a few times. It's Sweet Frawn. Speaker of Dreams is her second name. The one that's tied in with her spirit. She only gives that to friends or family and it's more for formality." He paused. "She'd have a third name, too. But that's not to be spoken. Adults choose those for themselves or ask their Thunder-Drummer to choose. She's the only one to know everyone's true-name, and no one else in the clan would know hers because of that."

Logan whistled. "What I wouldn't have given to have been with you. Hunting beside a Nitra clan, getting to know them, fighting their enemies, learning their names. Wow!"

Tani laughed. "You make it sound special. I thought you spent most of your time with the Shosonna. Aren't you adopted into their clan?"

She saw they were all looking at her and blinked. "Now what did I say?"

Brad explained slowly. "Tani, didn't Storm say anything about the clan?" He watched as the girl shook her head. "Well, my dear. You are only the second human in Arzor's history to be named as clan-friend to a Nitra clan. There are two types of native tribe. There are the Norbies, who are relatively civilized. Then there are the Nitra. They live the way their ancestors lived and they don't like humans. Mostly they don't come near human-settled lands, but when they do someone usually dies. Mostly it isn't Nitra, either."

Tani's eyes were widening as Brad continued. "My dear, the only other clan-friend they ever named was murdered in the early settlement days. The clan warriors rode into the port and hunted down his killers. Half the warriors in the clan were killed, but it was a debt of honor. They'd have kept coming until either they had the killers or there were no warriors left alive. Patterson was the first. It's been six generations since then. Now Tani, daughter to Bright Sky, is the second."

He smiled at Tani, who by now was staring at him huge-eyed. "The gods help us if anyone kills you, child. Your whole clan would paint for war. The more so as you seem to have a real friend in their Thunder-Drummer." He stood up. "Well, we all have things to think about. There's a lot of hot water waiting for you."

Tani made a small moaning sound. "Thank you, Mr. Quade. I won't keep it waiting."

She hurried for her bedroom and Brad stood listening as her footsteps died in the hall. Then he closed the door and turned to look at Storm.

"I gather there's more you didn't want to say in front of Tani."

Storm leaned back in his seat. "The medicine woman talked to me too, yes." He reported that discussion. "I know she did like Tani, that was genuine. So was the clan-friend naming. She saved several lives and I know Jumps High spoke for her. So did Stream Song and Swift Killer, after she saved their son. And no Thunder-Drummer would give her medicine-name casually. But the woman had an agenda as well. She wanted to bind Tani to the clan and Arzor."

"Why, what do they think a girl barely nineteen could do for them?"

"Save the clan, save the land. Destroy the Death-Which-Comes-from-the-Desert."

Brad snorted. "Would they like her to make the deserts

fertile and the mountains flat while she's about it?"

"Asizi." Storm hesitated and Brad saw he was serious. "They aren't so wrong. Speaker of Dreams said that I was a trained warrior. I'd fight an enemy where one was found. But Tani's not a warrior. She isn't trained and she isn't used to battle. They wanted her to love the clan and the land. That way she'd fight to save them. They said a knife needs to be honed. That isn't all. Tani's been hearing the killer when it kills. She may be able to lead us to it. A hunting party from another clan was taken the night before we left. It's where the sample came from."

Storm's face was hard. "A girl on her name-trial died too. I heard her dying while I slept and dreamed. I sent Baku out and she found the girl's skeleton in a hollow where she'd made camp. But Tani didn't have to search. She knew the direction for the other killing, and that bunch were more than twice as far away when they died. Mandy just flew a line out and called us when she saw them. Tani can hear the killers from a much greater distance and know from what direction they're coming. Speaker of Dreams was right. Tani could be what saves us in the end."

Brad sat in silence as he considered all of that. At last he stirred. "Her father was a Beast Master. Her mother, from what Brion says, was most probably a sensitive. Picking up the killers is so distressing to Tani that she shuts most of it off. Her team seems to help with that."

"Except that we need her not to. She has to open her mind, and we're asking her to live the death the killer hands out. At least long enough to get a direction. She needs to practice that, so we're saying she should do it maybe six, eight, a dozen times. As many times as it takes."

Brad nodded slowly. "So the Thunder-Drummer gave us a lever." He looked at Storm. "We'll use it if we have to. For now let her enjoy life. Oh, and you can tell her that filly is hers, too. I'll get Logan to take her to meet the Shosonna clan. She'll fascinate them and they'd keep her occupied. Once the Carraldos can tell us what we're facing we may have to use the lever. Until then let the girl build up her strength." His mouth tightened to grimness. "She's going to need it. Maybe we all are."

By the time Tani could spend a day with the Shosonna Logan had already told them her story. Krotag, the Chief, met her, his hands signing formally.

"We welcome one who is clan-friend to the Djimbut Ni-tra. Be at peace in our tents." His eyes shifted to the team. "One welcome holds for all of you. Share food, drink, and fire with the Shosonna of the Zamle clan."

Tani beamed. Her fingers flickered in answer. "Food and drink I bring to share as a guest should. My bird totem watches over me. My animal totems walk beside me. In their name also I thank you."

At her signal Mandy landed on a branch nearby while Minou and Ferarre sat down. Tani dropped to sit cross-legged by the flames and accepted the food offered. Meat was brought for the coyotes, who ate and then allowed themselves to be enticed into a game by the camp children. Tani smiled after them.

"Your children do not see what is strange as evil."

Ukurti, the clan shaman who had made certain to be present to speak with this strange human, leaned toward her. "Storm has visited us often. We know his totems are friends. Logan has said this would also be so with yours," he explained. He watched the children playing a game with the coyotes and gave the soft twittering that was Norbie laughter. "I see that he spoke only truth." His eyes met hers. "Did he speak also truth that you are small-sister to One-Who-Drums-Thunder in the Djimbut clan?"

"Yes. Why, is it important?"

Ukurti's face crumpled into a smile. "Such is always important, but some things are medicine. Since it is truth I may speak to you of dreams." Tani settled herself as Krotag quietly signaled the others to rise and leave them alone. She watched as fingers danced.

"I have dreamed that evil comes to the clan and the tribe. I have dreamed that the land rejects the evil. It is not of our lands."

Tani nodded. "So spoke the medicine woman of the Djimbut clan," she signed back.

"Yet the thing which slays comes from the heart of the desert. From the center of the lands you name the Big Blue. I have dreamed that behind lies hatred not of our kind, but of yours. That until That-Which-Hates lies dead also, the slayer will thrive. Find what lies at the heart of the desert and hates, Sunrise. Then will your arrows find the life of the enemy."

Tani nodded. "I thank you for your wisdom. May I speak of this to the Quades and my kin?"

"If there is need," the Thunder-Drummer accepted.

Tani returned from her day with the Shosonna very thoughtful. She'd seen enough in her life to believe Ukurti and Speaker of Dreams. Those of power had other avenues from which they might learn. She unsaddled Destiny, settled Mandy on her perch with a lastree nut, then went inside. Brion and Kady were there. Both looked exhausted and preoccupied. Tani knew they'd been working on the sample Storm had provided, since its arrival.

Kady was talking in a soft, tired voice as Tani walked in. "We have a very extensive range of materials in the Ark. We tested against everything there first. There's nothing. Jarro has contacted many of the planets that retained scientific data. Almost all agreed to download what they had. But it's a huge amount. We have everyone on the Ark running programs to either change the older different codes to something our computer can read, or run the altered programs looking for a DNA match with anything at all."

Brad was grim. "One of the Nitra clans has clashed with a Norbie tribe. There's a number of dead on both sides. Put Larkin has allowed the Norbies to move onto the edge of his range. It helps stop the fighting for a short time. But soon the Nitra are going to lose more to the killer, and they'll push deeper into Norbie lands. Once settlers start to die the Patrol will step in."

Brion looked even more weary than his wife. "I know, I know. But we have so much material to check. With the Xik attacks, many planets used whatever systems they could get at the time. Often new computer systems were wrecked and they brought old types back into service. A lot of the records have to be loaded by hand. Some systems are incompatible for automatic work. If only we could cut down the range we have to search for a match."

Tani's mouth fell open. The Xiks. The hatred that lives in the heart of the desert. Ukurti had said that it hated the settlers. Logan had told her about the Xik holdout group Storm had uncovered. She'd heard other rumors of such outfits herself. She cut into what Brad had begun to say with no regard for politeness. If she were right they could save time. A lot of time. If she were wrong, they'd lose none. They'd be checking and cross-matching everything anyhow.

"Check Xik material. Do we have any?"

Brion and Kady looked at her with annoyance. Brad intervened hastily. "What do you know?"

"It's something Ukurti told me. Do we have Xik records?"

"We do," Kady spoke thoughtfully. "Oddly enough they left records on Trastor when your father led the revolt that drove them out again. We hadn't got to those as yet. I can go and call the Ark to upload them all, then start checking for a cross-match." She was gone, almost running, and Tani heaved a sigh. Now they waited. There were times when that seemed to be life. Sitting about and waiting for something to happen.

She went to bed that night, still waiting. The results would be downloaded through the mobile laboratory link once the work was done. The whole Ark team was up there loading records, some of them by hand, and praying. Someone must have been listening. The call came at first light and Tani heard the shrill of the buzzer. She gathered in the dining room with the Quades and Storm. Kady arrived with Brion, both jubilant.

"The sample cross-checks with Xik material. It isn't Xik, but it seems to have been genetically altered from something on their home planet. The Xiks and the sample have too much in common for it not to be so."

Brad nodded. "Now we have a foot in the door. We know the enemy. With hard work maybe we can pry the door open." His face lit with his rare wide smile. Arzor might now have a chance to survive after all.

Chapter Fourteen

But while knowing a little more helped, they still knew only a part of the problem. Kady was talking.

"The material is from the Xiks' home world. It isn't from the Xiks themselves. We were lucky that one of the people who landed not long after first contact was a genetech scientist. He took samples from a number of organisms on the Xik home world and they've been kept in files ever since. When we asked for downloads on the subject we received that one along with the later material from Trastor. It came in after a lot of the other stuff, and the program was one of those that needed to be hand loaded and rewritten."

Brad Quade nodded. The history of human contact with the Xiks had been unpleasant. From the beginning the Xiks had been suspicious. When they found both species could live, if not always comfortably, on a similar sort of planet, trouble had begun. The Xiks believed that they were a superior race, that their way of life was sacred. What they wanted must be given to them. They saw Terrans as stupid, fools who weakly permitted native races to retain what was theirs. The initial permission for traders and scientists to visit the Xik home world had been revoked early. It was a small miracle Xik samples had been obtained and retained on file.

Brion took up the tale. "When Terra was destroyed, copies of the Xik files were still safe on Trastor. It's taken a lot of time and hard work to match the computer system they have with ours, but now that we've done that and run the files we're sure we have a match. We're running more comparisons with anything other worlds have but it may not be enough. I've started Jarro building three of the things from the DNA we found. Once we have a couple of living specimens we may learn a lot more."

"How long will that take?"

It was Kady who answered that. "A few days only. We're using forced growth, and from what Storm says and other evidence, they are likely to be small. We'll let you know as soon as we have viable specimens." She laughed grimly. "We aren't the only ones with problems. I had a spacegram from a friend on Ermaine. They had some odd sort of blight in the shallatoes. Personally I can't stand the things. They have that bitter aftertaste. But a lot of worlds are crazy about them and they're one of Ermaine's most important cash crops."

"What's happening to them?" Brad queried.

"They don't really know. Caryl is working day and night to find out, but all she can say so far is it's no disease they've ever seen there before." Kady sighed. "I'd help if I could, but with this business here we don't have the time." She headed purposefully back to her laboratory. Jarro should almost have finished the next part of the work by now.

The next event was two days later. Tani came hurrying in, waving a length of paper. "Mr. Quade, Storm, have you seen this?"

Brad took it from her and began to read. Storm leaned over his shoulder. They finished and stared at each other.

Kady entered and stood there listening. Brad offered her the message but she waved it away. "I saw it."

Storm started. "That's a very strange communication."

"I agree. It seems as if it's saying something important, but you can't be sure what."

Tani nodded. "I thought it was important. It's from Headquarters, after all. But it doesn't make a lot of sense. I think it's saying that there's trouble with Xik holdouts and sabotage groups still."

Brad grinned ruefully. "I think so too. It's the rest of it I don't get. It's so obscure that . . ."

"That you'd think they were trying to alert us to something without saying it," Brion finished, as he appeared in the doorway. "Maybe they are. Look at what they do say." He quoted. "A number of disasters on various planets that are rendering them financially nonviable. It appears this is occurring on predominantly human-settled worlds and settlers are warned to be on the lookout for anything that might cause major financial or life-threatening events on the planets of settlement. Read between the lines." He glanced at Brad. "I wonder if Caryl's shallatoes fall into that category?"

Storm was sitting comfortably in one of the large old armchairs. A thought came to him and he straightened.

"Kady, you can reach most human-settled planets from the Ark?"

"We can. Some of them take time to reach, but yes, we can. Why?"

"Will you send a couple of questions to all of them. Ask if they know of any rumors or actual events involving Xik hideouts or possible Xik sabotage. And also if any planets can report things like plagues, strange insects they've never had or seen before. Anything that looks like a major natural disaster but that could have been enemy action. Not that it probably was, but if they can think of a way it could have been made to happen. And suggest they check into the event looking for evidence of deliberate intent, just in case. We want everything they know. Even if it's just rumor, there may be information there. HQ can't risk coming out and asking that sort of question, but we can. It's important. Can you start now?"

For a moment Kady stared at him. "You think . . ." She broke off. "I'll send right away. I have friends in some places. I'll tag the messages personally to them where I can. They'll make it a priority." She was gone and Brion turned to look at Storm.

"You really believe this could be some part of another Xik plan?"

Brad answered him. "I fought the Xiks. They don't think the way we do in many ways. But they're good haters. And they learn from experience. They started a war with humans when they could have worked beside us. Not that they would have done so, they wanted everything we had. The planets we allowed autonomy, they would have ruled as autocrats. We were pleased when a settled world did well. They would have taken all the surplus and returned it to their home world so their ruling clans could grow fat. They lost the war in the end, but some of their hard-liners survived the surrender. Their politicians hint the population should wait, their time will come again. We know there were a lot of the small Xik groups left out there when peace came. Many of those didn't approve the surrender and didn't come in. We had one of those groups here—you heard about them?" He received a nod and carried on.

"They were one of the supply teams. They were sent in to steal food and supplies unobtrusively. They funneled them back to Xik worlds. There were also sabotage groups. Several groups like that were cleaned out of other planets. There were rumors that a lot of small self-contained Xik units had been sent out toward the end of the war. They were to dig into any human-settled world they could reach and continue the fight if possible."

"But that's crazy, Quade. The Xiks lost. We drove them right back to their home world. Destroyed their soldiers everywhere else, and where we could take them alive we sent their soldiers home again. If they start the war all over again they could . . . we could . . . well. Command surely would order the Xik home world destroyed this time. The same way the Xiks destroyed Terra."

Storm's eyes were hard. "They probably would. But the Xiks learned as much about us as we learned about them. One of the things they'd have learned is that we like to have evidence. They consider that a weakness in us. So if odd disasters begin happening on widely separated planets, and the disasters appear to be natural ones, then we may take a long time to even consider it enemy action. And then with no proof we may take far longer still to act in any way. Of course, once we have proof, their High Command will simply say that the unit found was a rogue one, operating in defiance of orders."

"As it could be," Brad added.

"As it could be. But it's unlikely." Storm glanced at the

two older men. "We cleaned out most holdout groups. It's been quite a while now since the war ended. Most of the groups gave themselves away within that first year. The bunch here lasted because there are big areas of Arzor still unexplored and the Native Treaty limits overflights. In fact, it's almost impossible to fly even the most powerful copter over the Big Blue because of the fierce updrafts. And they had one of the very few 'apers' ever created."

His mind went back for a brief moment to that. The Xik were humanoid, close enough to humanity's form to be surgically changed into a human replica. The Xik High Command had done just that with a few, a very few. One had come to Arzor as a paca-rat in the grain of Arzor's people. In the end the Xiks had been found, partly because the aper had feared a Beast Master enough to attack Storm once too often. After that Arzor had been scoured by humans and natives alike. At that time at least there had been no Xiks left.

Brad eyed him. "So, what do you think, son?"

Storm was thinking it out as he spoke slowly. "I think the Xik Command may feel that they've been quiet long enough to convince us they mean it. They could have sent out a few special units. Just to test the waters. If it's still too hot they'll deny knowledge, or claim the units are holdouts left over from the war."

"And if they get a toehold on a few worlds, if they can keep humans from getting the news out, then they could have new bases to begin building a war machine again," Brad said quietly.

"Yes. The same things that kept their first group unnoticed so long still apply here and they may feel they have a debt to settle with us."

Brad nodded, turning to look at Brion and Tani. "Tani, can you do a complete record of the problem here? Show it to me once it's done. I think we should send it to Headquarters."

"Saying what?" Brion asked.

Brad smiled. "Saying just that. Here is a report we thought you should see. The fact that the killers, whatever they are, contain Xik home world DNA will alert them. At the same time, Tani, show us any more disaster reports Kady receives. We'll condense those and pass them on, too."

The girl nodded. She returned with the report several hours later and Brad approved it. "Nice and lucid. All the facts followed by possible reasons and inferences clearly labeled as such. What's that you have?"

"A report that came in just now. It's from Lereene. I was going to add it to this one and send them together."

Brad scanned it quickly. A Lereene scientist was reporting in response to Kady's request. No plagues, no unknown diseases or strange insects. But things hadn't been well lately. There'd been a series of small quakes in a very isolated area. So far as they had pieced things together afterward, the quakes had caused a landslip. This had blocked the upper reaches of a tributary to the Jade River. Huge amounts of water had backed up over the weeks until at last five weeks ago they had broken through the landslip dam.

The flood of freed water had poured down into the Jade in one gigantic wave. There it had met the new Jade River dam. The sudden volume and the power with which it arrived had torn a great hole in the dam, and the water held back by the dam had been freed as well. It had rushed in a wall down the river and with only two hours warning had thundered over the capital city of Lereene. Deaths were estimated at close to ten thousand. Many more were injured and unable to receive proper medical care. The city had been almost destroyed. The scientist reporting suspected that in the emergency camps disease was beginning, but that wasn't what his friend had meant, was it? Kady knew how squalor bred disease.

Brad looked at Brion, who came forward. "This came in just now after Tani had left. Take a look."

It was another natural disaster. A fire that had started apparently from a piece of broken glass. Dropped, the authorities believed, by hunters in the massively wooded ranges of Merla. Many of the great stands of yellowwood, which had taken generations to grow, had been wiped out. This was not quite a disaster, although the wood was used to make a large number of beautiful pieces of luxury furniture, which brought in good revenue for the planet. The authorities had sent up a ranger team to investigate; meanwhile, hunting in the ranges was forbidden.

The real disaster had been the arrival of Astran jiggers on Merla. Somehow they'd appeared and were devastating the remaining forests. With no Merlan predator to prevent the explosion in numbers, the jiggers burrowed into trees all over the ranges. The weakened trees fell in storms and were also made useless for lumber. The jiggers were kept under control on their own world by the Krawk. It was thought that the jiggers could have come in with the luggage or cargo from a ship recently arrived from Astra. The authorities were frantically importing genetically sterile krawks and investigating the jiggers, yellowwoods, the ship, Astran immigrants, and apparently anything else they could think of. It hadn't occurred to them to investigate enemies. They still believed all events were natural accidents.

Tani was reading over Brad's arm. She took in a breath. "I should send that one too."

Storm nodded. "Yes. It's a beautiful plan. Nothing that would make a government suspect sabotage. But it could be easily done. With Lereene all they had to do was set off charges until the hillside slipped into the river. Add a few more to the hill behind that to make it really solid. I worked with a dozen first-in commandos who could have managed it easily. The rest would follow. As Kady's friend says. Disease is expected where people are living hand-to-mouth in flimsy shelters with no sanitation, and half of them already in shock trauma. But if there's no disease it's easy to help some appear.

"The same with Merla. All any team had to do was start a fire and listen to the port spacecom. Astra is in the same quadrant, and the planets trade regularly, so they wait until a ship comes in from Astra and release the jiggers. They get an added bonus if the Merlan authorities blame Astra and that starts trouble between the worlds. That may already be happening if they're hassling incoming ships and passengers." He looked at the papers. "Send them all, Tani. Include a description of that blight on Caryl's shallatoes, and any more that come in. All these could well be Xik mischief, but every world thinks their trouble is theirs only."

"Maybe it is."

"Maybe. But remember what HQ said. That suggests there's been a fair amount of this sort of thing already and someone is getting suspicious. You know the saying. Once is an accident, twice is coincidence . . ."

"Third time is enemy action," his stepfather finished. "I

think so many disasters all at once rather unlikely myself. Send it all. We'll see what Headquarters think."

What they thought was embodied in a spacegram that arrived late the next day. In clear and unambiguous language it stated that there was reason to believe Xik sabotage teams were operating on Terran worlds. Another planet had been racked with natural disasters. But they'd found evidence that indicated the disasters hadn't been all that natural. They'd dug further and happened on the Xik team. A number of innocent scientists had died, and the Xik team had blown themselves up rather than be taken. What evidence remained indicated a well-planned mission.

The message concluded, "There are strong indications that Xik social-disruption and sabotage hideout teams are using unfamiliar weapons and planned disasters to damage as many thinly human-settled planets as possible."

Brion read that aloud. "So now we know. We'll have more information coming in from Kady's friends tomorrow with luck. The Xik insects hatch then as well. I've sent a DNA profile to HQ asking if they can tell us anything. I don't think they can or we'd have had it in other material received. But they're alerted and they have the information. Tani, I need your help. I want you to see if you can read anything from the insects when they hatch."

Storm saw her face whiten slightly, but she nodded. "Can I bring Mandy in when I try? Having her with me helps."

"Of course. Don't worry. Kady and I will have weapons there. If these things are dangerous they won't escape. We're hatching them in heavy-duty clearplas containers for safety. Come to the laboratory around seven." He turned to look around. "That includes all of you. I'm sure you'd like to see what the killer looks like. You may be able to tell us something as well, Storm."

That was possible, Storm thought. He just wished the man hadn't asked Tani to be there. If he'd spoken to Storm first, Storm could have suggested Tani's help was unnecessary. It was too late now. If he said that after Brion had asked and she'd agreed already, the girl would feel that he didn't trust her, and he did.

He slept lightly that night and woke wondering what the buzzing was. It took only a tenth of a second to recognize it. Then he was up and running for the com as it flashed a light and sounded the alarm signal for an urgent message. The agitated face that appeared on the screen was familiar.

"Dumaroy? What is it, man?"

The big rancher's eyes were wild. "Nitra. They attacked the Merin clan near Put's western boundary. The clan fought a running battle onto my land. Put Larkin came over to my place and we used nausea gas on the Nitra tribe. They've cleared out again feeling mighty sorry for themselves. But there's a fair number of Norbie dead and wounded. Put called Kelson in as soon as it was over."

"What do you need?"

"Kelson wants to report to the Patrol. He says us Peaks ranchers should start moving off our land. I'm telling you, Storm. I ain't going and neither are a lot of the others. If Kelson or the Patrol wants us to move, then there'll be blood on the land. They can't pay compensation and I'm not going to live down at the Port with no money to pay off the boys or put a roof over our head."

"Is Kelson there?"

"Yeah. I'll put him on."

The tired face of the liaison man appeared on the small screen. "Storm. I'm sorry, but I have my job to do."

Storm nodded. "I know, but there's a few things you should know first. You haven't been back to your office since early yesterday, have you?" Kelson looked surprised as he shook his head. "Right. First up we had a spacegram from HQ. Not some computer jockey. It came from the General." He read out a copy of the first warning. "Got it? Then listen. After that Brad got suspicious. He had Kady Carraldo com every scientist she knew personally on other planets. We got a whole list of human-settled planets where odd disasters had hit. We passed the whole lot to HQ and got this yesterday." He proceeded to read the second gram.

Kelson's eyes widened. Storm held up a hand. "Hold on. That isn't all. I came back from a trip with fresh samples from a horse the death killed only hours before. The Carraldos managed to find a match with material from the Xik home world, and yes, they're certain. They checked it twice." From behind Kelson he could hear a blurred bellowing as Dumaroy passed on the information. That would slow down any trouble. Dumaroy had been a soldier and a good one. He didn't trust the Arzoran natives but he really hated the Xiks.

Kelson vanished for a few minutes, then returned. "So what you're suggesting is that calling the Patrol is likely to be a waste of time?"

"Yes. So I think," Storm told him. "On some of these other planets they're having food riots and close to civil war. We haven't got to that as yet and we won't if we can keep our heads. Why don't you come to the ranch and bring Dumaroy and Larkin. We may have something to show you all by the time you arrive."

He got hasty agreement from all three before switching off. Storm turned and found his father behind him.

"You heard?"

"I heard," Brad said soberly. "You say we haven't got war yet, but son, we will have if we don't crack this thing soon. That's the second Norbie tribe the Nitra have taken on to get further away from the killer. The Norbies are pressing onto settler lands. So Dumaroy knows the Xiks could be behind it. That may not stop him shooting when his frawns start to get killed for food. The Lancins and Larkins in the Peaks are good men. They'll hold off, see what can be done. But even they have a breaking point." He sighed. "And Mirt Lasco up there lost his boy. Dumaroy's raw over it as well. He feels he was to blame in some way."

Storm sagged into a chair. "We're doing all we can. I got samples the Carraldos could identify and build specimens from. We know the Xiks have to be behind this and a lot more stuff on other planets. If only we knew what the things they're using are." He stood again. "And where the Xik team is hiding. Well, it must be about time to see what Kady and Brion have built in the mobile laboratory."

"When are Kelson and the others arriving?"

Storm looked at the chrono. "Soon, I should think. He was leaving in a copter a few minutes after we talked." Brad moved to the door.

"We'll go now. I'd like to know what the Carraldos have managed in advance. If the news isn't good we can meet Dumaroy and calm him down before he starts yelling."

Storm smiled grimly. "The trouble is that good news may not be so good. Let's go."

They walked briskly across to where the Ark's mobile

laboratory stood. Brad tapped politely and the door was opened by Kady. She motioned them inside in silence. Brion was bending over a small machine and Tani was running readings on a computer. Now and again they conferred in low voices. Storm and his father found places to stand where they could watch but be out of the way. At last the readings seemed to satisfy the workers. On a perch in the corner Mandy also waited silently, but to Storm she was savagely alert. He could feel her tension in the back of his mind.

Kady glanced over to her niece. "Can you read anything?"

Tani's voice was faint. "Hunger!"

"For food? Is it the killer?"

The girl's voice came slowly, she sounded sick. "It wants blood and flesh. It enjoys pain. It knows me." She jerked backward in horror.

"Let's see what it looks like." Brion stepped back, moved a lever, and something scuttled out into the high-sided clear-plas box. It moved incredibly fast so they had only a brief glimpse. Brion was reaching for the lid—too slowly. The thing leaped for the edge, kicked over, and was racing across the floor toward Tani. It was perhaps two inches long, barely half that across. In front a mouth, much larger in proportion to its size, gaped in anticipation.

Tani flung herself back as the thing reversed and headed for her again. From her perch the paraowl stepped forward, dropping on half-open wings. Her massively powerful beak snapped shut. There was a crunching crack and her prey stopped its struggles. Mandy gave a reassuring croon, offering the thing to Tani. Tani's face went whiter as she started to sway. Brad grabbed her.

"Head down, child. Storm, get water. Brion, I wouldn't

let any more of those things out just yet. Kady, persuade Mandy to give it to you."

There was a flurry of activity that ended with Tani sitting up drinking the water as Storm supported her. Brion was standing by the bench as Kady tried to persuade the paraowl into parting with her prey. She was unsuccessful until Tani turned to look. Then, sulkily, Mandy handed the thing over. Kady took it in a hand well protected by a metal-mesh glove. She looked down at it.

"Now," she said in a voice that rang. "Now, we get some answers."

Chapter Fifteen

They wrenched answers from the tiny body over the next day. Kelson arrived with Dumaroy and Larkin, who sat, watching and listening as the information poured out. The dead specimen yielded many secrets over that time. Kady prodded it toward late afternoon.

"They have very hard exoskeletons. It takes direct opposing pressure from something very powerful to crack one."

Dumaroy looked at the killer in disgust. "So a kick or something wouldn't do it. You'd have to stomp?"

"Even that might not crack the shell," Kady told him. "It might if you jumped on it, but they're fast. In the time it took for you to do that they'd probably have their jaws into you."

Dumaroy shuddered.

The liaison man leaned forward. "What's the poison?"

"Nasty. It paralyzes involuntary muscles but allows the autonomic functions to continue. You breathe, your heart continues to beat, and you don't lose consciousness. You are just unable to move no matter how desperately you try."

Dumaroy half snarled, his face working in rage. "Are those things natural or did the Xiks fix them up to be that way?"

Brion turned from where he was running more checks. "Both, Mr. Dumaroy. We've been cooperating with Command HQ and they've accessed records civilians never saw. The killer seems to have started with a hive type of insect on the Xik world. It was wiped out there in the wild but specimens survived in zoos, and in research institutes, we believe. The poison of the originals was weak. For the Xiks it was a painful bite that often festered. For one of us it would have made us ill and sluggish for a couple of weeks. The original insects preyed on small animals. For evolutionary reasons the insects preferred to eat living prey. To do that they evolved a specialized series of subspecies."

He paused to check his results as Kady took up the explanation. "There is the front-runner. They have the poison, they also have the ability to spring quite sizable distances either forward or straight up. The others are workers. They eat, dissolve the food into a semiliquid paste, and feed it to the front-runners. They do this because feeding them appears to produce a sensation of pleasure. Very strong pleasure. That ties in with the eating of live prey. Apparently they have a weak ability for empathy. They enjoy any emotion, the stronger the better."

In the background Storm felt sick. That was what he and Tani had felt. The joy in eating the quivering living flesh that gave off agony as it was devoured. The Xiks had modified that ability. The insects chose the more powerful emotions. That meant they killed people in preference to animals. Humans with any trace of the same abilities in preference to those with none. He'd thought Tani might have stronger abilities than him, even if hers were untrained. The insect's actions confirmed it. That was why the thing had made for Tani first.

The girl was standing behind him and he could feel the horror in her. He thanked the Great Spirit that Mandy had known the danger. They'd run tests on the paraowl, too. It seemed that her species could kill and eat the insects without harm—not to the paraowls, anyway. DuIshan was due a consignment of paraowls shortly. Brion and Kady had made the decision that they'd clone Mandy. With forced growth and from actual tissue they could have a flock of the big birds in days.

DuIshan could have their birds later on, if they were no longer required on Arzor. It was necessary work either way; DuIshan wanted the birds, Arzor needed them, but if another way was found here, the birds could simply be held in stasis for DuIshan. Storm hoped they wouldn't be needed on Arzor. He stepped outside to breathe in the cooling air. Brad joined him to look up at the stars.

"Seems hard, looking up at them, to think of all the evil they can hold." Brad's tones were tired.

Storm looked at his stepfather. "You were a soldier. Nothing is always as it seems. But we have part of the puzzle."

"Maybe. We know what the damn things are. We know where they come from, what they can do, and what changes the Xiks made in them. We don't know where the Xik team is. We don't know if there's other things they can unleash, and we don't have a way of dealing with those things yet."

"Mandy's clones . . ."

"Will undoubtedly kill a lot of the things. I talked to Brion. It's certain the Xiks can pour out hatchlings faster than paraowls can kill them. We have to find the direction the killers are coming from. Brion says their metabolism is high. So far their pattern has been to leave the hideout at dusk and hunt. Then return just before dawn, he thinks. Originally there was only one, well, I suppose hive-group is as good a description as any. Now we know there are two. How long before there's five, six, and spreading?"

His face in the moonlight looked suddenly old. "Kady heard from her friends on Lereene and Merla. Their situation is going bad fast. Astra has stopped their ships landing on Merla and disease has hit the refugee camps on Lereene. People are rioting."

Storm shook his head slowly. "That's because the news about the Xiks hasn't got there yet. It will have been arriving just about the time Kady was hearing about the problems. Look, Asizi. People love to have an enemy they can blame. So long as their problems appear to be natural disasters, they fight with each other. But you wait. Once they hear the Xiks are back and all their deaths, everything they've lost can be blamed on Xiks, they'll focus their anger there. The riots will stop and the people will sit back and see sense."

"You sound very sure, son."

Storm laughed shortly. "I am. Our problem here is Tani. The thing made straight for her. That means she has the strongest abilities, but she's so terrified of the things she's blocking any ability to hear them. Once the meeting in there breaks up, try to get her to bed early. I want to take her riding in the morning. Away from the laboratory and the things, I may be able to persuade her to try listening for them."

"Kady said young Jarro built three. Were they all the same type?"

"No," Storm told him. "The other two were workers. They're slower, not so aggressive, and they don't have the poison. Maybe I can convince Tani that trying with them is safer."

They returned quietly to the laboratory to find everyone studying the two insects scurrying around the plascrete container. Both made a small clicking as they moved. On some of the isolated frontier planets batteries were not always available. Clockwork watches and clocks had come back into fashion. The insects sounded like overwound clockwork. But with a clicking rather than a ticking. Tani was still in her chair in a corner. She looked greenish-white under her tan, and miserable.

Brad nodded to her, spoke briefly to Kady, then swept the girl out. Storm followed. Let the rest of them stay up half the night talking over the clickers. He knew Brad would give the girl something in her swankee to make sure she slept soundly. To help that he collected Mandy, taking her and the perch to Tani's room. He checked before she reached it. The coyotes were there lying lazily on a corner. Good. With her team about her she'd both feel and be more secure.

Tani slept solidly. The drugged swankee, the team presence, and the exhausting events of the previous day combined so she simply let go of everything and slept without dreams or waking. When she was slept out she woke slowly. Dawn light was streaming in through her window. She felt rested and calm again. It would be good to ride, to get away from the laboratory and relax with Destiny and the land.

She slipped into the kitchen, snatched bread and frawn cheese, then padded toward the corrals. Destiny greeted her enthusiastically. The girl spent some time merely leaning against the rails and petting the filly before reaching for saddle-pad and bridle. Tani felt lazy, the sun was warming her back, Destiny was happy, and already her team was encouraging her to ride out. She'd have a peaceful day. She swung onto the silvery back as Destiny pranced. They moved out toward the Basin rim, half a day's ride away.

Not that Tani intended to go that far. She smiled at the thought. She hadn't meant to go so far last time. But she'd ended up almost three days' ride away in the valley where the Djimbut clan had welcomed her. She thought of them all. Small Bird and Jumps High. The Thunder-Drummer, Speaker of Dreams. Stream Song, her mate Swift Killer, and their small son who owed humans his life. Her thoughts darkened slowly. How safe were they in that small valley on the edge of the Peaks?

They'd been forced out of their own desert territory by the deaths of their people and fear of the clickers. Well, she knew how that could happen. She'd read the old books. Her father had told her of the way their people had been driven from their lands by another race. In some ways it had been something that had given her mother and father a tie of understanding. Both had come from a people who'd had their lands taken from them. She'd thought it wouldn't happen here. There were laws.

But clickers didn't listen to laws. If they kept coming the Nitra would have to keep moving away from them. Tani knew the pattern. Even if the Patrol made the settlers leave it wouldn't help. The clickers would keep coming, and the natives would keep moving, until at last there would be no-place left to go or hide. Then they'd die. She remembered how they'd die and began to shiver. All of them, her friends who'd welcomed her, given her gifts, and shared laughter.

Puzzled by the feeling of a rider who let the reins go slack, Destiny halted. Tani dropped to the ground and huddled by a sun-warmed rock. Her shivering became worse. She had to do something. What kind of clan-friend let her friends die just because she was scared? Behind her, Storm, who had followed her from the ranch, slowed the spotted stallion. Rain-on-Dust was following the filly's scent as horses can do. They'd rounded the trail bend to see the filly standing motionless ahead of them. Storm dismounted, dropping the reins. Rain would wait until called.

He walked quietly forward. Tani noticed nothing, sunk in her fear, misery, and disgust at her own cowardice. She was huddled against the rock, her whole body shuddering as she tried to force herself to accept what she must do. The coyotes cuddled close, while on her shoulder Mandy crooned comfort in vain. The team knew Storm. He was safe. They allowed him to approach without alarm. He reached the girl and understood.

There was the terror of a trapped animal in the way she huddled, shivering violently, into the rock. From her mind he could feel the fear radiating in waves. She knew her fear and despised it but still it drove her close to madness. She must help, but she could not. She had to face her fear and could not turn to see. Her mind stretched further and further, torn between two irreconcilable forces. The desire to help her friends, and the knowledge that she could only help by doing the one thing she could not force herself to do.

Storm's intentions were swept away in a wave of pity. Without thought of what he should do he moved toward her. He lifted Mandy, allowing the bird to set her claws in a rock crevice. Then he sat, drawing Tani into his arms. He cradled her, whispering words of comfort. All would be well. She must not fear so, here was one who would be a blade at her back. A shield across her breast. Here was kin, here was strength to lean upon, to share as she shared with her team in need.

The shivering gradually stopped. He felt her racing pulse slow, her body grow limp, and he turned her gently. Utterly overcome by the force of her fears and emotion, Tani slept trustingly. A warmly gentle smile tugged at the corners of his mouth. He knew this sleep. She'd wake in an hour or so. It was the body's refuge from unbearable strain once that strain was released. He shifted her to a more comfortable position for them both and relaxed.

The coyotes relaxed too. They trotted off to hunt, secure in the belief that Tani was safe. Destiny moved away to crop some of the grass nearby. She wasn't so sure but she'd watch. Storm looked down. Tani's face had smoothed out as she slept. It was a vivid face. It showed all her emotions when she was awake. The eyebrows arched like wings, the mouth was a warm curve. A generous face, Storm thought. The face of one who would give to her friends, to her kin, without demanding a return. A strong heart. Strong to fight and to give.

The body in his arms was slender yet there was a wiry strength in the muscles. He had seen her ride down the hours and miles, seen her tease and spin before Destiny's probing horns. There was speed of reflexes there. He'd talked about her since his return and come to understand many of the events that had shaped her, and the security that she had lacked. Brion and Kady loved her, but in an absentminded way.

They were different, with other drives and desires. They didn't understand this girl who had ridden out to tear her mind apart with her own demands. She was courage and fear, fire and ice. She had the gifts and the love of her team. Tani moved in her sleep, making a tiny whimpering sound. Storm bent his head. He'd planned to blackmail her with her love of friends and land. He'd have broken her to harness and forced her to a load that, with her unwilling, would have killed her.

He sighed. He couldn't do that. And what would it profit them, anyway? They'd end with a girl retreating into mindlessness and the clickers still to find and stop. His head bent lower until his lips touched the corner of her soft mouth.

"I won't let it happen," he assured her quietly. Her eyes opened slowly. Her voice a whisper.

"What won't?"

"No one will make you hear the clickers."

"You wanted me to listen to them."

"Until I saw what it cost you."

Tani closed her eyes. Within her mind the other words he'd spoken echoed still. Her mind spun, considered, recalled. She'd heard once of this usage of gifts. It was rare but possible. They could try. She would not be so afraid if she had another to help. At least she hoped that would be so. And she would be trying. She wouldn't feel that she'd allowed her friends to lose everything, even life, without Tani putting up a fight. She was the daughter of a warrior, a man who'd died trying to save friends. That bloodline went back to Wolf Sister of the Cheyenne. Could Tani be less?

She opened her eyes and looked up. Softly she quoted, "Do not fear so, here is one who would be a blade at your back. A shield across your breast. Here is kin, here is strength to lean upon, to share as you share with your team in need." Her eyes held his with a savage intensity. "So you said. Did you really mean it?"

He nodded, not knowing what she intended, only that in the seconds of silence she had conceived a plan.

"You have heard that sometimes, using a willing team, Beast Masters can link?"

Storm bit back his dismay. That was madness that she spoke. He'd heard rumors that it had been tried. In all cases rumored, the Beast Masters had died or burned out their gift. Those who had done the latter had killed themselves. Was he to die, leave the team alone to mourn without him? Tani saw his immediate rejection of the suggestion and guessed at some of the reasons.

"The team won't be left alone," she told him quietly. "You have a mate for Hing. I can decant the other meerkats soon. And eagles breed very slowly. One pair won't cause problems here. The surplus adults would be welcomed on Trastor. The Xiks spread a poison there that killed the Mallan hawks at the end of their food chain. They are very strongly allergic to it and with so much in the land we can't simply replace the hawks again. They have already approached the Ark for eagles or something similar."

Storm's face twisted. "What about Surra?"

Tani laughed, a small rippling sound. "Surra is the least problem. Survey is starting again. They'll want dune cats for first-in teams. She can have all the kittens she wants. The survey people will take them at six months and find suitable people to match them with. I can have mates for Baku and Surra in less than three months." She sobered, waiting.

Storm released her, gently holding her arm until she was steady on her feet as they both rose. "Slave driver. But if you can provide mates for the team I guess I can risk this link. What about your team if anything happens to you?"

"Minou and Ferarre could go with Mandy to DuIshan. They'd be freed there. Your father said to me that Destiny could join the breeding herd when I left Arzor. That she'd never accept another rider." She giggled. "He said he wasn't too sure she'd accept any stallion, either, but she'd be free and she could make her own choices. Any foal she did have would be worth its weight in credits as breeding stock."

He stretched. Beside him the coyotes returned, copied the leisurely movement. Wordlessly, Tani unhooked Destiny's reins and settled into the saddle. Storm whistled. Rain arrived as the silver filly pranced. Minutes later two riders pursued by a large bird and two small four-footed followers were heading back to the ranch. No one was about as they unsaddled, leaving their mounts in two of the smaller corrals. It was clear to Storm that Tani meant to try linking at once, before her determination failed. They slipped silently into the house and made for her rooms. Both teams joined them there.

Once inside Storm lifted the bed while Tani removed the lower spare kept beneath. With the beds in parallel they lay down, held hands, and began. On the corner perches Mandy and Baku eyed each other. Minou and Ferarre had joined Tani on the bed while Surra lay heavily across Storm's legs. Both teams were restless. They sensed urgency but were unsure what was required of them. Slowly, carefully, with a mixture of pictures, emotions, and the occasional word, the Beast Masters explained.

The team must link with them as usual. With that established the humans would try to bring each other's teams into link. With each human linked to all the teams' beasts, they would then attempt to link with each other through their teams. If the try was successful they could allow the teams to drop from the linkage. The question hung in all their minds. Not in words from Surra and the others, but in a simple emotion-query. Danger?

"Yes," Storm sent, as Tani was also warning her team. No danger to the team but to the humans, yes. Emotions rumbled through the team's linkages. They were unhappy but they could feel the need, the urgency. They agreed. Storm clamped his fingers shut. He would hold until they had succeeded or failure was certain. Touch would help the linkage establish. They allowed their eyes to close. Behind the lids both envisioned their teams. One by one each team member dropped into place.

Storm gathered in Baku, Surra, and Hing with the casual ease of long practice. He tightened the link until it was as if they pressed against him. He held that and reached out cautiously. Tani loved the strength and the calmness that Mandy emitted in link, the merry quick minds of Minou and Ferarre. To her surprise she felt Destiny seeking her. She reached, gathered the filly in, and settled the team in balance. There was a fiery power in that extra addition to the group. A drive to live, to fight and win.

With her team secured Tani reached out again, slowly. She knew Surra best. She could taste the big cat with her mind: the unbreakable pride and swift power. The quick killing skills tasted like metal in Tani's mouth. She linked, adding Hing—warmth and love of kin, enjoyment digging into Tani's mind. And Baku—fierce joy in the downward stoop, the clench of claws on prey. The affection for the humans she trusted. Then, within the link she stretched out again to touch Storm.

It hurt. Pain searing through her mind. With an effort she kept it from the team. She tried again, then again. Each time the pain drove her away. Touching the edge of Storm's mind was like placing fingers into fire. She winced back. They'd agreed it should be Tani who tried. Storm had insisted. He'd endured pain before. He feared that if it were he who made the attempts he would continue too far, that Tani would break under the lash of his demands before he realized what he had done.

Now half linked, he knew her pain. Still she tried stubbornly. In the back of both minds he could feel the teams watching, supporting where they could. Tani winced back again and into both minds slashed silver fire and inflexible purpose. This was what the human wished? This, Destiny could help her do. Fire burned, searing across the bridge. The filly's fury rose. She would fight, she would! Better to die fighting than to live broken. She forced the link. It held. She could feel the pain grow less, then fade. Her will relaxed. It was done as her human wished.

Feeling as if his mind had been bruised by trampling hooves, Storm tightened the link. Down it and back again flowed feelings of gratitude that the pain was gone. The link remained. Storm reached out, gathering the team back in again; Tani added her team and they relaxed. It was well, very well. They had the link. Quietly Storm broke it, allowing the teams to drop away one by one. Then he reached, taking them back and linking again with Tani. That was the final test.

He opened his eyes. Tani had a grin that matched his own. Storm unclasped cramped fingers and grimaced over slowly darkening bruises on her wrist.

"I'm sorry." Her gaze followed his and she laughed.

"If that's the only price I'm lucky. You did know what we risked?"

"I did. I didn't know if you knew."

Tani shook back her hair. "Bright Sky was involved in some of the first experiments. The other man died. Father was ill for weeks. Alisha told me about it a few months before she was killed. She said it was another example of how Command wasted people." She took a deep breath. "Father wasn't burned out, though. But Alisha said that usually happened if a Beast Master lived. I think she almost hoped it would happen. She was sure she could have kept my father from suiciding and then she'd have had him to herself. I think I was so afraid to try in case I burned out and then didn't have the courage to die."

Storm clasped her hand. "You have the courage to live. That's more important. And now, I'll get us food. We'll practice linking a couple more times and get a good long sleep. In the morning I'll get Kelson here."

"Why him?"

"Because with our link we stop running. Now we find the clickers and hunt them, for a change. We may even find the Xik team." His eyes gleamed ferally. "I'd like that."

"So would I," Tani said, the teams echoing the desire to have their enemies in sight. "I'm starving," she added, as her stomach growled. Storm grinned.

"Don't move. I'll be right back." He returned bearing plunder from the ranch kitchen for humans and teams. They ate ravenously before Tani found her eyes starting to close. Storm smiled and stood, signaling his team to follow. "Sleep. I'll call for you in the morning once I've commed Kelson. He's going to be a very happy man to hear what we can do."

Tani yawned hugely as the door shut behind Storm and his team. Inside her there was joy. She had taken the next step. At least they could now find the clickers, maybe destroy them and save her friends. And she owed half of it to a Beast Master. Alisha had been wrong. There were good Beast Masters besides Bright Sky. She believed now that Hing's mate hadn't been thrown away.

Well, Tani would provide others. Hing would be matriarch of a meerkat clan. Tani grinned as she undressed and washed before slipping into a sleep robe. Storm was a good man. She hadn't been asleep all the time in his arms, either. Her finger went up to touch the corner of her lips. No, not all the time. She fell into bed, asleep almost before she had stretched out. On her face a small grin still lingered. Life was becoming more interesting by the hour. Tani found it frightening and exhilarating.

Chapter Sixteen

Both were awake again early.
For some time Tani lay in her bed, luxuriating in warmth, the presence of her team, and the link she could establish. That thought nudged her. Idly she reached, yes, she could feel Storm. She couldn't link. She required physical touch for that, but she had the sense of him. She knew where he was, how far away and in what direction. She reached again. She could do the same for his team as well. That could be useful one day soon.

She knew she'd taken a huge risk when she insisted on the linking. Those who tried went mad for one simple reason: they were unable to cope with another's thoughts. Not just as intrusive thoughts, but in a complete overlay. A doubling of everything they were in their head, with the link's thoughts laid on top. They became lost inside their own heads, driven mad by thoughts that were not their own.

She wasn't sure why she and Storm could link without that happening. It could have been the addition of Destiny to the link; they hadn't been able to complete the original tie without her forceful assistance. Perhaps it was because they were of a different blood. Maybe those who were wholly or partially Indian had better defenses against madness. After all, her father had attempted the link once; he'd failed but survived the try. She grinned to herself. That was racist, but it wasn't impossible. Once this was over she might talk to Uncle Brion and Aunt Kady about running tests. If they could find out why Storm and Tani could survive linking, it would be useful to others.

At the back of her mind, as she mused, she'd kept light contact with the feel of Storm's mind. His direction shifted, he was heading toward her. Tani scrambled out of bed, flinging on her clothes. She was brushing out her long black hair when Storm tapped on the door.

"Come in, Storm."

He entered, his eyes warming as he looked at her. Tani grinned back as the coyotes went to greet him.

"They approve of you."

"It's mutual."

The girl was plaiting her hair swiftly as they talked. She tied off the long fall of plait and turned. "Let's do this before I lose my nerve again."

His hand brushed lightly down her arm. "You won't. I asked Kady to leave the clickers out in an escape-proof container. No one will be there but us. If you and I can hear them close up, then Brad will help us make experiments. We need to find out how far away we can hear them and if we can get the direction. Dumaroy and the others will copter back once we have anything solid we can show. Dad says they were still frothing about Xiks when they had to leave."

Tani laughed. "I liked Mr. Dumaroy."

Storm looked at her in surprise. "Why? Oh, he isn't a bad man, and he was a good soldier. He's a loudmouthed hothead, though, and he doesn't like the natives."

It was the girl's turn to ask why.

Storm snorted. "The sort of thing that happened in the early days. His father was sick so his mother rode out to check the frawn herd. She was thrown and badly hurt. Norbies found her, cared for her, but she was left crippled. Her husband blamed them. Said they let the Thunder-Drummer try healing when she should have been brought in at once. Rig would have been only small. All he knew was that his mother went out fit and happy one day and came back a week later in pain, a permanent invalid, and his father said the natives had done it.

"She was never well again. She lost the baby she'd been carrying and Rig ended up as the only child. Mind you, I don't know this myself. It was what Brad told me once when I was more annoyed than usual with Dumaroy and his stubbornness. Brad said the man adored his mother. She didn't blame the Norbies but Rig took his father's word for it." Storm grinned. "He got shaken up a while back, though. He went off half-cocked, listened to the wrong person, and made a fool of himself.

"Then a while later he started a fuss about the natives and it turned out the trouble was started by a human. Since then he's been a bit less keen to jump to the conclusion that everything that goes wrong is tied to the natives. He still isn't fond of them, though, and I guess he never will be. He refuses to use them as riders like the rest of us. So, why did you like him?"

Tani was seeing the story as he told it. The small boy who loved his mother. The woman injured and cared for by Norbies who did their best. The father who felt that if he hadn't been sick in bed his wife wouldn't have been doing his work. The father who blamed the Norbies because he couldn't blame himself, and passed on his guilt to a small child. She looked up at Storm as they reached the laboratory door.

"He feels something like you." Storm was still open-mouthed as they walked in. He sought for words to deny he was anything like the big bellowing rancher from the Peaks and gave it up. How Tani could say that he'd never know. Tani hid a smile. That had pushed him off balance. She took a last step inside and came face-to-face with the clicker container. She shuddered.

The clickers, too, seemed agitated. Storm reached for the container and positioned it in the center of the bench. He closed a gentle hand on her unbruised wrist.

"Now. Link." They slid awkwardly into contact. Tani reached toward the clickers slowly. The feel of them was like a blow as she reached. Hunger! Flesh. Pleasure-pain. The hot salty coppery taste of blood remembered. Hunger! She jerked her mind back, shutting down on the reading so fast that Storm felt it, like a door slamming in his mind, then easing open just a crack again.

Storm gave a soft grunt. "Right. No trouble with that. Let's go outside. I want to check something." He walked out and shut the laboratory door. Then he turned to the girl, taking her by the shoulders. "Shut your eyes." Tani obeyed. "Don't open them until I say." He left her briefly, then returned. He began to spin her around. At last when he stopped she was dizzy. "Don't open your eyes yet and don't try to touch the clickers. Think of it as if you're feeling heat. Not close enough to know more than the change in temperature before you feel it as actual warmth. Now, where are the clickers. What direction?"

Tani could feel his fingers around her wrist. She reached. There! A faint sensation of distaste, something unpleasant. Her free hand came up to point. She opened her eyes to find she was pointing in the direction opposite to the laboratory.

"Oh, it's no good. Storm, it didn't work."

"Yes, it did. I moved the container. I wanted to check that you didn't just feel the direction of the laboratory and point at that."

"Then—we did it?"

"Yes." He raised his voice, "Dad!"

His stepfather walked out from behind the tack-shed. "I'm here, and yes, I saw that. Okay, we'll try the next stage. Take her inside and have a mug of swankee. This will take a few minutes."

Tani relaxed as she sipped the hot chocolaty flavor. After ten minutes or so she was ready. They walked out and Storm grinned down at her. "Dad's taken the clickers about ten minutes' ride away. Tell me which way."

His hand closed on her wrist, Tani's eyes shut and her mind swung out, like a restless compass needle as she revolved. Then—there! That way, where she could feel a kind of disgust as her mind recoiled. Her hand rose up to point. She opened her eyes to find she was pointing down the road toward the port.

"Is that right?"

"Let's see." He lifted the handheld com. "All right, Asizi. Come in now." They waited until Brad came into view up the port road. "Looks as if we were."

His stepfather arrived smiling. "Well?"

"Very well," Storm informed him. "We'd better call in Kelson and the copter now. I want to find how far away the clickers can get before Tani loses them. She felt them feed ten miles out."

"When I was asleep," Tani objected. "Maybe I can't do that well if they aren't feeding."

"And maybe with our link you can do better. We need to know. That way we don't find we can only read them a couple of miles and we're walking right into the Xik team with no warning."

It made sense. Tani nodded and followed him inside, listening to the comcall. Kelson was almost glowing with enthusiasm when he shut off. He'd be there in an hour. He was as good as his word. The liaison man exploded from the machine at a half-run.

"Brad? Is it true, you can find the clickers?"

"Looks like it. Calm down, Kelson. We want to run distance and direction tests using the copter today. We need to find out if Tani can tell how far away as well. If the results are effective and consistent, then we can call up some of the boys and head out."

Kelson's face was hard. "I'd like that, Brad. I really would. And so would they. You know there's been more trouble. Down at the port this time. Some idiot saw a new ship in and decided it was the Patrol. We had a riot when he started yelling they were coming to drive settlers off their lands. There's ten people hurt and six more in jail. I've got my hands full. If we can give the people something else to focus on it'll do wonders for morale."

"Then we'd better get on with the tests," Brad stated.

"Storm, you and Tani go inside. I want earplugs in so you don't know the direction. Don't try for it until I say." Half an hour later he was looking at them with satisfaction.

"That was the ten miles Tani could hear last time. The right direction, too. Let's try again. Tani, see if you can get an idea how far away the things are, not just direction and that you can hear them."

Two days of hard work followed. Brion had matured another of the front-runners. This time it was hatched into a heavily secured container and they found that Tani could hear the more lethal emotion still further and more accurately. The greater the distance, the deeper her link must be to find them, and that made her ill, but she persevered. Each attempt left her retching, but with Storm to give her an anchor she could make the contact, give direction, and approximate distance. The range of her ability seemed to be about twenty miles.

Brad took Storm aside. "How bad is this for her, son?"

"Bad," Storm said briefly. "She was sick again last night after we finished. She's pretty much stopped eating, because she can't keep anything down. She won't quit now she's started, though."

He turned to look at his stepfather. "You're Cheyenne. She mentioned something a couple of times about her father being from the line of Wolf Sister. It sounded as if that had been important to him and she thought it was to her, too."

Brad stared. "Wolf Sister? Yes, that's important." He thought while Storm waited. "The old story, so far as I can remember, goes this way. Wolf Sister probably lived in the early seventeen hundreds, and wasn't originally named Wolf Sister, but Brown Deer. She was one of those they called

Berdashe, one sex behaving like another. She began as a hunter and was so successful, she chose to become a warrior. She was renowned for her ability to steal horses, to begin with.

"Then in a fight with a party of Kiowa, her brother was shot from his horse and injured. Brown Deer rode back through an arrow storm to rescue him. She suffered a minor wound herself, but succeeded, and her brother lived. After that she became a regular part of war parties until there was a great raid on the Kiowa. The Cheyenne took many horses and Brown Deer killed a noted Kiowa warrior in a hand-to-hand fight while she stood protecting a badly injured friend."

Storm nodded. "Was that when her name was changed?"

"It was. Her family gave a dance for her and Brown Deer had all the horses she'd taken brought up. Then she gave them all away. As my grandfather told me, she'd taken more than twenty herself, so it was a great show of generosity. After that she told her story of the fight and the chief did a rare thing. He rewarded her with a new name. From then on she was called Wolf Sister and regarded as one of the great warriors."

"She married?"

"Yes, later on. A warrior who was as well known as she was. She had two children, a boy and a girl. Her father had been killed in later fighting, so she took her mother into their tent to care for the children while Wolf Sister went back to the war trail. Our oral history says she died some years later, but not how, only that it was bravely, in battle. There's a suggestion she died trying to rescue a dismounted companion, as she'd done with her brother."

"This is significant to Tani," Storm said slowly. "Wolf

Sister gained acceptance as a warrior, not by fighting at first but by saving someone she cared about. Then she may have died trying to do the same thing years later. I think it's that part of the stories that is most important. Bright Sky died trying to save a friend as well. The Thunder-Drummer was right. We bound Tani to friends and this land and she's willing to die to save it and us. Her mother taught her it was wrong to fight, but right to save people. Finding the clickers fits everything Tani believes in."

"How well is she doing?"

"It looks as if twenty miles is her limit, but I'm not so sure." Brad waited to hear the remainder. "We're using three clickers. Out there the swarm is a lot more. She may be able to hear the much greater numbers from further away."

"I hope so. The further away, the better chance we have to take somebody by surprise. Kelson's calling in the ranchers who'll fight. Logan rode in last night. Ukurti says the Sho-sonna tribe stand ready as warriors. He's talked with other Thunder-Drummers. If we are truly going out to fight the Death-Which-Comes-in-the-Night, then the peace poles are up for us. They'll even allow copter overflights anywhere we are following the death. Another of the Nitra tribes lost a hunting group two nights back. Tani's friend Speaker of Dreams has been talking, too. The peace poles apply to the Nitra as well."

Storm whistled softly. "They have to be losing people to agree to that."

"So Logan says. The Nitra tribes are right in clicker ter-ritory. Nothing much comes out of there, but the fact that several of the tribes are shifting out indicates they're losing heavily. Add an agreement to peace and overflights and it says they can't find the clickers or fight them, either. If we can they'll go along with anything that works."

Storm looked thoughtful. "What sort of a force is Kelson planning?"

"You two," Brad informed him. "Tani wants the teams. She says you need them to help the link. They'll go in the copter with you two, but I'm just thankful she'll let Destiny stay behind for this particular trip." Storm grinned at the idea of trying to fit the duocorn filly in a copter. "Yes, it does have its funny side. You, Tani, and the teams will go with Kelson and his pilot in the small copter. The port is providing two larger ones. We can get twenty men in each. A few will be ranchers, the rest are security men from the port."

"Think that'll be enough?"

"Who knows. Kelson has reserves standing by. The copters will take it in turn to shuttle back to the port for more men if it looks like we need them. At least that's the plan."

"No plan ever survives first enemy contact."

"True. But Kelson's done his best. Find Tani, get her to eat something, and then go to bed. Drug her if you have to. We leave before dawn."

Tani was already in bed and asleep from sheer exhaustion when Storm found her. Her face looked thinner, and there were dark marks under the closed eyes. They had to end this, Storm thought as he stood there. She hadn't been able to keep anything down for almost three days. The link they had was a balance. He provided the strength and stability; Tani provided the delicate sensitivity and actual contact. Any emotions he received from the clickers were filtered through Tani so that it was the girl who bore the brunt of their hungers.

He went to check on Hing next. Tani had decanted an Ark-bred meerkat soon after she returned from the Djimbut clan. He was an attractive young adult male and Hing had accepted him eagerly. She'd had a litter of two kits three days ago. Tani had promised that the others for the clan would be ready in just a few more days. Storm smiled at the thought. He'd have a full meerkat clan just when Hing had her new litter of kits. The meerkats could learn together.

The Ark had held a number of full-grown or almost grown beasts in stasis. These were the breeds used for Beast Masters and now likely to be wanted for survey. Once this business was over Tani had arranged that Surra and Baku's mates should also be provided. Tani! He'd started by disliking her for her rudeness, when he went to the Ark to ask for help. Then, gradually, he'd come to change his mind about her, and finally to trust the girl. He'd watched how valiantly she struggled to control her fear and disgust of the clickers. He'd seen her stagger away to vomit after another test and return to try again.

She saw herself as a coward, afraid to touch even the emotions of an insect miles away. Storm saw her differently. He was only now beginning to see how differently, and once this was over . . . he snorted wryly. They'd all been saying that a lot lately. There were times when it felt as if he'd said nothing else since he landed on Arzor. Once this was over, and there always seemed to be something else that had to be over before he could reach for his desire. But not this time.

He wanted what others had. Land, a home of his own, and a mate. The land he had; as a veteran of the war he was entitled to twenty squares or over three thousand acres. He'd added to that when he discovered the Xik holdout group, and the Government had added another ten squares and lowered import tax for ten years as a reward. Storm had taken up land in the Limpopo Range, where it curved around closest to the Basin and his stepfather's holdings. He'd built a cabin there, added stock, and hired Norbie riders. He had a part of his dream but there was more. He looked down at the girl in her exhausted sleep. Could she be the last part of his dream?

He went to his own room to check on Hing, cuddling her briefly before allowing a sleepy meerkat to snuggle back into her bedding beside her mate and babies. Hing was fine. She could stay behind tomorrow. There was nothing she could do. She wasn't a fighter and they'd have no need of any digging Storm could imagine. He left them, climbing into his bed to sleep lightly.

He rose in the early hours and donned his clothing, adding the concha belt, necklace, and ketoh bracelet. He'd have need of his medicine today. He went to wake Tani.

An hour later three copters swung out over the Basin. They rose in a line, heading for the desert fringe. There they landed. Storm and Tani linked as the others waited in silence. Even Dumaroy, leading the small rancher group, was quiet. Tani shut her eyes, reaching out. There! The impact was sickening. Images of tearing out mouthfuls of warm bloody flesh, of rolling in the emotions, the agony of the prey eaten alive, like a dog rolling in filth. The delights of the final spring that would hold the prey for those who followed.

With a savage effort she held back her sickness as she pointed. "That way. At least ten miles, but it could be more. There's a lot of them."

She straightened as Dumaroy walked over. He patted her shoulder kindly. "You're doing good, girl. I know it ain't easy, but you're doing fine." He stomped off toward his copter as Storm stared after him. He wouldn't have thought to see the day when Rig was understanding. But then Tani had said she liked the man, it was possible Rig liked Tani as well. The copters rose again, heading out obliquely into the Big Blue. Ahead was one of the most barren areas. It wasn't quite within the part of the desert where the winds played havoc with copter flight. But it was on the edge of that.

A good place to hide out, Storm considered. Too barren even to be claimed by a Nitra tribe but encircled by territory that was. Right on the edge of the no-fly areas, and a vicious jumble of weather-worn rock spires, canyons, and heaped boulders. It was wicked land and wouldn't be easy to fight through. Not if the enemy was well dug in. By hopping the copters forward for small distances, and landing where they could, they worked their way forward. Each time Tani was able to keep them on track and say they were closer. But at last she shook her head.

"Here, somewhere very near. I get the strongest reading from there." Her finger pointed, the unprotected flesh sending a signal to that which waited. Even as she lowered her hand something came up from the ground. Poised on the girl's shoulder, Mandy had been ready. Her beak shot out, there was a satisfying crunch, and the clicker was dead. Kelson had planned well and the fighters were waiting. They had flamers and stunners, and their clothing, including throat scarves, had been drenched in a scent Brion and Kady had found repelled the killer insects to some degree.

The clickers came in waves and died the same way. Stunners on full killed the much smaller clickers wherever they struck. Storm guarded Tani, with Mandy as enthusiastic backup. The last of the clickers attacked and died. There was a long pause. Dumaroy broke it.

"Storm, you an' the cat sense Xiks?"

Surra indeed had her head up and was giving vent to a low, soft snarling. She'd fought Xiks before and would be happy to do so again. Storm linked. At the back of his mind he was conscious that Tani had joined him in the linkage. Yes, there. He considered the area. Gradually, out of the jagged jumbled rock an outline coalesced. It was well camouflaged, but he'd been taught what to look for a long time ago. He waved Kelson and Rig over, pointing out the possible door.

"Right." Kelson was prepared. "Jackson, here, see that door. I want it blown in. Just the door. Storm says there's likely tunnels behind and we want to use them."

Five minutes later, as they all sheltered behind rocks, there was a loud flat bang. The port security were out from behind their rocks with a whoop, the ranchers right behind them. They poured into the largest tunnel, fighting their way through a small group of Xiks and out into the cave at the end, Storm and Surra behind Kelson. Tani waited, the coyotes guarding her. Mandy employed her time happily eating clickers. So far as she was concerned, the clickers were an easily solved problem. Within the tunnels the fight was dying. Surra was sniffing her way down a side tunnel and Storm called the liaison man.

"Kelson, who'd you leave on guard out there? I think Surra's found a back door."

There was a horrified silence as they realized no one had

remained behind apart from the girl and her team. Without thought Storm found he was running. Ahead of him Surra was hurtling down the tunnel. She found a concealed exit and they erupted from the rockface to stare wildly about. From behind spires to their left, there was a scream of fury. Then the sound of a Xik weapon. A confused snarling mingled with cries and screeches. Storm saw Baku appear briefly as she rose abruptly on powerful wings, then stooped to strike. He leaped for the battleground.

Surra was racing ahead, her muzzle wrinkled in a ferocious snarl. They rounded the rocks to find Tani struggling with one of three Xiks. A second flailed weakly at Baku, having been battered almost insensible by the powerful wings, his head streaming green-tinged blood where her beak had reached him. The third was fighting off Minou and Ferarre while overhead Mandy waited her opportunity. Surra took Baku's victim with one swift rush. But as Storm arrived, the Xik struggling with the frantic girl managed to free himself with a vicious blow. Tani staggered back half dazed, for the moment unable to fight.

It was then that Storm saw. Tani had not been attacking the alien, she had been holding his gun back from her team with a desperate strength. Surra was turning from her victim. Mandy was dropping in the terrifying strike of the Ishan paraowl. In seconds the Xik the coyotes held would die. But for the leader of the hideout there were whole seconds of time. He could destroy the animals. His gun came level and Storm leaped in a flat dive toward him.

His hand struck the gun as it fired. He felt the wash of flame over his upper arm but his knife went home, once, twice. Behind him he heard a dull thud and a crack. Mandy had taken out the other enemy. Storm was on his knees, his arm cradled in his other hand. It hurt, the pain burning into his mind. Tani, must find . . . Storm staggered to his feet, his gaze searching the rocks.

At his feet the Xik moved, groaning something. Tani was running toward them. Storm stooped low, his voice sliding into the terse form of combat speech the Xiks used.

"Report!" Tani arrived to stand silently. Storm turned to hiss to her softly. "Go back by the tunnels. Make sure they don't interrupt." He turned back to find hate-filled eyes staring up.

"Report, First Leader!"

The alien glared, then uttered the harsh sound that was Xik laughter. Storm leaned closer still, listening to the labored breathing and the rough guttural sound of Xik language. It was fortunate they taught Beast Masters and first-in commandos the language. It hadn't been so long since he heard it that he'd forgotten.

The dying Xik was still muttering. "You lose after all. This was the outpost, just to destabilize the population. Our laboratories are elsewhere. The insects you destroyed were only the first experiments. In breeding vats millions wait. They breed at many times the speed."

Storm sneered. "You Xiks aren't that good. We'll find these labs, destroy your pets and your friends with them. No one shall awaken your soul with the naming of names."

The alien eyes were glazing; blood ran from the corner of his mouth. He muttered, then laughed again. "No friends, only soldiers. Two places to guard and automatic relays. You find, they hatch, not find, they hatch anyhow. Try to blow the labs and you make matters worse, there are safeguards."

He paused to cough. More blood ran. "Too bad, you lose this world. Lose many worlds. My son shall take up the four rights after me."

Tani moved and the alien's gaze lifted. He spat the mouthful of blood at her weakly. Tani's hand closed hard on Storm's wrist. Then her free hand went out to lie across the enemy's forehead. Storm spoke in a piercing clear voice. It broke through to the dying Xik.

"Where are the laboratories?" The Xik glared up at Tani as she crouched, hand laid on his flesh. He spat at her again and died. Storm felt all the pain he'd been holding back pour over him. His arm was burning until it filled his mind. Vaguely he was aware of Tani calling. Someone pressed a patch against his bared shoulder and the pain ebbed. Brad was helping him to his feet, guiding him to the copter. Storm was trying to explain that they had to stay, to search for the laboratories.

Tani was on his other side. He turned to her. Her smile was very lovely. She would leave Arzor now. He didn't want that. She had to stay. He needed her. He found he was mumbling at her. He could see his voice made no sense; from somewhere he drew strength for seven clear words.

"Love you, stay with me on Arzor!" Blackness reached out and he fell gratefully into it.

Chapter Seventeen

He woke to an arm that was still achingly sore, but the burning agony was only a memory. Tani sat quietly in an armchair nearby. Surra curled up on one side of her, the coyotes on the other. She must have felt the tiny movement he made. She looked at him and smiled.

"Awake?"

"Barely. What happened?"

Tani grinned. "You passed out. Mr. Dumaroy caught you and carried you to the copter. The medic said you were exhausted. He put you out for forty-eight hours. I helped with the cleanup, then he put me out too. I woke up a while back and had breakfast with your father and Logan. The medic treated your arm while you were unconscious. He said the clothing you wore saved you from real damage, but it's a nasty burn. You're not to use that arm for at least two weeks."

The events just before his involuntary fade from the scene came back to Storm in a rush.

"I have to. Tani, you were linking with me to read that First Leader, weren't you? Did you get anything?"

"Yes, but I need you to interpret what I saw."

His eyes met hers. "I need you too, Sunrise—for

more than interpreting." He took in a slow breath. What if he was wrong? Maybe she didn't feel the same way. He tried to sound calm. "But that can wait a little."

Tani chuckled, a small merry gurgling sound. "Not too long it won't. Your father is talking about holding the wedding here. Logan is demanding to be best man, and Aunt Kady is asking about your own land. Will it feed us both or would money be a good wedding present?"

Storm's mouth opened. After a few seconds he got out, "How did that happen?"

"How do you think? You can't tell me you love me and ask me to stay on Arzor in front of more than forty people without having it talked about."

He remembered his last words and a faint flush showed across his cheeks. "I did, didn't I? Well, I guess I'll have to marry you. I wouldn't want a Cheyenne mad at me." He held out his unbandaged arm and Tani settled lightly into it on the side of the bed. His gaze met hers. "Will you marry me, Tani?"

She leaned over, her mouth soft and warm on his. The kiss lasted some time before she straightened up, still holding his hand.

"I guess I will. I wouldn't want a Navaho mad at me, either. But we'd better talk about the clickers right now."

His face became serious. "What did you get in the link when you touched the First Leader?"

"A picture. It was as if he was standing looking out across real desert. It was horrible land, dry, barren, and with dust blowing. He was higher. Not on flat land. I can't draw and it's just desert, anyhow. I can't show it to the others."

"But it was in his mind as he died," Storm said, thinking

about it. "Right after I asked where the clicker place was. A clear strong picture which I got across our link, because he was so sure we'd never find the place he'd seen. That picture was from where he'd stood and looked out across the land, probably from the main entrance. If I'm right about the other things he said, there's two more sites. Both near to each other but both deeper into the Big Blue. One to breed more clickers, and one to guard against people entering the desert from the settled lands. If we can trace the picture and go back to where he must have been standing we may find the clickers. Show me!"

Tani shook her head firmly. "No, first you eat, and your father wants to see you. So does Logan. I'll get food and you can talk to them." She trotted out and Storm heard her speaking to someone outside the door. His stepfather came in.

"How do you feel, son?"

"I'll live," Storm said briefly. "What were the results of the raid?"

Brad looked angry. "They had a real Xik nest there. We don't think any got away. Tani said only three came out of that back exit. Once the fighting was done we went back and combed right through. Tani came with us. Minou found us a hidden room with another Xik and a lot of interesting equipment and information. Seems they had plans for Arzor." His grin was half snarl. "If we finish the job they won't be carrying any of them out. We cleaned out all of the information and records and copies are on their way to HQ. A lot was in code. They'll crack it and let us know anything back we need to hear."

Storm nodded. "I don't know how fast they can crack the codes and get back to us, but it may not be fast enough. That was a First Leader I killed, I've seen the rank badges before. They wouldn't waste somone that highly trained on the simple installation we raided. That was just to start destabilizing the natives. I'm sure from what he gabbled as he died that there's more than one. How many Xik soldiers did we kill?"

"All up? Twenty-nine. That's counting the clerk and the three outside."

"Did you take the clerk alive? He'd be able to tell you a lot."

Brad sighed. "He probably could have. That'll be why he took poison as we broke in. He was dead before we could do anything. The coyotes were sure he was the last one and we left guards. Kelson went back again with equipment and looked for hollow areas. Rooms, cupboards, anything like that. He found a couple but there was only gear, no more Xiks. After that we doped Tani, too. You've both slept the clock round but she woke up first. She wanted to sit with you until you were awake." He looked the question he didn't want to ask aloud.

Storm smiled. "Yes, Asizi. You can start arranging a wedding. But not until after we get this mess cleaned up." From the doorway Logan gave a war whoop that set Storm's head ringing. He glared at his brother. "And yes, you can be best man, but only if you don't do that again."

Logan's grin widened knowingly. "Bet you don't know who Tani wants at the wedding to stand on her side?"

Storm looked at the wicked amusement and guessed. His voice was calm. "I suppose a Nitra or two can be fitted in. We may have to ask a few favors of them, anyway." He turned back to Brad. "Tani saw a picture in the First Leader's mind as he died. We think it shows the land in front of the entrance to their clicker laboratory, or if not that, then the separate guard installation. Tani says it's just desert to her and she can't draw, anyway. I'll link and see what I can tell you. But we may have to call in the tribes to search."

From the door came a soft rattle of a tray. Tani came in holding it as delectable aromas preceded her. She smiled down.

"Eat all the food on this tray, then you can talk again."

Storm reached to help her, finding as he smelled the food that he was quite ravenous. He ate and drank steadily as his stepfather continued with his tale of events. Now and again Logan or Tani added details. Storm finished, polished the plate, drank off the last drops of swankee, and sighed.

"That's better. Now, did they find anything to say where the other hideout is?"

"Nothing. HQ says the codes the Xiks used are new. They could take a few days to break. Did the Leader give you any idea of how long we may have before the new clickers hatch?"

Tani nodded. "Not in chrono. But I had the sense of 'soon.' Not this minute but not too long either. If I had to guess I'd say no more than fifteen days, no less than ten. Don't forget what else he said."

Storm quoted some of the First Leader's dying triumphant words slowly. "No friends only soldiers there, they guard. Automatic relays. You find, they hatch, not find, they hatch anyhow. We have safeguards. Too bad, you lose this world. Lose many worlds." Storm looked up. "What's the word on those other worlds?"

Logan laughed shortly. "HQ got all the official stuff, but Kady made up a gram for her friends and sent that. We've been hearing back ever since. With reason to think Xiks were on those worlds and causing the problems they were having, most of the worlds went hunting for Xiks undercover and sabotage groups with a real fervor. A lot of settlers died where they found them, but they think they've shaken every single Xik out of hiding. The Governments on those worlds aren't pleased about it, either. High Command will have to do something this time. It turned out that only one world had real natural disasters. The Xiks caused all the others."

"Asizi?"

"Logan's right. The governments of the damaged worlds are kicking up a fuss, including ours. They're demanding reparations to repair all the damage caused and compensation for the families of the dead, and for the injured and those who lost property. On top of that they want punitive damages. The amount will set back any Xik expansion plans for generations. And that's if Command settles for just the credits. With a dozen worlds yelling it's likely to be more." He looked at Storm. "How do you feel now?"

"A lot better. I think we should try for a picture of this clicker place." He took Tani's hand again. "Show me, Sunrise which flames across my sky."

Tani smiled at him as she closed her eyes. The picture formed in the link, just as she'd seen it in the dying alien's mind. She held, allowing Storm to study the land it showed. When he signaled she broke the link and opened her eyes.

Storm was cursing under his breath. Brad raised his brows in query.

"How bad is it, son?"

"Tani's right. It's real desert. I can recognize some of the land, enough to know it's well into the Big Blue. We can't copter in. There's a glimpse of mountains a good distance away and in the corner of the picture. You're standing higher than the desert, though, which may mean he was into the foothill fringe of the mountains. A place where the foothills run out a long way into the lower desert."

He looked at Logan. "Is that anything you recognize?"

His half-brother grimaced. "Not in Shosonna territory, I'm sure."

Tani made a small noise in the back of her throat. "The Blue is mostly Nitra territory, isn't it? I can go to the clan and ask them if they know the place. They'll search and get the other tribes to help."

"It may not be that simple," Brad said.

"Why not? They've lost friends and family. Logan said they've put the peace poles up even for overflights. Let me go and tell Speaker of Dreams all about it."

Storm turned his head to her. "You can't describe the place. I need to go with you."

Brad queried her with a look and she nodded. "He's right. We could move him carefully. Strap the arm up and copter him in."

Logan headed for the door. "I'll com Kelson. See if he can arrange it. I'll come back when he's set a time."

The door clicked shut behind him and Storm lay back. His arm was beginning to hurt again and he felt as if he'd been up for days. Tani saw the growing weariness in his face. Gently she indicated first Storm, then the door. Brad smiled at her and nodded. Storm was drifting into sleep again as they left him. He half woke when Tani returned to give the pain and sleep shot. Long enough to feel her kiss and to stroke her cheek with his fingers in reply.

This time when he woke he was completely rested. Tani was asleep on a bed set up by his. Ferarre was watching him and the coyote nudged Tani at once with his nose. She sat up.

"Storm. Good, I'll bring you food. Kelson says he can have the copter here as soon as we let him know. The government doesn't care what it costs. They have to stop the clickers. Kelson's going crazy about that and so is Logan. I'll just be a minute."

Storm was left there wondering why his brother and the liaison man should be so excited. Tani returned with a tray bearing enough to feed four men. She handed it over and sat down. Storm asked the question even as he reached for a fork.

"Well. The government's agreed that there should be a ranger force. It won't fall through this time. They've already drafted the parameters and got it passed by law. Kelson's asked Logan to head it. Kelson will stay as liaison man for all the departments dealing with the natives and just add the force to that." She giggled as she expanded on the rangers and Logan's pleasure. Storm finished his meal and listened. "Logan's running about trying to do everything at once. I told him you were awake again and looking a lot better. He's commed Kelson and the copter will be here in a couple of hours."

Her expression hardened. "I dreamed last night. The clickers hatched and they were a new kind. All of them are poisonous instead of just a few. They're bigger, and they breed every few weeks. They prefer people, but they'll eat anything, even plants if they can't find flesh. I dreamed there was nothing left on Arzor, the whole planet was clickers. Then they killed each other and there was nothing. Only rock and the dust blowing." Her face was haunted. "Storm, it isn't going to happen, is it?"

He'd felt chilled listening. It could, if they couldn't find and destroy the Xik time bomb.

"It could happen," he told her quietly. "I won't lie to you. But we'll do everything we can to fight it. A warrior can do no more than his best."

And their best was starting to look good, he thought some time later, as the copter dropped toward the Nitra camp. He remained hopeful as he described the scene to the clan's Thunder-Drummer. It had taken a while to disentangle Tani from her friends and to explain why a forbidden machine came, but now the clan sat patient. His arm hurt as he signed but he continued. This was more important than a little pain. Speaker of Dreams watched, her interpreter passing on the information in soft twitterings to those of the clan who did not read the finger-talk so well.

After that it was question and answer until both Tani and Storm were wrung dry. The Thunder-Drummer considered. Then she spoke.

"This is a matter for Those-Who-Drum-Thunder. I have sent out a message. The five great tribes of the Nitra shall meet. I will pass on your words and I think they will search as you wish. I think they will search very hard. Our clan has been fortunate thanks to Sunrise. Others have not been so. Many are dead and their clans mourn. That this enemy is yours as well as ours I will so-say."

"How long before the Nitra search?"

"A day. Two days. No more. Time is short, that I understand." Her gaze traveled over him, noting the weakness and the bandaged arm. Her interpreter signed as she spoke again. "Rest, warrior. The fight is now ours but you shall not be cheated. I will bring word. Let Sunrise return here to-morrow and each day until I have news."

Kelson and the pilot had remained in the copter. Tani and Storm were surrounded by the clan as the Thunder-Drummer rode out. The girl laughed, her fingers flickering in the signs as she talked of what had happened. They visited for an hour, then rejoined the machine that rose to head for the ranch. For four days Storm rested. By then his arm was healing well and he was restless. The Thunder-Drummers had cooperated. None were so blind or stubborn that they could not see the possible extinction of their tribe.

Into the area settlers had named the Big Blue, small groups of Nitra warriors now fanned out. They knew not to approach the place too closely. They must recognize it, then ride swiftly to the Djimbut clan. Twice warriors came with news. Each time Tani rode with clan-friends and each time the place was not the one she had seen. The third time she was almost sure. She rode across the front of the foothills and the scene changed. It too was wrong. She bit back her fears. There was so little time left. She could feel it.

The next day Storm was well enough to return with her. They were talking with Stream Song when the warning call went up. Tani looked, then stood up hastily.

"More warriors with another place they've found." She ran to join Speaker of Dreams as Storm followed more slowly. Both watched intently as the interpreter signed of the place found. Now and again the girl nodded. It fitted, every bit so far. One of the warriors turned to Tani. His arms and partially bared chest were seamed with scars, red tattooed lines emphasizing his warrior status. His fingers moved slowly.

"I am a great warrior. I have fought enemies many times. Always I win. I know how the enemy thinks, and I feel when enemy is near. I feel the enemy in this place."

Tani faced him. "I see the scars of a true warrior. If you will lead us, I will ride with you to see the place you have found. But let us ride very carefully. A wise warrior does not ride into ambush where enemies wait. Will you lead us?"

The warrior studied her. He had heard of the human female who was clan-friend to the Djimbut. It was said she could feel the death. Warn of it. She wore the ornaments of the thunder-flowers. The clan would not give those for no cause. He nodded.

"I lead. You listen for the death. Who rides with you?"

Storm stepped to join Tani. His fingers signed. "I ride with one who will be my mate. I too can hear the death. Together we hear even better, very far. We will follow you, warrior, find this enemy. We speak with tribes then."

They followed, to a place where Tani cringed back once they had linked. The clickers swarmed there in the thousands. Hidden inside rock tunnels and great rooms. The old breed to guard, as the dying Xik had said. And further in the distance, the faint touch of the new breed waiting to rise up and devour a world. In the end the dying Leader had spoken truth, there were other safeguards as well. They returned to the ranch, leaving Speaker of Dreams to give further orders.

Kelson was worried. "I don't know, Storm. Letting Nitra do most of the fighting."

Tani spoke quietly. "Mr. Kelson, there isn't much choice. I talked to Speaker of Dreams. Under treaty humans have no right to enter native lands. The Nitra don't want hundreds, or even dozens, of humans swarming into their tribal areas. They will permit a few of us. But not nearly the numbers we'd need to fight the Xiks on our own. The First Leader said there were safeguards. The teams scouted for us. They say there are about another thirty Xiks in the guard post. They're holed up in an area that overlooks the laboratory where they have the clicker breeding vats. Storm thinks he knows what system they'll have used to connect the two hideouts. Hing can cut that."

"Cut?" Kelson looked surprised. "Won't they use radio impulses of some kind?"

"Something like that, and they'd have to run regular checks to make sure it works," Storm informed him. "If a copter was in the air on the desert fringe it might pick that up, or if planet security had the wave detector on they'd pick it up at once. The Xiks prefer to do it the simple way in something like this. They'll have run a couple of buried wires."

"But the Nitra?"

Tani answered that. "It's their kind of country. The tribes don't usually go there, it's too barren. But they're used to fighting in that sort of land. It's going to be a brutal scrambling fight in land where you can't use anything but your own feet. Besides," her eyes glittered at him, "my people had a saying. The enemy of my enemy is my friend. Don't you think the tribes might look more kindly on the rangers and settlers if they'd fought beside them? If they help to fight a mutual enemy?"

The liaison man stared, then grinned. "I suppose you'll be with us, and your clan too?"

"Of course."

"Storm?"

"Tani makes sense. Logan's picked a dozen temporary rangers who'll come. The ones who survive can join up permanently."

Kelson winced. "We lost seven good men in the last fight."

"Good men die the same as bad ones," Storm said. "Maybe more often. They'll risk more to do what's right. If we have your okay I'll com Logan. The word will go out. Speaker of Dreams says she can have some warriors arriving at the Xik hideouts, and ready to fight against the Xiks, in less than twenty-four hours, and others will be riding in later." He paused. "Kelson. I think we have to go with it. The only other choice is to saturation-bomb the whole area. Even then the laboratory is so deep, and so well shielded, we'd have to use massive bombing to be sure of wiping everything out down there. If we do something like that in tribal lands, it will bring the tribes out—against us. And Tani's been listening . . ."

Kelson's head jerked up. "What? What's she hear?"

"The new clickers hatch very soon now. She thinks it could be as close as thirty hours."

Kelson sagged into the chair. "Then there isn't a choice. I don't like having the natives doing so much of our fighting for us, but you've made some good points. We go with the Nitra. Com Logan. Tell him the pilot is to swing by, collect us and whichever of the teams you're using. We leave tonight for Tani's clan camp. In the morning we can run relay with copter and horses if the clan will agree."

"We guessed you'd offer. Tani talked to Speaker of Dreams, the Nitra agree, and Brad sent our horses on to the clan a while back. They should just arrive in time for us to ride with the main war party. The first group of warriors will leave with most of the horses tonight and keep moving. We explained to the Nitra that they'd be safe. The loose swarms were cleaned out. There could be another at the laboratory, but there shouldn't be any loose clicker swarms running about the desert. As for the Xiks, there's soldiers at the guard post and maybe a few scientists and clerks in the hidden laboratory, with the breeding vats. Logan talked to the pilot earlier and they checked the map. A copter should be able to get to within twenty miles safely. The air currents don't pick up until after that. I'll go com Logan."

Kelson was gathering his gear. Tani helped, then fetched the two small packs she'd prepared. Surra and the coyotes would remain at the ranch. Mandy and Baku would act as sky-eyes and air cover. The erratic currents wouldn't bring them down as they did copters. The other passengers would be meerkats. Hing was eager to do her old job of sabotage. Her kits to her original mate were barely adult, but Storm had trained them as well. Somehow Hing had conveyed events to her new mate; he was coming with them, eager as she to hunt and dig.

The clan welcomed them soon after dawn. The copter hopped the odd assembly ahead and returned for more. Waiting were the mounts for several clans and their riders. Destiny had been led along with Storm's mount, first to the clan camp and then to the waiting warriors. The twittering deepened as the girl swung up. The warrior who had found the Xik hideout pointed to Destiny, then signed to Tani.

"They say that is a warrior horse, and a warrior rides her. We ride with the Djimbut's clan-friend. Is it good?"

"It is good," Tani signed back. "The enemy of my enemy is my friend. We hunt enemies, kill them together. With them dead we feast, show our scars afterward to the clan. Is it good?"

The warrior gave his high twittering laugh. He translated it to the others.

Storm grinned as they too twittered in amusement. "Little diplomat," he commented.

Tani smiled at him. The warrior turned to sign to them both. "They say it is very good. Do you hear the death yet?"

They were perhaps ten miles away. Tani reached over to touch Storm's arm. They fell into link and listened. The clickers were there.

Chapter Eighteen

They rode forward with caution. This battle would be twofold. There was the guard post where the main body of Xik soliders lived and worked. It was closest to the edge of the desert, and the layout, they believed, was simpler in construction. From it an underground comline ran to the hidden laboratory, which bred and hatched the clickers, before loosing them on the people of Arzor. The laboratory was more complex, with subsidiary tunnels and rooms but far fewer inhabitants. Storm wasn't certain there was anyone living there on a permanent basis. It could be that the Xiks went there only to work. That would be something they'd only discover when they attacked the second target.

Tani and Storm led the war party onward, Hing and her new mate perched in front of them. Overhead Baku and Mandy spiraled upward, watching the land below. It had been only a short time but already the link was strong. Behind them rode the warriors of five Nitra tribes. The ranger force was much smaller, but they had something no Nitra would own. Lasers. It had been discussed at Government levels and agreed. For safety the weapons were matched to user prints. Only the handprints of their operators allowed them to work.

But the five lasers, while only handheld weapons, would lay down a deadly covering fire against clickers. The killers literally exploded, cooked in an instant in their shells. Storm carried one of the weapons, Tani another. Both were cross-printed so that both could use either weapon. Kelson carried a third, while two other picked rangers carried the last pair. Dumaroy rode with them, carrying a laser pulse rifle. He'd been a marksman in the war, and a very good one. His rifle had returned to Arzor with him, something that had been semi-legal at best, but right now no one was objecting. The weapon was stunningly accurate, well-worn but still deadly.

The horses plodded on into a land increasingly barren but not so empty as it appeared. The two who were linked could read life ahead. An avid greedy life that swarmed, waiting, hungry to kill and gorge. It hated the bright burning sun, but where it waited the light was dimmer. The prey would have to approach and it would be ready.

The com Kelson carried chimed softly. He opened a channel. "Kelson here?" There was a long silence as he listened, then he spoke. "Thanks, I'll pass that on." He turned to look at those who rode with him. "Gather round, people, and listen. That was Brion Carraldo. He's had some of the coded scientific papers back with a translation. The clickers at the laboratory are a new type. All of them have poison, the front-runners and the eaters both. Be careful once we find the lab, Brion Carraldo thinks that the poison destroys nerve tissue as well. If you're bitten but get away from the swarm, you could still lose a limb if that's where the bite is, or if it's near an organ, you'll die in a few days. That's all." Storm led the group on again, Tani's hand in his.

In an hour they had covered only a short distance more, but from overhead Mandy's huge golden eyes saw a flicker of movement. She relayed the picture to Tani. Baku saw it at the same instant. The overlapping images filled the human minds. A Xik had showed at the edge of a tumble of boulders, just for a few seconds, but it had been enough for the predators who hovered far forward of the war party, and high overhead, watching for a movement. Tani and Storm paused to speak softly to those who followed. The group rode on another mile before halting. Warriors slid from mounts, younger hunters caught up the loose animals, running them to shelter to wait. Destiny and Rain-on-Dust stood together unfettered. The filly was alert just in case.

Tani paused to pat Destiny in reassurance. Both mare and stallion had been led by one of the Quade riders, to the edge of the Djimbut clan land. From there Speaker of Dreams had ordered them brought to where the copter would land at the desert's fringe. Neither Storm nor Tani wished to ride to war without their most trusted mounts. The Big Blue area was the harshest of all desert lands; riders needed a mount they could trust not to run off if the rider was thrown.

Storm's burned arm was half healed. It hurt only if handled roughly, but under his sleeve lay a protective bandage. He hoped that would stop further damage. If he could avoid it he had no intention of allowing rough hands to be laid on him. Tani pattered quietly beside him. Both carried a meerkat laid along their shoulders. Other rangers carried Hing's adult kits. At last they were almost to where their sky-eyes had seen the incautious enemy. Storm halted and signed vigorously.

"Everyone waits now. The spirit animals go forward to

seek out the thing that warns the enemy. They destroy it, then return to us. After that we hunt out the enemy."

The warriors squatted in silence in what small amounts of shade could be found. Storm placed Hing on the ground. She squeaked to gather her clan, then sat to groom her stomach. Storm dropped to his knees to hold her gaze with his. It took little effort. Hing had been his sabotage expert in the days when they had fought from star to star. She and her mate Ho had been responsible for much damage. Now Hing trotted out again. She knew the signs of buried wire; the scents of such man-made items. She conveyed them to her clan and they scurried silently into the rocks.

They need have no fear of clickers as yet. The lethal insects were confined to the hidden laboratory, this was only the guard post for that. Storm worried silently over what they would find at the laboratory; the First Leader had spoke of safeguards. Storm was sure he hadn't only meant the Xik soldiers. Breaking the comline should be safe for a short period. No doubt it was regularly tested, but out here in the desert there were a number of ways in which a comline could temporarily fail. Falling rock was one; in the desert lands, here in the foothills of the mountain range, large rocks often cracked away and fell. The Xiks would be used to that, and they'd send someone to check before they assumed they were about to be attacked. That was, if they noticed quickly. If they didn't notice for some time, then the Nitra and human war party would have attacked by then, anyhow.

The sun rose higher. The heat would be stifling soon. Storm touched Hing's mind. She had found something, sharing the picture. Yes, he encouraged her. Yes, dig. She dug.

The others, seeing her interest, came to dig with her. Tani grinned, signing rapidly.

"Our spirit animals find the big secret our enemy hides. It is a pity the enemy does not hide great wealth."

From around her there were subdued chuckles. With the wire uncovered in several places and then broken Hing led her tiny clan back to Storm. They were petted, praised, then tucked to wait in a small rock hollow. Storm signaled a general advance. The warriors slipped forward in slow silence. They fanned out ahead of the humans, skins blending with the same reddish-yellow as Arzoran earth and rock. They encircled the area where the Xik's hidden guard post lay, and waited. Kelson took a deep breath.

"Jackson, Larkin. Blow that door in." The lasers were poised and ready. Twin rays converged silently and the door was gone. Into the gap poured the waiting Nitra. They ran in silence but their eyes glowed fierce and ready. They raced down the entrance tunnel, killing as they ran. Here and there fire was returned and a man fell. The human force ran with them, giving each other covering fire. Human shouts or screams of pain mingled with the Nitra's high-pitched cries.

In the tunnel dust boiled, drawn from the rock walls by laser fire. The stench of musk from the Xik soldiers, the stink of burned flesh, the copper smell of human blood, and the sharper overlay of Nitra blood caught in the throats of those who fought. The blue overhead lights shone through a growing mist of dust and smoke. They had to finish this fight before the laboratory became suspicious about the comlink being silent. Tani jigged from one foot to the other, anxious for her clan-friends. Speaker of Dreams came out of the dust to smile cheerfully at Tani.

"Kelson so-say we are to share all the enemy has. We have found very many blankets, much food, Swift Killer finds a corral. The enemy had horses also. I think they dressed as Nitra, ride out in the land and you do not see they were an enemy. The five tribes sent ten warriors each. I think the warriors will have fine plunder to take back to their people. This is a good war trail."

The noise from the tunnels was subsiding little by little. "How many horses?" Tani signed.

"Maybeso twenty. Good horses, and there is much gear with them."

Tani looked at Storm. "I wonder where they stole those. Unless . . ." She was remembering the story she'd heard from Storm's stepfather. How human renegades had helped the first Xik holdout team when Storm had gone up against the Xiks here on Arzor soon after his arrival.

"I don't think so," Storm said slowly, knowing what she must be thinking. The same thought had initially occurred to him. "There's been no signs of renegades. No, this section of the land is dangerous. Perhaps some of those who vanished near it didn't die so accidentally."

Tani signed that to the Thunder-Drummer, who agreed. "I think so. This enemy was an enemy to all of us. They would kill your people or mine, it would be all the same to them. This is a good hunting, it is their turn to die."

The noise from the tunnels had died down to moans of pain and quiet voices. Tani and Storm turned their attention to the sound of approaching footsteps, as Kelson plodded up-slope to where the three sat. He had a torn shirt sleeve and a ruffled look. Blood was splashed across one shoulder. He saw them looking at that and nodded.

"That isn't mine. The casualties aren't good but Mirt's taking care of them. He was a medic in the service. Mostly those who got hit square are dead. We lost twelve out of the fifty Nitra and two of our boys." His face twisted in grief. "Damn it all to hell. I hate losing men even if we have killed two of theirs for one of ours."

"Who was killed?" Storm queried, a sudden fear in his heart. Not Logan; not his young impetuous half-brother? Logan had been one of the first into the tunnel, along with the leading warriors of the clans. If anyone was likely to be killed, it would be those front-runners.

Kelson saw Storm's fear and allayed it quickly. "Logan's okay. But Dumaroy's cousin Mason is dead and Put Lancin's young brother, Dade. Shen Larson is hurt bad. Mirt says Shen'll make it but he won't be riding with us this season."

They were beginning to carry the dead out of the tunnel now. The Nitra were mourning quietly as Speaker of Dreams carried out the rites, releasing the dead warriors' spirits. Kelson went back to help carry out the human bodies. These were laid on blankets as the men stood around them. Dumaroy leaned down to close his cousin's eyes. His chest heaved once in a dry sob.

"He always rushed into things. I shoulda been there for him."

Kelson gripped him by the shoulder. "You couldn't be everywhere, Rig. He died clean; no long dying, no agony, and he died fighting." He managed a rueful grin. "You knew Mason, he was always fighting. If he had to choose, I reckon he'd have liked it this way."

"Maybe. Maybe so, but I'm going to miss him."

Speaker of Dreams came to them quietly, a clan blanket

over one arm. She signed, her gaze direct into Dumaroy's eyes.

"I bring a blanket that your kin may sleep the sleep of a warrior. If you wish me to release his spirit for its return, I will do so."

Rig Dumaroy stared at her. Most of his life he'd hated the natives. Now a Thunder-Drummer offered warrior tribute. She named Mason as one who had died fighting, and should lie in a warrior blanket, should have his spirit released to return in the body of a newborn who would be a warrior in turn.

Wordlessly he nodded, tears in his eyes as he watched her kneel, lay the blanket out, and roll Mason within. Her hands swept over the blanketed shape as she twittered softly in the Nitra tongue. Speaker of Dreams stood up again and her hands flickered.

"It is done. Once this is over, let you take the warrior home. Watch for the return of his spirit, which will surely come." She walked away to continue her work over the bodies of other dead while Dumaroy looked after her, tears in his eyes.

Tani had seen and heard it all. The pain of the living, the sorrow for the dead. Blood spent to buy Arzor's future. She sucked in her breath. It hadn't been quite real to her before. Now it was. Her mother had said war was wrong. It was acceptable to fight if you were attacked, but not to seek out war. She would have protested this invasion of the desert lands, seeing it as aggression.

Tani had seen what was happening on Arzor. It didn't take two to make a fight. Only one who didn't care. If they let the Xiks have their way, far more people would die and

Arzor would be a desert everywhere. She'd dreamed that, and she wasn't going to let that happen in real life. She rose slowly.

"Let's go find the clickers." She whistled to Destiny softly, turning to look at Storm as he mounted Rain, who had also obeyed a summons.

"We'll ride until we get close. It'll take less time and we don't have time to waste." Her hand went out as the filly walked forward.

Storm took Tani's hand, holding firmly. The link tightened as they moved forward, searching in their linked minds for the feel of the lethal insects. Several times they lost the line but always they came back to it. In the back of Storm's battle-trained mind, seconds ticked away. If they didn't find the entrance soon, the Xiks were almost certain to notice the comline was broken. If they sent one of their soldiers to seek out the break and he saw the war party before they saw him, it could be disastrous. Finally, they halted their mounts near where a cliff face rose above them.

Tani nodded toward the cliff face. "In here!"

The war party left their mounts to move quietly to the cliff. Kelson ran his hands over the rock and nodded. He called Logan, who ran an echo-sounder over a lower edge of the rock face.

"Hollow behind there, all right. But no entrance I can see."

Storm turned. "Bring Hing and the others, they're good at this, and hurry. Tani's getting worried."

He looked to where she stood, her hands against the harsh surface. Her face was intent, listening. This close to so many of the small killers she could read them without the link. She was sweating, her face white and strained. Logan looked and ran, calling in soft bird-cry signals to several of his men. They were back shortly, each with a clinging meerkat. Storm took Hing. Gently he reached out to tell her what was required. She understood and trotted busily away; her mate scurried off with her and Storm turned to the kits.

It was harder with them. But at last they, too, knew what they hunted. A way into the hollow places behind the rock. They would search. They vanished, intent on the hunt. Storm sat abruptly. Impressing his request on a team, most members of which were untrained, was exhausting. Tani still stood, her fingertips against the rock. Her face was twisting slowly into an expression of fear. Hing was back. She'd found something. Storm ran to look. Then he moved away. He spoke, keeping his voice very low and signaling the others to do the same.

"Kelson, Hing can get inside here. It looks like an air vent. What's the rock thickness?" Time was growing very short. He could read that from Tani. The echo-sounder was brought and used. Logan nodded, moving away before he answered.

"I think it's an air vent above a major tunnel. There's a fault in the rock there. We could drill a hole big enough for one at a time to go in, but it can't be done without some noise."

He moved close to the vent and something leapt. Instinctively Storm struck out. The clicker landed and leapt again. Kelson stunned it in midair and moved back hastily, waving the others back as well.

"The guards seem to be rather alert today. Lucky they didn't get your meerkat."

Storm was feeling the same way. But Hing had known the danger. She wouldn't have entered if the clickers had been too close. They must have moved up the vent, most likely following the sounds she'd made.

He recalled the First Leader's words. "Kelson, have your boys check for anything else they can find. Sample the air, use everything you have. That Xik said they had other safeguards for the laboratories. We could just drop a flame bomb down the air vent but I'm worried they may have a counter to it."

"Okay." He turned to give quiet-voiced orders. Equipment was moved up, nothing large; all of it had come on horseback, but even on technology-poor Arzor that could be some really sophisticated gear in small packages.

Storm saw that one of the instruments was attracting increased attention from Kelson. He padded over quietly to touch the liaison man on the arm and mouth the words.

"You've found something?"

Kelson moved back some distance to where he was less likely to be heard. "Oh, yes, we've found something, all right. First, the instruments say the few Xik personnel in there are deep underground beyond the breeding vats. If we get in without making too much of a noise about it, they may not know we're here until we're tapping them on the shoulders. They could be relying on the guard post to alert them. Apart from that, they prefer a world that is less bright. Here they'd sleep most of the day. It's right at the brightest hottest part of the day now, so they could be asleep."

"A lot of could be."

"It's what we have."

"Go on."

"The instruments aren't certain of this, either. But from the emanations, it's possible the Xiks have a bomb down there."

"What sort?"

"The sort that drills downward once it's set, then explodes."

Storm shivered. "I know that sort. If it's big enough it can reach magma, then start a volcanic eruption when it blows."

"Exactly." Kelson's expression was grim. "But there's a couple of things going for us. If the instruments are right, that bomb is placed nearer to where we are here than to where the Xiks are now. Tank Kilgariff thinks it will be on two systems. One is manual; any Xik with the codes can set it off, but that could take several minutes. He thinks it's probably on an automatic system as well, one that will set it off if we drop a flame bomb down to clear out the clickers. In other words, if we can go in without alerting the Xiks and get between them and the bomb, they can't set it off manually. If we don't use flamers of any type it may not go off on automatic, either."

"They could still fire something toward it. If they picked the right weapon to use, the bomb's automatic systems would detonate it."

Kelson nodded. "We'd not be around to worry about it, if that happened. But what's the alternative? Leave them here to overrun Arzor with clickers?"

"I know. Right now we need more information about the clickers." Then we can decide what to do." Storm crossed to Tani, who had been maintaining a light link with the deadly creatures, and laid a hand on her arm.

"How many clickers do you hear?"

Her eyes were vague, her voice quiet and almost inaudible. "Many. Like a living carpet within the walls. They wait. The little ones can't hatch until it is time or they will die. They must guard them. They will not harm the Xiks, they've been programmed to leave them alone, but they will kill any other who enters. They wait. They hunger." She started to shake. Her gaze lifted to focus on him. Her voice strengthened. "Storm, the new ones hatch tonight. We have to laser the vats before that happens."

"Why?" Kelson blurted. "What's the hurry?"

"The clicker guards. They're held here until the new breed hatches. Once that starts they're free. If we're still here then in the dark . . ." She broke off as Kelson also took on a sick look.

Logan looked at them. "How do these things breed?"

Tani roused. "Kady says they have a queen."

"Can you sense one in there with the guards?"

"Not a guard queen, no. There's ones in the vats for the new clickers."

"Then if we can get in now and laser the vats, if we kill most of the guards, the ones left can't breed?" She nodded, her eyes on him. "Then that's it. We get it done and be out of here by dark just in case. What sort of a life span do individual clickers have?"

"Weeks." Logan opened his mouth again and Storm cut him off.

"Yes. Kelson, get your men to blow the tunnel here and here." His hands sketched out the areas. He turned to Tani; she muttered something emphatic and he held up a hand in surrender. "Tani and I will go in to laser the vats." There was an inarticulate sound of protest from the rangers. "You'll have work to do as well," Storm snapped. "Cut us a path through and then sweep the sides of it away from us."

Dumaroy's bull voice echoed. "Sure, but some of the clickers are gonna get through. It only takes one if they've got a deadly poison now."

Tani smiled at him. A small weary grin. "We'll douse our clothes in the repellent. It will make them reluctant to attack us but it won't hold a whole swarm off. Some will ignore it. It's just the best we've had time to make so far. Storm and I think we can link tight enough to stop the others attacking us. If it was the whole swarm we couldn't. But if it's only a few trying at a time we should be able to persuade them we aren't there at all." She saw the horrified, mutinous look the big rancher wore and walked over to him. "Please, Mr. Dumaroy. Storm and I are the only ones who have a chance." Her voice lowered so that only he could hear her.

"I trust you. Storm said you were a marksman in the war, and you're one of the best shots on Arzor. The guard clickers are poisonous. But it may take five or ten minutes to die even if they bite somewhere vital. If . . . if any of them bite us, I want to die before the others hatch. Please, promise me. I don't want to die the way your hand did."

He looked at her a moment. "You remind me of my ma. No size an' all courage." He looked at the laser rifle he held. "Yeah. I know how Jarry died. You go in there and I'll keep them off you. And . . . I promise."

Her fingers went out to touch the back of his hand where it rested on the rifle. "Thank you."

Her terror lifted a little as she turned to rejoin Storm. She was afraid, so afraid. But she couldn't let Storm go alone.

He'd die without the link they shared. It was the link they could use. They'd tried it once with the laboratory clickers. Pretended to be not there, shut down the feeling of human and substituted it for that of rock. If she stayed back Storm would go anyhow. Watching him die would be worse than dying with him. And she trusted Dumaroy. He'd keep his promise. She wouldn't die, screaming silently, unable to move as she was eaten alive.

Chapter Nineteen

The rock face between the tunnel and the outer air vaporized, and the lasers were ready. They carved an explosive path through the clicker guards as they streamed out to face the invaders. Each ruby fan exploded clickers by the dozen. Dumaroy wasn't firing yet. A laser pulse rifle's power pack had a finite amount of power time. He had a spare power pack, but it took a few seconds to change them; someone could die in those few seconds. It was better to wait for the right time to start shooting. When he'd been discharged he'd taken his top-line laser pulse rifle with him. Like many of that type it was geared to his handprint. It was useless to anyone else. He'd been allowed to keep it because of that, although according to the letter of the law it should have been taken from him. For the last five years it had lived in a locked cabinet in a hidden cupboard.

Now he knelt, staring straight down the tunnel. Behind him Logan held steady the light from an atom light. Something in the loss of the tunnel's integrity had also put out its internal illumination. Many of the clicker guards had died, others milled at the edge of the blazing path of light. Kelson produced the container of repellent and doused the two waiting figures.

Storm smiled wryly as he turned in place, making sure his exposed flesh and clothing were all coated with the repellent. "Thanks be it doesn't smell too bad."

Tani took her turn and winced at the scent. It smelled bad enough to her. She opened her mind cautiously and fought back the urge to retch as the feel of the clickers, only yards away, invaded her mind. Storm took her hand.

"You don't have to do this."

She shivered, then straightened, chin setting in determination. "Yes, I do. Brad said he told you about Wolf Sister. She was a warrior and my father was proud he was descended from her. My father didn't let Trastor die, I'm not going to see the enemy that murdered him win here. Now let's move before I'm shaking so hard I fall over instead."

Storm's fingers tightened. Steadily he walked forward, the link between them beginning to project. Rock. There was nothing edible here. Just the reddish-yellow unchanging rock. Tani wrapped herself in it. Rock. They were rock, nothing more. The clickers closed in, confused. Rock? Rock did not move, but these things felt like rock. Dumaroy knelt, beginning to fire, smoothly, expertly, in single laser pulses as he picked off any clicker that came too close. One leaped and exploded with a tiny acrid puff and pop in midair.

They were rock. See the crevices in the rock, the dust across its surface. Rock!

Logan moved, as another flashlight joined his. Together the beams lit up the tunnel length. Far down it they could see the dull gleam of metal. The breeding vats? Both Tani and Storm cradled the short-barreled, widemouthed lasers. Sweep those across the breeding vats; miss nothing, do it over and over, and it was certain the internal liquid would heat sufficiently inside the vats to cook their occupants. She looked straight ahead to where the vats must be. If she looked to either side and saw the waiting guards she might lose her nerve. If she ran screaming from the tunnel Storm would die. Her clan-friends, the Quade ranch, then Arzor would follow. She gritted her teeth, fought down the sickness trying to drain her courage, and projected savagely.

They were rock. Just rock. Rocks did not move, therefore she did not move. It was an illusion caused by the strange lights. She was—they were—rock!

So far the repellent was working, but they were moving deeper into the tunnel. The clickers were programmed not to permit that. Rock was not supposed to move and this rock smelled bad. The clickers were confused. Dumaroy fired and a clicker that had decided to test the rock died. He swept a pulse to each side of the moving figures so that more clickers died. He didn't know how that pair were doing it, but no one could say he didn't do his part. The kid had trusted him. He wasn't about to fail her, not Rig Dumaroy.

Step, and another step. A small door caught Storm's attention. It was an ordinary-sized aperture, and half open. He moved them on a diagonal as they continued to walk slowly down the tunnel. He could see past the door as they approached. There was a chair, the deep, soft, comfortable type an officer might choose. In front of it was a screen and keyboard with a set of buttons. One was red, secured under a heavy clearplas cover. He noted it in the back of his mind as they moved on down the tunnel, one pace at a time.

Tani was holding the illusion with all her strength. Rock. They were rock. Several clicker guards were becoming anxious. There'd been no rocks in the tunnel. They were here to prevent anything approaching the breeding vats. Maybe that included strange rocks? They closed in—and died. The scent of their dying roused others. Maybe the rocks were a danger? Dumaroy swept another pulse to either side of the figures. They were nearing the cave at the end of the tunnel, the breeding vats were in there.

Tani's every pulse-beat said she was rock. She was rock. Laid down by ancient seas. Perhaps prehistoric shells lay within, fossils of things that had once lived. No, nothing that had ever lived. She was rock! Unliving, never-living rock!

At the end of the tunnel, the long tube opened out into a vast room. The light flooded down, leaving shadows around the edge but illuminating the vats. They bulked large. Panels along the sides showed where they would break open for the hatching. Tani allowed a thread of her mind to reach out. The impact was so great that she almost lost the projection. She gripped. Dragged it back over her as the clickers moved closer.

With her face set in a grimace of effort she dragged Storm back to the door of the room, turned to face the far entrance. It was hard but she managed to hold the link and project her rockness, even as she signed with her free hand. At the mouth of the tunnel they'd set up a vid-relay; it would send back the picture of her signals.

"Quickly. Hatch now very soon. Very very soon!"

She couldn't manage more. There was no strength to explain that there'd been still other safeguards no one had expected. The new clickers would be slightly immature. But they could be decanted a few hours ahead at need. That need had been triggered by the change in pressure in the tunnel, as they vaporized a portion of the tunnel wall. Storm raised his gun from where they had remained in the hatching room's doorway and began to sweep the nearest vat methodically. They could see and hear nothing of any reaction. They could only hope it was working. He continued as Tani took up the strain of projection. Most of the guard clickers were staying back, but not all of them.

They were rock. She was so tired of rock, why not be a horse, a silver three-quarter-bred duocorn filly? The clickers converged on her and from the entrance the laser pulsed again and again. Rock! She was—they both were—rock! Tired rock. Tani grabbed at her slipping projection. They had to be rock. So tired, her mind seemed to blur, but she was rock. She'd always been rock. She couldn't remember being anything else but rock. Rock that walled out danger, kept Storm and her safe. Rock, always and only rock.

Storm, too, was faltering. His arm was hurting. He'd brushed it against the rock. Or was he rock? No, rock didn't hurt. He shut down that line of thought hard. He was rock. Rock felt nothing. He was rock. The laser died and he took the other laser from Tani's hand. The second vat seemed to take forever. He must be certain to cover every inch. The clickers inside had to die. All of them. But it must be in the lowest tech way possible so as not to trigger the bomb.

Tani felt herself fading. She—no—rock did not get tired. She was rock. She felt Storm turn her and give a small tug. They could start the long walk back down the tunnel to safety. To the daylight and green growing things. To friends and clan, to Destiny and—no, she was rock. Rock did not care, it had no one and nothing. They were rock!

She faltered again. Her spirit was fighting still but the drain on her strength had been impossible. Storm hooked his good arm under her shoulder. They were halfway back. In the light Logan could see what was happening. With a muffled, desperate curse he thrust his flashlight into Kelson's hands.

"Keep that lighting up the tunnel."

He trotted down past clickers beginning to turn toward him. Laser pulses swept them aside in puffs of death. Before the confused clicker guards reacted, he had reached Tani and Storm.

"Tani, we're rock, all of us!" Storm's tone was sharp as Logan scooped her up.

The link was wearing thin. The girl's strength running like water through the crevices in—rock, yes, they were rock still. She held grimly, despairingly as Logan carried her pace by pace toward safety. The clickers closed in. At the entrance Dumaroy moved up to the center of the opening. He knelt and began to fire like a machine. Clicker after clicker died. He'd been the best. At the back of his mind he'd known he'd never been this good. Now and again he'd missed. Here he couldn't afford that. If he missed one of the clickers he'd have to shoot the girl.

The laser rifle pulsed silently, each pulse another hit, more dead enemies. Storm and Logan moved on. Ten steps to go, then five. The laser rifle's charge was running down, too. The pulses had that first touch of raggedness. Dumaroy swore and kept shooting. By him Kelson was hissing orders. Logan swung Tani clear and two Nitra seized her, running her to safety away from the tunnel. Storm staggered another five paces and collapsed on the warm rock.

As he cleared the opening Kelson and his rangers moved in. Lasers swept the tunnel again and again. If only they could have done it that way to begin with, Storm thought. But they dared not take the risk. Too much laser fire could have triggered other warning systems. Now they held the tunnel, and hatching tanks held only dead bodies. Clickers died until at last there were no more to be seen.

Kelson signaled some of his people forward. "Rater, take a look at the small room halfway down the tunnel, on the left before the room with the breeding vats. Storm thinks the bomb controls are there." A small, wiry man, with graying hair, nodded and trotted briskly down the tunnel to investigate. Rater had been a UXB-tech in the Xik war before he returned to Arzor to ranch frawns.

A Thunder-Drummer joined Kelson, his hands moving in interested question.

"There have been no enemy people, only Death-Which-Comes-in-the-Night. Where are the enemy? Are they in hiding?"

"Maybeso. Wait." Kelson was studying one of the screens Logan had set up. Put came up behind them to peer over their shoulders. It was he who spoke first.

"There, see. Two or maybe three of them. The heat signatures overlap, it could be three. Move the angle." Logan obeyed. "No one anywhere else. I'd say those two or three are the afternoon shift and that's all."

The medicine man, who had been watching, might not have understood most of the discussion, but he understood the moving heat shapes. He turned to Dumaroy.

"Gun die?"

The big rancher was snapping in a second charge. Now that there was a lull, he could do that without fearing Tani would die if he paused.

Dumaroy grinned, his hands flicking through fast signs. "No, Gun lives again, why?"

"My warriors. We tempt out Death-Which-Comes-in-the-Night. We bring any left from hiding. You kill them."

Before there could be any objections, he twittered. A warrior trotted deep into the tunnel opening, past the door to the bomb room, and posed. From near the vats, a clicker leapt and died, its imperative to guard the vats still alive. Bit by bit the warriors teased—as they said—the enemy from hiding. Dumaroy continued to shoot. Finally no clicker came to the gun. Kelson straightened.

"Bring the flashlights. We have to check the vats, I want the inside broken open and the contents re-lasered just to make certain. While some of us are doing that, I want a squad to shake out those Xik scientists, or whatever they are, the ones the heat screen shows in the lower rooms.

A mixed group of human and Nitra answered his demands. The vats were lasered over and over until the contents were ash. At the same time a second group had padded their way silently down the tunnels. The three Xiks below might have been scientists, but they fought like mad beasts, reported Dumaroy, who'd led that attack. They couldn't be taken alive, and his men were bringing the bodies out now. He'd had two men injured, but both should survive.

Kelson returned an hour later to where Storm and Tani lay on blankets. Storm was awake again but Tani slept, curled peacefully into herself, holding Storm's hand. Speaker of Dreams nodded to the liaison man.

"They are only tired. Let them rest a little, drink water, eat something. They'll be strong enough to ride back to our camp soon."

Kelson dropped to a squat and nodded to Storm. "Looks as if you did it. Everything in the vats is ash, and we can't persuade another guard to show its feelers. If the Ark scientists are right, any guard clicker left will die without breeding in a few weeks, anyway. There were three scientists in the lower levels of the laboratory. They fought to the death but we have the bodies. High Command is likely to lean hard on the Xik home world over this business. They have more than enough proof to make further sanctions stick. We'll start for the copter in an hour. I'm sharing out the loot as we promised, then the Nitra will head back to their own tribes."

Storm nodded wearily, looking at Tani. "Leave us until last, Kelson. Let her rest as long as she can." He summoned up a tired smile. "The clan will want to celebrate when we get to camp. She'll need to be awake for that."

The clan did, and Tani was. One of the Nitra warriors was already leading Storm's and Tani's mounts back toward the Quade ranch by the time the celebration was slowing down. With dawn the copter carried Storm and Tani to the ranch, where, once Tani had slept herself out, Kady entered her bedroom to talk.

"You're staying here, aren't you?"

Tani took her hands. "It's where I belong now," she said gently. "I'll miss the Ark and you two. You will stop off at Arzor sometimes on business. I'll see you then. But I can't leave Storm." She giggled suddenly. "I'm a landowner too. The Government voted me fifty squares alongside Storm's land. He said Destiny will like that. He gets five years free of tax, so we'll both manage very well."

"What about the others?"

"The humans all get five squares of land or something equivalent. The Nitra left really loaded down with loot. They'll all be big warriors when they get back to their tribes. Kelson's men have a list of stuff. I don't think anyone feels they weren't well treated."

Kady looked at her niece. "So how long do Brion and I have to hold the Ark?"

"Why? Oh!" Tani flushed, then laughed. "Not long. Storm says we'll have the most mixed lot of wedding guests Arzor has ever seen. Brad says it's okay. It isn't every day a Cheyenne-Irish clan-friend marries a Navaho Beast Master. He's looking forward to it. I just hope the weather's okay for the ceremony. There's far too many guests coming for us to have it inside, and it's so close to the start of the Big Wet."

The day was clouded but not wet. The guests crowded the area near the ranch house where Tani stood with Storm. Through their feet played Hing, her mate, and a positive meerkat clan. On perches Mandy and a male paraowl eyed each other thoughtfully. They were still undecided. Baku and Surra were nowhere to be seen. They'd already decided and were off celebrating those decisions.

Those gathered to hear the oath were as mixed as Brad had said. They had one thing in common, however: approving smiles as they listened. After oaths were given and taken, Logan amused those who spoke one-speech by teasing Mandy into replying to trick questions. Such as "What do you think Xiks should do on such a lovely morning?" The guests found the answers amusing . . . until an indignant Tani put a stop to it. Later they watched as two riders cantered away across the mauve and green landscape toward the Basin rim.

A day later the shuttle rose toward the Ark. Below, Tani opened an eye to watch, then shut it again and snuggled closer. That felt odd. She groaned and opened her eyes to look properly. Between her and Storm, Minou and Ferarre were finding it pleasantly warm. Two humans were a lot warmer than one on a chilly early morning. Storm watched her eviction of the coyotes and laughed.

"You'll have to get used to that. It comes with being a Beast Master."

Tani pounced and he rolled as she tickled mercilessly. Above, unnoticed, the Ark swung out of orbit, heading away for the next world. Below, Storm and Tani were otherwise occupied. Their world was enough—for now.

One of the best-loved and most famous science fiction and fantasy authors of all time, Andre Norton was named Grand Master by the Science Fiction and Fantasy Writers of America and was awarded an H. P. Lovecraft Life Achievement Award by the World Fantasy Convention. She has written over a hundred novels, which have sold millions of copies worldwide, including her Witch World, Beast Master, Solar Queen, and Time Traders series, among others. She lives in Murfreesboro, Tennessee, where she presides over High Hallack, a writer's resource and retreat. More can be learned at www.andre-norton.org.

Lyn McConchie has written many novels, including collaborations with Andre Norton, *Key to the Keplian*, a Witch World novel, and the forthcoming *Beast Master's Circus*. She lives in New Zealand, where she writes—and runs a farm.